Mombasa Nights

An English Safari Mystery

Rick Dietrich

RADAR BOOKS LLC

Cover designed by MiblArt

ISBN: 979-8-9860310-2-6

To all the security professionals who toil
in anonymity to keep us safe.
Thank you.

Swahili words in Mombasa Nights

Asante sana – thank you very much
Bibi - grandmother
Bora – excellent
Bosi – boss
Habari – hello there
Habari gani - How are you doing?
Habari na asante – Hello & thank you
Habari za asubuhi – Good morning
Hakuna matata – No problems
Hapana – No
Jambo - hello
Karibu – welcome
Kwa heri – goodbye
Matatus – minibus
Mbambakofi – type of Kenyan hardwood tree
Mbuzi – goat
Mzungu – white person
Mzuri sana – very good
Ndiyo – yes
Ndugu – brother
Nimekuelewa? - Understand?
Nyati – buffalo
Rafiki – friend
Samahani – sorry
Samahani bwana – excuse me, sir
Shillings – Kenya currency
Tafadhali – please
Tangawizi – brand of ginger beer soda
Tusker – Kenyan beer
Tuk-tuks – auto rickshaw

Italian words in Mombasa Nights

Perdonami – excuse me
Scusi – excuse me
Perfetto – perfect
E tu – and you
Eccellente – excellent
Signore – gentleman
Signori – gentlemen
Buon pomeriggio – good afternoon
Perdonateci – forgive us
Molto bene – very good

CONTENTS

Rick Dietrich

CHAPTER 1

Elijah Botsole leaned against a small palm tree as he struggled to catch his breath. Sweat stung his eyes, but panic kept them wide open as he stared at the pale green tsavorite ring he held clutched in his hand. He nearly laughed; it was such a small trinket to get killed over, even if it represented such terrible things. Elijah shook his head as he wondered why he had ever turned honest. When he opened that cargo container, he should have turned away. Just a few short years ago, he would have done so, maybe even earned a few shillings to keep his mouth shut. Damn that man, Safari, and his principles. Of course, in his heart, Elijah wanted Kenya to be free from corruption. He wanted it for his wife, his children, and his country. But it would never come to pass. Too many powerful men relied on corruption for their livelihood, money, and power.

I should have known better, Elijah thought to himself. The one thing these vile men would never give up is their power. In fact, the more power they have, the more they crave. It is a hunger never sated, and feeding it creates an evermore ravenous appetite. Elijah had wanted to believe in Safari and his dream of a better Kenya. He had embraced these ideals enough to turn over a new leaf and join Safari's team. Now, those beliefs were going to cost him. There seemed to be no escape. He needed to find a way out, so he ran while maintaining his vice-like grip on the ring.

The dark, cloud-covered night sky prevented Elijah from getting his bearings. He had always hated the dark. Shapes were distorted into nightmarish figures as sounds amplified by the surrounding quiet had him on edge. Long moss-covered branches clawed at him as the warning cries of monkeys and feral cats fighting in the distance screeched through the air. One sound above all made him catch his breath. He suddenly heard his pursuers shouting behind him in the distance, and fear drove him further into the darkness ahead. Elijah stumbled over unseen roots and rocks. He fell to the ground hard but quickly bounced back up into a run. The tumble sent searing pain through his body, but Elijah refused to cry out lest the sound give him away. He looked into the night sky as he cursed Safari again and prayed for an escape.

Elijah lowered his eyes back down and caught sight of an enormous granite pyramid-shaped boulder, and hope found a toehold. He knew this place; he had played here as a child when his parents had brought him to see the mythical rock. The pyramid's origin was a mystery, and many people came to rub the stone for good luck. This place was only about two hundred meters from the banks of Kilindini Harbor and the thick mangrove forest that lined it. He might still have a chance. He could hide among the mangroves till dawn. If he stayed motionless in the maze of roots, the crocs, let alone his hunters, would not detect him. These men would not be so bold as to attack an officer of the Revenue Authority in broad daylight. The country could not have fallen so far that the people would allow such a brazen offense.

Elijah picked up speed, propelled by this newfound optimism. He was a strong runner. His tribe prided itself on producing the fastest people in all of Kenya. The dark void ahead could only be the water, and it spurred him faster still.

A distant peel of thunder rang out just as he reached the shoreline. A stinging sensation burrowed through his back and exploded from his stomach. He put his hands to his gut, but only warm stickiness met his probing touch. Elijah realized he had been shot as he splashed into the deep, salty water. The open wound prickled with a stinging burn, but he was unable to feel or move his legs as he sank. Tucking the ring into a hidden pocket of what was left of his shirt, Elijah struggled to the surface using only his arms. He suppressed a cough when he breached, knowing any sound meant certain death. Elijah managed to pull himself into the thick roots of an extensive mangrove tree until his upper body became wedged. He was too weak from blood loss to use brute strength to break free, and it was too dark for him to navigate an escape path. So, he resigned himself to being quite stuck.

Elijah heard voices and footsteps approaching his location. Suddenly, lights from the men's torches began searching the waters. His dark skin blended easily with his surroundings, and the roots made it virtually impossible for them to see him. He almost sighed in relief when the lights stopped scanning the waters, but the men were now close enough that Elijah could make out their conversation.

"He is not here!"

"I hit him!"

"You lie! You just want the reward money."

"How dare you impugn me. Hang the ten thousand shillings. That is nothing to me."

Ten thousand shillings? Elijah thought. He nearly laughed. Everything he had–his work, his family, and his life turned out to be worth only ten thousand shillings.

His breathing was becoming weaker, and he struggled to keep awake. Discovering how little these men were being paid to kill him drained much of his will to survive.

"Bah, let us be gone from here," roared the man who had shot Elijah. "I am certain I hit him. If I killed him, then good. If not, the blood will attract the crocs, and he is finished either way."

Elijah knew it to be true. The crocs from all around would smell his blood and swarm to see if there was anything left for them to scavenge. He realized in horror the distinctive splashing he heard was the sound of the large crocs heading into the water, already being drawn to his scent.

"If I missed like you say, we will never find him in this muck on a night like tonight." The man spit loudly into the water to emphasize his point. "Besides, I have lined up two fine young ladies for us."

"No lie?"

"No lie. They are waiting at the Miami Bar."

The men raucously laughed as they slapped hands in anticipation of their coming conquests. Their voices faded into the distance as Elijah's consciousness slipped into oblivion. He was blissfully unaware as the colossal croc tore his lower half from his trunk and swam away to gorge itself on his flesh, far from its competition. The eviscerated stump of Elijah's body remained wedged in the roots, with his arms spread wide like some gory marionette putting on a show designed to induce nightmares in its audience.

CHAPTER 2

English Safari sat at his desk in the Kenya Revenue Authority Southern Region Headquarters. Sweat was forming on his brow, but he wasn't sure if it was because the old a/c unit had conked out again or if it was the berating he was receiving on the phone. Safari had been promoted to deputy commissioner of the Southern Region of Kenya less than a week ago. It was a great honor and a sizable promotion, especially for someone as young as he was, but Commissioner Sambu was expecting him to perform miracles. English had known her since she was a deputy commissioner for the KRA, and he had made his first big bust as a field agent. She had promoted him against everyone's advice and reminded him at every opportunity that he needed to make progress, and quick. He decided it was the a/c making him sweat. The commissioner had always liked him; she just knew that he needed results to keep the job.

English had finished setting up his new office late the night before, arranging everything in its proper place. The new uniforms arrived only yesterday, too, but he was already sporting his whites with perfect military creases that he had ironed meticulously this morning. English felt uniforms not only showed outsiders that you meant business but also reminded those in the uniform of their duties. It was a small detail, but since the last Deputy Commissioner was imprisoned for corruption, he felt those who had worked closely with him might need a reminder. Besides, English thought, as he caught his reflection in the mirror across the office, he looked quite fetching.

"Yes, Commissioner," Safari replied as he cradled the phone between his shoulder and ear. He was taking notes with one hand while using the other to push his wireframe glasses back up. He had bought this new expensive pair to go with his new position. The glasses looked good, but they seemed insistent on sliding down the bridge of his nose. The constant slipping did nothing to help create the image he was striving to project. If they kept falling, he would be forced to revert to his old black pair. They weren't as fancy, but they stayed put.

English looked up from his writing to see Michael Tsumbe smiling at him through the now-ajar door. The huge man was head of security for the port and had constantly dropped by Safari's office since his promotion. English held up his hand for the man to wait, then grimaced when he realized he had missed part of what the commissioner had said. He would have to piece it together later from his notes. English knew from experience how she hated to repeat herself.

"Yes, Commissioner Sambu. I will see to it. Goodbye, kwa heri, Commissioner Sambu, asante sana." Safari hung up the phone and quickly read through his call notes. Hearing shuffling sounds from the doorway, he looked up to see a chagrined Michael staring at him. Safari suppressed a sigh. He really didn't have time for this.

Tsumbe's feigned sadness deepened. "What, no welcome for your old friend, Michael?"

English smirked internally. *Old friend?* The man hadn't spoken two words to him before his promotion. *Just play the game English, just play the game*, he thought to himself. He stood up with as big a grin as he could muster.

"Yes, Michael, samahani, of course, you are welcome," he lied. "Welcome, welcome, karibu, my friend," he said as he ushered the big man to a chair across from his desk. "Just on the phone with my boss. You know how that goes."

"Haha, hakuna matata. Yes, my friend, I know how that goes, especially with one like that commissioner of yours."

Safari held his tongue. Was Michael testing his loyalty to Commissioner Sambu? *No, English, stop being paranoid*, he admonished himself.

He leaned his head out the door. "Kelly?"

A spritely young woman popped up from behind her desk. "Yes, Deputy Commissioner?"

"Some tea and biscuits, tafadhali."

"Of course, sir," his assistant replied, then headed down the hall.

Safari came back and sat down heavily in his padded leather chair.

"So, how is your new job treating you?" asked Michael.

English looked up to see the hulking man holding his brass name placard ham-fistedly in his meaty grip.

Wiping the sweat from his brow, Safari barely managed to hide the cringe he felt when he looked at the empty spot where his name had rested just moments ago. He leaned back in his chair and met Michael's eyes. The head of security broadly smiled as he stared intently back at him.

"As well as can be expected. HQ wants big changes here, but it is not as easy as they think." English tried to judge Tsumbe's response, but the massive man kept smiling. Safari paused as Kelly returned with the tea. Michael leaned into his chair so he could take in her backside as she bent over to pour each man a cup. He raised his eyebrows lecherously at English to get his reaction, but Safari remained stone-faced.

"Anything else, Deputy Commissioner?"

"That will be all, Kelly, asante sana." Kelly did a slight curtsy before turning to go.

Michael picked up his tea and a biscuit as he turned to watch the girl leave. He made a throaty sound after she closed the door. "You sure know how to pick assistants, my friend." The man's deep chuckle elicited anger from English, or was it disgust? Maybe both. He couldn't quite tell, but he worked hard to keep it from showing on his face. They drank their tea in silence, which was occasionally broken by Michael, eagerly enjoying his biscuits. Except for when Michael looked down to locate another biscuit or find his cup, he held that wide smile directed at Safari. Finally, the big man stood with a stretch.

"Well, I must get back to work. Thank you for the tea."

English walked over to shake the man's hand and escort him out of the office, but Michael pulled him close when he took his hand. The man was more than a head taller than Safari (who was no small man in his own right) and nearly double his girth.

"Things can be easy for you, Deputy Commissioner," Michael whispered down at him. "You just have to learn how to make friends. Say what you will about your predecessor, but he did know how to make friends." The big man slapped Safari hard on the shoulder before turning to go. Michael paused briefly to ogle Kelly again as he slipped on his shades. She pretended not to notice until he left, then gave English a wide-eyed look. He shook his head in apology. She smiled before resuming her work.

English returned to his office, closed the door, and sat back at his desk. He laid his glasses on the highly polished, ebony-accented teak wood surface and buried his face in his hands. "Make friends," he thought aloud. *What exactly did Tsumbe mean? Was he implying I should follow my predecessor's example? Did my predecessor start as an honest deputy commissioner, only becoming corrupt under duress?* English assumed the previous deputy commissioner had been crooked from day one. It was a reasonable inference since most appointees in Kenya had bought their positions. However, Safari did not and reluctantly admitted to himself his predecessor might not have either. He peeked at his reflection in the mirror. Safari realized everyone he dealt with would make the same suppositions about him. His goal was to avoid not only corruption but even the slightest appearance of corruption. He leaned back in his chair and looked up at the ceiling. *How am I ever going to enact all the changes needed?*

It was hard to find trustworthy employees in the system. That was why English had brought his team with him when he was promoted and placed them in leadership positions across the Southern Region's Headquarters. They were people he could count on and held the same ideals he did. Their performance was almost as responsible for his promotion as his own. English had made some enemies by displacing those who held positions of power in the previous deputy's staff, but there was nothing for it. He had not let those employees go, just shuffled them to other jobs where they could do little harm. Over time, if the displaced staff proved trustworthy, he would welcome them back, but not before he was certain. Too much was at risk to move hastily.

English needed to know what kind of man Tsumbe was and what he meant by "make friends." His paranoia saw it as a thinly veiled threat. "Play by our rules or end up like your predecessor or worse." Many officials went missing in Kenya. Sometimes, it was because they were incorruptible. More often than not, it was because a corrupt official's price for cooperation was becoming too expensive for their own good. It was a fine line to walk for a dirty official; they had to get enough money to make it worth the risk of prison, but not so much that the criminals would eliminate them. Safari would need to discretely investigate the Port of Mombasa's head of security. English had just the man for the job—a man who had connections everywhere. Many of them were not law-abiding citizens but had proved helpful from time to time. Safari went to the door and cracked it open.

"Kelly, have Elijah come to my office at his earliest convenience."

"Yes, Deputy Commissioner."

"Please, Kelly, I have told you to call me English when no one is around."

The young woman smiled at him. "Yes, Deputy Commissioner, you did, and I mentioned you needn't come to the door each time you want something. You can just intercom me."

"Yes, Kelly, but there is a difference. You know how to say my name, but I do not know how to operate that blasted contraption." The pair laughed, and Safari returned to his office to tackle the mountain of paperwork that had built more rapidly than he could have imagined in his inbox. He had disliked writing reports in the field, but he quickly learned that reading someone else's documents was far worse than writing his own. Unfortunately, he wasn't familiar enough with the job or the officers to know which reports he could skim or which he needed to read thoroughly, so he read them all to their fullest. His compulsive nature led him to make corrections down to the spelling errors he came across. He drew thin lines through every modification to keep the original text visible. The final touch was adding his initials to the documents to show he was the one who had made the changes.

English thanked the heavens when the phone rang, giving him an excuse to take his eyes off the monotonous papers.

"Habari, Deputy Commissioner Safari speaking." He felt sudden pride at introducing himself so formally. He hadn't spoken his new title until that moment.

"Yes, Deputy Commissioner, it's me, Kelly. There is an Alex Stoney on the line for you. Would you like me to patch him through?"

English laughed. He now saw it was indeed the intercom button that had lit up, not the phone. *I really need to learn how to use this phone system.*

"Yes, Kelly. Please patch my old friend through."

"Yes, Deputy Commissioner." Suddenly, the intercom light turned off, and the phone rang again but with a subtly different tone. He would have to try to notice the difference next time.

He punched the lit button and heard someone on the line. "Habari, Alex. How's my favorite mzungu?"

"Mzuri sana, English. Mzungu? I work outdoors, unlike desk jockeys such as yourself. After a whole week of you working indoors, I'm probably blacker than you are, my friend." The pair laughed. Alex was a third-generation Kenyan but was still a Brit to the natives. He had the strange accent all Brit expats seemed to acquire in Kenya after a few years of living in their region of Mombasa. Alex's grandfather started the massive construction company, Constructicon, after WWII; his family has run it since. By his casual dress, movie star looks, and relaxed attitude, he seemed more likely to be surfing off the shorelines of California or Australia than barking orders at people while wearing steel-toe boots and a hard hat. But that is exactly what he did, day in and day out. Despite his constant complaining, he loved every minute of it. It also helped that Alex was exceedingly good at his job. Since he took over as VP, Constructicon's profits have more than doubled and are looking to double again in as many years.

"So, to what do I owe the honor of receiving a call at work from the great black mzungu?"

Alex laughed easily before his voice took on a more concerned tone. "I wanted to know how you were doing. Habari gani, my friend?"

English paused before answering. "Mzuri sana, but very tired. Asante. It has been a long week, as you can imagine."

"Yes, I can imagine. But it might get longer still."

"Oh?"

"Yes, I wanted to call to congratulate you on the promotion, but I also wanted to warn you."

"Warn me of …?"

"Your name has been coming up in conversations between seedy men, or so I've heard."

English thought for a moment. Alex had one of the best flows of information in the region. He had a massive workforce with many connections throughout the business community as well as the rumor mill of his workers' family connections.

"Asante sana for the warning, my friend. I knew taking this job might put a target on my back, but I didn't think it would be this soon. Believe me, if someone else could do the job, it would have been my pleasure. Unfortunately, no one else qualified and honest enough, or maybe I should say dumb enough, was available."

"That's true," Alex said with a chuckle before turning somber again. "Just promise me you'll be careful, Safari."

"You have my word. Believe me. No one wants me to remain safe more than I do."

Both men laughed.

"I don't know about that, English. After all, where would I find another bowler as apt as you? They may play cricket here, but only someone who's played in England can truly appreciate the game."

"Thank you for your concern. I will keep my eyes open, but I must run now, my friend. I am scheduled to meet with the new police commissioner. I do not want to get off on the wrong foot with him by being late, and you know how Mombasa traffic is."

"Indeed, I do."

Like most European cities, Mombasa's roads were established before the invention of the automobile. Even though the port brought in a large portion of the country's income, there never seemed to be enough funds to expand the roads sufficiently for the traffic. Driving through Mombasa also meant dealing with the other causes of congestion. The enormous pedestrian traffic, bicycle and hand-cart deliveries, the golf-cart-like tuk-tuks, and the crazy matatus (their sudden swerves to pick up and drop off their passengers always created chaos) were all likely to cause accidents. Thus, one should leave plenty of time to get through the city no matter how short your intended trip.

"Oh, and English, be careful with the new commissioner. I've heard he is young for the post. Good luck!" Alex hung up the phone to leave Safari wondering about his upcoming meeting.

Young meant one of two things: either the man was related to someone in power (and therefore likely corrupt) or extremely good at his job. Alex's warning made it evident which one he assumed was the case. English was running out of time before their meeting. He was waiting on a background check on the police commissioner from his right-hand man. A quick online search about the commissioner revealed nothing of substance. English could typically count on Elijah to thoroughly vet someone, but he hadn't heard from him since Friday. Taking a deep breath, he grabbed his umbrella before stepping out of his office.

"Kelly, have Elijah meet me in the garage. I need him to update me on the drive to police HQ."

"I'm sorry, Deputy Commissioner, Mr. Botsole

hasn't arrived yet."

English thought for a moment. Elijah considered office work the least essential part of the job, but he was extremely reliable. In frustration, English shook his head quickly and muttered, "I was sure he would have been in early this week." A little louder, he added, "Do you know if he has a meeting or site visit scheduled for today?" Kelly shook her head as she raised her shoulders. "Do you have his new mobile number?"

"No, I am afraid not, Deputy Commissioner. The list has not been updated. Shall I have him call you when he arrives?"

"Yes, please do. If he gets in before my meeting, at least it will be of some help."

"Shall I have your driver bring the car around, Deputy Commissioner?"

English, planning to take his own car, stopped in his tracks. He had forgotten the KRA had assigned him a car and driver. It was considered unseemly for a person of his stature to drive themselves.

"Yes, Kelly, I will meet him up front." The woman nodded before hurrying to call down to the garage. English realized he probably would not need the umbrella with a driver to drop him off at the front door but did not want to look foolish by returning it to his office. Instead, he put the end of it to his brow in salute to his secretary and headed for the stairs.

One of the security guards was getting onto the elevator as Safari passed and held the door for him.

"No, asante. I need my exercise," English lied. The man shrugged his shoulders and let the door close. Truth be told, he hated enclosed spaces, and with all the power outages caused by the drought, he feared becoming trapped in the tiny elevator for hours. Not for the first time did he lament his city's dependence on hydroelectric power. Safari hurried down the stairs and nodded to the security guard disembarking the lift.

His driver, Sammy, must have been waiting at the SUV for Kelly's call because it was already parked out front when English exited the building. The driver opened the back door and saluted when he saw Safari approaching.

"Good morning, sir." The young man wore the broadest smile his face could support.

Well, English thought, *sir was easier on the ears than Deputy Commissioner* as Kelly was insistent on calling him.

"Good morning, Sammy." He thanked the man as he sat in the back of his new Landcruiser.

Sammy closed the door and raced around to get behind the wheel. He turned to face English. "Where to, sir?"

"I'm meeting with the police commissioner at their headquarters. Do you know where it is located?"

"Of course, sir. Sammy knows where everything is in Mombasa."

"Excellent. Then let us be off. I would hate to be late for my first official meeting as deputy commissioner."

"Hakuna matata, sir. Sammy will get you there in no time." The man spun around and drove to the gate, flashing his official badge to the guard. The guard idly lifted the steel drop bar, and Sammy launched into the flow of traffic. Safari had been a little leery of letting someone else drive him. He had always liked the feeling of control, but how this man expertly weaved in and out of the cars began to ease his concerns.

"Do you mind if I ask how old you are, Sammy?"

"Not at all, sir. I have just turned 20 years old, sir."

"Really? Where did you learn to drive so expertly?"

"Sammy has been a taxi driver here in Mombasa for four years and two years before that in Nairobi."

"Taxi driver for six years, eh? You started quite young."

"Yes, sir." The man smiled at English in the rearview mirror as he wove through the crowded street.

"Well, since you are such an adroit driver, I can catch up on some of my paperwork."

"Of course, sir. Have no fear. Sammy will get you there safe and on time." The man gave English another big smile in the mirror before directing his full attention back to the road.

Safari thought to himself, m*aybe this will not be so bad after all,* as he pulled some files from his briefcase. He managed to get into a good rhythm reviewing and signing paperwork. Before he knew it, they were pulling up to the guard shack at the police headquarters. The guard was obviously not informed about English's appointment and was trying to refuse them entrance, but Sammy wasn't having it.

The young chauffeur began a tirade in Swahili about how important Deputy Commissioner Safari was and how dare he refuse him entrance. The guard's eyes shifted several times from the list in his hands to English sitting patiently in the back seat. English nearly suggested he get out and walk up to the entrance but was curious to see if Sammy prevailed here. After another speech from the small driver, the guard nodded. He did a cursory bomb check under the car with his angled mirror and raised the steel drop bar.

English unbuckled and leaned forward as Sammy parked. He patted the driver on the shoulder, exclaiming, "We made excellent time, Sammy. Had I known it would have been so quick, I would have had another cup of tea." The man broadly smiled again at English's praise. "I did not think the policeman was going to let us through. Good job again."

"Thank you, sir. I have found most guards in Kenya will back down when you are adamant. Only powerful people are usually so bold, and guards almost always yield to powerful people."

"I do not think that bodes well for places needing guards, but at least we got in. Give me your mobile number so I can call you when I am finished here."

"No need, sir. I will wait with the car."

"Are you certain? It is quite hot today."

"Yes, sir, that is why I will park under that Mbambakofi tree over there," Sammy assured him as he pointed towards a shaded area. "I will be quite comfortable. Thank you for your concern, sir."

"Ok, then. I imagine this will take no more than an hour."

"Take as long as you need, sir. Sammy will be here."

When Safari reached for the door handle, Sammy sprang into action and raced around the car to open it for him.

"Appearances, sir, are everything," he whispered as he looked at the windows above them.

"Of course, Sammy, thank you again. I am unaccustomed to such things."

English's eyes flashed up to where Sammy had looked and saw someone quickly turning away from one of the top-floor windows. He put on his customary wide grin and pushed his glasses up. "Well, wish me luck."

"Good luck, sir. Remember, they know everything about you already, so carefully consider your responses to any questions."

English felt woefully unprepared for this meeting due to the demands imposed by the transition to leadership. This man could be his biggest ally or worst enemy in the fight against corruption, and he was going in blind. "Damn it!" Safari whispered angrily through his teeth to chastise himself. He could not make mistakes like this again. It was far too dangerous now to be less than perfect. If it had been possible, English would have postponed this meeting. Unfortunately, this last-minute appointment was the police commissioner's only availability for the foreseeable future, and they needed to meet. He chided himself once more, then hid it behind his grin and headed to the large double doors. The burly guards at the entryway had automatic weapons hanging nonchalantly from their shoulders and eyed him suspiciously as he approached.

"KRA Deputy Commissioner Safari to see *local* Police Commissioner Abasi Chongoi." English emphasized his title while minimizing Abasi's. Things would go easier for him if it were apparent to the guards he was more important than their boss. The man he had addressed looked him up and down once grimly before he walked over to the small booth to the left of the door. Picking up a clipboard, he scanned the top page before nodding to the other guard, who opened the door in response. The burly man moved slightly out of the way. English cocked his eyebrow slightly as he tilted his head at the man. The guard jerked his head in the direction of the door. Safari forced himself to walk at his usual pace to show the guard he was not intimidated. As he passed the man, he saw his lip curl up angrily in his peripheral vision, and the door nearly clipped Safari as it slammed shut the instant he crossed the threshold. He found the commissioner's office with minimal effort and knocked once before hearing a call to enter.

The police commissioner was standing near his office windows. He had a youthful appearance and a strong jawline. It was evident that he took his physical conditioning seriously. The commissioner took a long look at English as he methodically tucked his polished stick under his arm and removed the bright white gloves that were part of his impeccable uniform. English's father had always warned him it wasn't the man with the gun you need fear, but the man with the stick who ordered him who to shoot that was the real danger, and his father's warning sang in his ears now. The commissioner sat down behind the impressive desk and gestured to the tea cup in front of Safari. The police commissioner picked up the phone when English nodded.

"Yes, tea for myself and the Deputy Commissioner." He hung up the phone and smiled at Safari without speaking as they waited. English sat back comfortably in a chair and returned his best smile. It was considered a breach of etiquette for any discussions to occur prior to refreshments being served in any interagency meeting. Both men wordlessly adhered to the tradition. Their shared silence was soon interrupted by an elderly man, hunched over a tea tray, entering the room. As the server approached English, he noticed his left eye was missing, replaced only by a scar where the socket had been sewn shut many years ago. While the server arranged the tray on the table before English, his body obstructed the space between him and the police commissioner. English took the opportunity to look around the office. It was filled with Kenyan artifacts, all as highly polished as the commissioner's command baton, displayed in places of honor around the office. The rest of the bookshelves were stocked with large tomes of law codes and other appropriate reading materials for a police commissioner. Safari wondered, *were these books here before the new commissioner's appointment, or had he brought them with him? If he did bring them, are they for show? Maybe Chongoi is actually concerned about the law and Kenya's welfare.* The server's gruff voice cut off his thoughts.

"Black or white tea, sir?" The gravelly intonation attested to years of near-constant smoking.

"White, tafadhali." The elderly man chose one of the insulated pitchers from the tray and poured hot milk into a cup containing a tea bag. English politely waived off the proffered sugar and took the cup that was extended before him.

"Asante sana."

The server muttered "karibu" and nodded as he poured a cup of black tea for the police commissioner. After setting the pitcher down, he placed two biscuits neatly on each saucer. English grabbed the more precariously perched one and dunked it into his tea. As the grizzled man shuffled away, English used his half-eaten biscuit to point around the room.

"You have quite an impressive collection, Commissioner Chongoi."

The man paused as if he were carefully considering his response. "Do you refer to the books or the artifacts?"

"Both. Your shield is one of the most ornate I have ever seen." Abasi turned slightly to admire the piece. "And your books appear to be a plethoric law library."

The police commissioner smiled broadly. "You may be the only other government employee in the Mombasa region who appreciates the value inherent in books. I suppose that is the benefit of being *English* Safari, isn't it?"

English paused a moment, perplexed. "I'm not certain I get your meaning, Commissioner." He had a sinking feeling he knew what Abasi was implying but did not want to jump to any conclusions.

"I think you very much *get* my meaning. Your parents named you English because it would endear you to the Brits. It looks like it worked. According to my sources, you received a full-ride scholarship to the University of Oxford. If only all of our parents had such forethought. That's a nice perk for a bit of teasing, wouldn't you say?"

Safari suppressed a frown and worked to keep an even tone in his voice as he replied. "I do not believe they put much forethought into my name, Abasi. They just liked the sound of it. I worked extremely hard to get into Oxford. If I had not had that opportunity, I most likely would have attended the University of Nairobi and still might very well be sitting here across from you."

Abasi raised his hands noncommittally. "Possibly, but that would mean you believe the knowledge gained is more important than the location where it is learned."

"The knowledge gained is *the* important part of the college experience. The two advantages Oxford granted me are the experience of a different culture and a network of friends and colleagues. Still, neither of those has proven advantageous in my career path. They have greatly enriched my life outside of the office, however, and for that, I am deeply grateful. If that is due to my given name, then I am indebted to my parents for a lifelong blessing."

A grin appeared on Commissioner Chongoi's face, and English knew he had been had. The man raised the issue to see if Safari could be goaded into a response. "Indeed, we must all be appreciative of our parents for the opportunities they provide us. Just so you know, even though I did not attend Oxford, it does not mean I am neither well educated nor well informed."

English nodded his concurrence, and the two men began discussing the state of Kenya and the Mombasa region. Each tried to read the other's face, looking for signs in the subtle dance of determining if they would be friends or foes. English began to feel hopeful about the man sitting across the desk from him during this exchange. After an hour of discussions, a knock came at the door.

Abasi held up his hand to halt the conversation and barked out an order. "Come!"

A well-dressed officer entered the room. "Excuse me, Commissioner, the interrogation is about to begin."

Looking at his watch, he exhaled his discontent. "Indeed it is. My apologies, Deputy Commissioner Safari. Urgent police matters require my attention."

English stood up and extended his hand. When Abasi took it, Safari spoke. "I am certain we will have many opportunities to work together, Police

Commissioner Chongoi. I look forward to a long, fruitful partnership."

"I do as well. Until next time."

"Kwa heri, commissioner." Abasi nodded, and English headed for the door. Safari could have sworn he heard the officer holding it open let out a low growl as he passed.

English left Chongoi's office not nearly as frustrated with the results of this meeting as he was with his run-in with Tsumbe. Even though he had gained a slight sense of the police commissioner's values, English decided he would continue to be cautious until he observed the commissioner's actions. *Talk was cheap, as they say.* As Safari hurried down the stairs, he reviewed everything he learned in the meeting. He discovered Abasi was an extremely organized man who took his physical fitness and appearance seriously. That in itself was a far cry from the slovenly man he replaced. The entirety of Chongoi's office was placed with purpose and impeccably clean. Indeed, everything about the man himself, from his boots to the well-oiled stick he carried tucked under his arm, made a statement that this man was serious. But, serious about what? Was he a good cop who planned on making a profound, tangible impact? Or was he a wannabe dictator who, on his deathbed, everyone would decry what a tyrant he was but comment on how well his shoes were polished?

Chongoi's appearance of being an honorable man gave English a glimmer of hope. The police commissioner had spoken well of the need for cooperation between their two departments. English knew he would soon find out what type of cooperation

Abasi intended—actual law enforcement cooperation or the more nefarious kind he suspected Tsumbe desired.

Safari, engrossed in thought, reached the ground floor without realizing it. He would have to write notes of his meeting while his memory was fresh. Not knowing if he had just met a new friend or a future enemy, English planned on researching him thoroughly. He fixed a broad grin on his face as he passed officers on the way to the front door and thanked the guards on the way out before hurriedly waving for Sammy to bring the car around. He kept the smile plastered on his face until they drove a reasonable distance from the compound, where he let it fall with a slight huff.

Sammy took the sound as a cue to speak. "Back to headquarters, Deputy Commissioner?"

"Yes, Sammy, asante." English leaned back into the leather seat. He rested his elbow on the armrest and watched the traffic crawl by. After a moment, he closed his eyes and rubbed his temples, trying to release some of the tension this new position had laid upon him.

As the car inched along, the incessant honking of nearby traffic seemed to fade to a low din. Some part of English's mind noted how relaxed he was becoming, and he forced his eyes open. It would be all too easy to succumb to sleep, and he had far too much work to do. Safari pulled out his phone and was relieved to find no messages waiting for him when he switched it on. A blessing of having new phones was no one had their mobile numbers yet, but it also meant they couldn't get hold of one another either. He quickly dialed his office, where Kelly picked up before the first ring ended.

"Department of Taxation and Revenue, Southern Region, Deputy Commissioner Safari's office. How may I help you?"

English reflected momentarily on how much he liked the sound of his new title and how pleasant Kelly always sounded, no matter how difficult the day was.

"Yes, Kelly, it's English."

"Oh, hello, sir. How may I help you?"

"Has Elijah come in?"

"No, sir. I just received the list of the new mobile numbers but have not reached him successfully."

"You got the list? Excellent, let me have Elijah's number."

"Certainly. Are you ready, sir?"

"Just a minute."

Kelly waited while English retrieved a pen and paper out of his briefcase.

"OK, Kelly, go ahead."

Kelly rattled off the number, and English again made a mental note of how nice it is having a driver. Before today, he would have had to memorize the number or struggle to write while holding the steering wheel and weaving through the chaotic traffic.

"Great, asante, Kelly."

"You are quite welcome, Deputy Commissioner. Do you require anything else?"

"Were there any calls for me while I was out?"

"Yes, sir, you had several calls from people wishing you well and congratulations on your new promotion, and Thomas called from the port site office wanting to speak with you. None of the calls seemed urgent."

"Asante sana, Kelly. I will take care of those calls when I return to the office. Kwa heri."

"Kwa heri, sir."

As soon as they hung up, Safari was dialing Elijah's mobile. After several rings, the phone picked up, but it was merely a "this mailbox has not yet been set up" message. It was unlike Elijah not to answer. Over the years, English had to reprimand him multiple times for taking calls during meetings. Like most people in Mombasa, Elijah had no home phone; the infrastructure simply did not exist, and with the advent of cell phones, no one felt the need for a landline anymore. English frustratedly hung up.

Since joining Safari's team, Elijah had not missed a day of work. Something was not right. Elijah would not be absent during such a critical time. Before moving to Mombasa with English, Elijah had been heavily involved in one of the many street gangs that ruled Mathare, Nairobi's second-largest slum. When Elijah met his wife, Aailyah, he wanted to clean up his act, but it wasn't until he met English that he discovered a way to do so. English had seen that Elijah wished to put his past behind him, but getting out of one of these gangs was difficult. Still, English gave him a chance, and no one had bothered Elijah since moving south. Suddenly, English was fearful for his friend. There was nothing for it but to go to Elijah's house and check on him in person.

CHAPTER 3

"Sammy?"

"Yes, sir."

"Change of plans. Do you know where Mwabundu Road is?"

"Of course, sir. As I've said, Sammy knows where everything is in Mombasa."

"Excellent. I know it is in the other direction, but let us head there now. I need to find out what is going on with my second-in-command, Elijah. I am significantly disadvantaged without him at the office this week."

"No trouble, sir. Sammy will have you there as quickly as the traffic will allow."

After a tortuously slow commute, Sammy turned the car into a neighborhood of squat houses that were practically on top of one another. Many of the homes would classify as only slightly better than ramshackle, and some were little more than shanties. On the plus side, the neighborhood was within Mombasa's city limits and was safe enough for children to play in the streets. Elijah's home was located in the middle of his block and was distinguishable for being immaculately maintained. The paint looked freshly applied, and Aailyah had an impressive flower collection in their front garden.

As soon as the car came to a stop, the front door opened. Aailyah came out carrying her and Elijah's youngest son, with their older child trailing behind, practically attached to her right leg. Her bright smile was infectious, and English found himself broadly smiling back at her as he walked to the house's stoop.

"English, what a pleasant surprise, habari. What brings you around?" Then, her smile quickly turned to a look of concern. "Is Elijah all right?"

English stopped in his tracks. With that simple question, unwanted thoughts materialized. *Either Elijah had returned to his gang roots, or something had befallen him.*

"He is not here?"

"No, of course not," Aailyah replied. "He is on a special assignment for you." Bewilderment showed on her face as well as in her voice.

English paused. *Could that be correct?* He scoured his cognizance for any recollection that Elijah was going on a special assignment, but nothing came to his mind. Was he spread so thin he had wholly forgotten sending his second-in-command on a particular assignment? English knew he had been under a lot of pressure, but such an oversight was inconceivable.

"He is?" Safari asked. "My new position is pulling me in so many directions I am afraid I do not recall any mission."

Realizing English wasn't here to deliver bad news about her husband, Aailyah returned to her usual demeanor. "Elijah only told me he had a special assignment vital to national security, and he would not be able to contact me until it was over," she informed him. "Well, come inside and take a load off of your mind. Maybe if you sit a moment away from your work, it will come back to you."

English nodded. "Perhaps you are right. It would be good to clear my head. Asante sana." Following Aailyah into the house, he noted all the work she and Elijah had put into fixing up their home. "The house is coming along nicely. You and Elijah have done an amazing job in the short time you have lived here."

Aailyah smiled with pride. "Every moment Elijah is home, he is working on a new project around here. We hope to be *completely* finished with our renovations by the end of summer. We look forward to simply living in our home rather than laboring on it." She pointed to one of the chairs in the parlor. "Tafadhali, have a seat. Would you like a Tangawizi?"

English smiled. Everyone knew he liked nothing better than an ice-cold ginger beer on a hot day. "You remembered? I would love one, asante."

Aailyah let out a slight giggle. "Certainly, I remembered. You got Elijah addicted to those silly things. Would you mind…" she said as she proffered her younger son to English.

"Of course." English raised his arms to receive the squirming bundle.

When she returned, he traded the youngster for the drink she passed to him, condensation already covering the bottle's cold surface.

"Asante."

He took a deep draught of the refreshing elixir and let out a satisfied "ahh" as he lowered the drink.

Aailyah's easy laugh filled the air again. "You and Elijah are two peas in a pod."

English smiled widely. "With all the pressures of this new position, it certainly makes you appreciate the simple joys of life. I remember when Elijah and I shared our first Tangawizi after working so hard to capture that smuggler. It seems like such a long time ago, but I can still recall how crisp and thirst-quenching it was after inspecting those containers all day in the hot sun. Since then, each time I have one, I relive that victory if but for that one moment. Now that my life consists primarily of paperwork, I don't know if such sweet moments are lost to me forever."

"Nonsense! You and Elijah have built a good team together. Each time one of your officers stops a criminal, a piece of that victory belongs to you."

"Of course, you are right, but it never feels quite the same, does it? When someone compliments your lovely flower garden, do you think you would beam with the same pride had you hired a gardener instead of planting them yourself?"

Aailyah leaned her head to the side while cocking an eyebrow and pursing her lips. English knew this was the only sign acknowledging his logic that he would receive from the woman. Safari put his drink down and thanked her for her kindness.

"Resting and enjoying my favorite beverage certainly helped me get out of my head, asante. Unfortunately, I fear I am no closer to remembering what Elijah was working on."

"Have you tried his phone? You know he goes nowhere without it."

Safari nodded. "I have. I do not know if you were aware, but we switched to the new phones today. I only received Elijah's new number a short while ago. Unfortunately, his voicemail has not been set up yet."

"When Elijah left on Saturday," Aailyah said as she thought aloud, "he had his old phone on him. There is a cellphone-sized box on his desk. I can check if it is in there."

"He has not contacted you since Saturday?" English's mind raced. *What investigation could put Elijah out of contact for days?* Again, he came up blank.

"No, but as I said earlier, Elijah told me he would be unable to call until his work was complete."

"Well, that makes me feel a little better. First, Elijah did not show up for our meeting with the new police commissioner. Then, when he did not answer his phone, I feared his old life had caught up with him."

Aailyah laughed. "Elijah has been the straightest of arrows since you hired him."

English chuckled, "I think you had more to do with straightening him out than I did. I am just glad my fears were unfounded. Does Elijah keep any work files at the house? All of our documents were boxed up and are being shipped to our new offices. If he has some here, they might point me to where I can find him."

English found it increasingly difficult to believe he had forgotten Elijah was on an assignment of such importance as he expressed to Aailyah. Still, he didn't want to worry her if it wasn't warranted.

"He keeps some files in his office. You are welcome to look at them. Come with me."

English could detect no sign that Aailyah had picked up on his worry or was worried in her own right. He attributed that to her naturally positive attitude. Here was a woman whose thoughts would remain optimistic about any circumstances unless confronted with irrefutable facts. Even then, she would find a way to spin the situation into a positive. He could not remember any point in his life when he was not a realist or pragmatist. At least, that is what he considered himself. Others labelled him a pessimist, but he rarely found an occasion when something or someone proved his viewpoint wrong.

He trailed Aailyah down the hall to a small office and stepped past her as she gestured for him to enter.

"Call if you need me. I must put the little one down."

"Asante," he absently replied as he looked around. There wasn't much to the small space. An old wooden desk with a single pullout drawer accompanied by a simple chair was in the center of the room. A four-drawer metal filing cabinet occupied the far corner. The only wall adornments were the award they had received for "exceptional service," and a cork bulletin board displaying a map of Kenya held up with push pins. English pulled open the desk drawer and found several file folders neatly stacked inside. He tossed them onto the desk and sat down to peruse through them.

English opened the first file and found a handful of newspaper clippings. The top one was about the Vice President awarding the navy for its efforts to combat Somali pirates. He remembered this story when it came out. Instead of seizing entire ships, the pirates stole what they could from containers and were forced to flee before the navy could catch them. While the pirates were still able to get away with some goods, it was significantly less costly than the ransoms they had commanded for an entire ship. If he recalled correctly, the shippers whose containers were hit had only nominal losses. The world heaped praise on Kenya for its efforts to protect the Indian Ocean and the trade routes within it.

The following article was about the Vice President's inauguration speech. The speech was a typical political tripe in which he promised to stamp out corruption and improve the living conditions of all Kenyans. Elijah appeared to have been more interested in the photo than the article. He had circled two men sitting on the dais behind the Vice President. Safari did not recognize the white man but felt that the other man was familiar. English was fairly certain he had seen him at the Port of Mombasa in one of the administrative buildings.

There were a few other clippings in the file. They all seemed to deal with hunting rights on public lands. The government had been reducing certain tribes' traditional hunting grounds, which had caused great consternation among those tribes. There were no great outcries from the general public, only those affected by the mandates. Indeed, one of the clippings covered skirmishes between the Waliangulu tribe and some miners. English failed to connect these clippings and the first two stories beyond the government's involvement. He pushed the file away to make room for the next one.

It contained a dozen or so shipping manifests. English scanned the documents, but nothing remarkable stood out to him. They were all different types of goods. As far as he could tell, there wasn't anything impressive about the contents. Nothing high-dollar or likely contraband was listed. He noted household goods, wood crafts, and foodstuffs. None of these items would usually trigger an inspection.

English could see no connection between any of these containers. None of them were from the same shipper, nor were they headed to the same destination. The only link he noticed was they were all shipped around six months ago.

Elijah must have thought otherwise. English then found a sheet of yellow, lined paper listing each container number corresponding to manifests in the file. It was Elijah's handwriting, and Safari's number two always carried a yellow legal pad wherever he went. Whatever Elijah felt was suspicious about these seemingly innocuous cargo containers, English could not see upon first look.

In addition to the manifest data, the folder held two X-ray scan images of containers from Elijah's list. Even if Elijah had not circled the anomalies in red, English would have picked up that something was amiss. While X-ray scans can sometimes be challenging to read, common sense can lead to discoveries. Most of the X-rays seemed normal, with various household goods visible in the images. Peculiar to both scans, however, were dark square blocks near the container doors and on top. An item that could block the X-rays so thoroughly would have to be extremely dense and heavy. No shipper in their right mind would place such an object on top of other items. Here, two shippers did it in different cargo containers. English finally felt like he was on to Elijah's trail, but still, he could not see where the path was leading.

The third folder held another handwritten list of container numbers with corresponding bills of lading. The lack of manifests told English that the containers hadn't shipped yet or hadn't when Elijah last investigated them. The bills of lading typically showed up at the port a few days before the official manifests so the paperwork could be started. Sometimes, the official manifests never arrived. The containers could still be shipped as long as the shipper signed that the bill of lading was accurate. They weren't supposed to operate that way, but until the infrastructure improved, the government allowed this practice. If they tried to hold firm on the requirement for official manifests, commerce would likely be cut in half. No government would be willing to answer for that.

English found no relationship between these containers and the previous list, but he was confident Elijah had found one. The man was indefatigable when he had a hunch. "Like a dog with a bone" was how he was often described. Elijah's gut feelings were responsible for much of their combined success. His criminal past gave him great insight into the mind of the criminal element they were trying to inhibit in Kenya.

The seemingly innocuous nature of this investigation was giving English great pause. There seemed to be no reason this investigation would take Elijah away from his family for so long. English began to wish his friend had returned to the gang life that suddenly seemed to be the less dangerous possibility.

"Aailyah!" English called out as he gathered up the files.

"Yes, English?" The bubbly woman said as she popped her head in the doorway.

He held up the three files. "Would you mind if I took these files to the office? I want to make copies; then I can return them."

"Of course. I'm certain Elijah would not mind.

Did you figure out what he was working on?"

"I am afraid not. Elijah was always better at seeing connections than me. His talent was instinctual. I fear I will need to ponder on this for quite a while before grasping its meaning."

"I'm sure you will figure it out. Elijah always says he's never met a smarter man." She pushed on before English could protest, placing her hand gently on his arm. "Please have Elijah call me when you locate him. The children miss him, and I miss him, *dearly*."

"I will, Aailyah. You have my word. My second-best man is on the case now."

Aailyah smiled. She knew he meant that he would investigate. English always referred to Elijah as his best man. "Thank you. I will rest easier knowing that."

English wrote down his office and new cell numbers. "If you hear anything or need anything, do not hesitate to call me. Nimekuelewa?"

"Yes, asante."

"Kwa heri."

"Kwa heri."

English jogged out to the car. Sammy was wiping down the vehicle with a damp rag while drinking a Tangawizi. English smiled. Even with everything she had going on, Aailyah had made sure to bring a drink out to the driver. As English ducked into the door Sammy held open, he said, "I need to go to a copy shop to copy these documents and then bring them back."

The slightly puzzled look on his face did not dampen the driver's enthusiastic reply. "Of course, sir. Sammy knows such a place not far from here."

English knew his request would seem odd, but he also knew that not all of the corruption from the previous regime had been stamped out. That meant some business had best be done away from the office. It would not pay to have the wrong person look over his shoulder to save a few shillings making copies.

After returning the originals, English poured over the copies. He felt frustration building. He was certain Elijah had singled out these containers for a reason, but the manifests held no clues as to their connections. The same was true for the newspaper clippings. Beyond their government-related themes, they seemed unrelated. The only clue English could glean from any of it was he had seen the man Elijah circled in the photo at the port. He would have to find an excuse to snoop around. Maybe it was time the Deputy Commissioner of Customs Southern Region toured the port, *officially*. He could see if his "friend" Tsumbe would arrange it. He didn't want to get too entangled with the sycophantic man, but it might be the only way to proceed.

With at least a modicum of a path forward, he locked the documents in his briefcase. The straightforward approach would be to call the paper or the office of the Vice President to see who those men were, but that might alert someone. Until English knew where Elijah was, he dared not raise any suspicions. English remained preoccupied until Sammy parked the car and opened his door.

Still distracted, English climbed out of the car and headed to his office. Vaguely aware of greetings, he absently nodded in their general direction. English had a gut-wrenching feeling that Elijah was in serious trouble. Powerful government officials plus cargo shipping implied a corruption scandal at the highest levels. It explained why Elijah was investigating the issue personally instead of delegating it. It also explained his secrecy and the lack of his usual prolific notes. Unfortunately, it might also explain Elijah's sudden disappearance.

By the time English reached his office door, he had decided that he had better keep up with his everyday work until he found a connection between Elijah's clues. His current position may be his only hope of helping his friend.

Kelly stood up as he entered. When he saw all the messages in her hand, he waved her off.

"Jambo, Kelly. Please hold my calls."

"Of course, Deputy Commissioner."

The woman had always been good at reading his moods and sat down without further interactions. English sat at his desk and pulled out the papers from his inbox. He had to force himself to re-read the documents before him multiple times. His eyes kept sliding toward the locked briefcase on the other side of the room. *Forget this*, he said to himself. He knew he would never get any work done at this rate and pressed the intercom button. "Kelly, get Michael Tsumbe on the phone for me, tafadhali."

"Yes, Deputy Commissioner."

A moment later, the intercom button lit up. Kelly's pleasant voice sounded through the speaker as soon as he pressed it.

"Deputy Commissioner, Mr. Tsumbe is on line one for you."

"Asante, Kelly."

English took a deep breath to prepare himself and loaded the friendliest voice his throat could muster.

"Michael, my friend, habari gani? I think it's high time I officially toured the port. When can I pay you a visit …"

CHAPTER 4

The following day, at nine a.m., Sammy dropped English off at the Port of Mombasa's security office. Michael Tsumbe greeted him with a great grin and a firm handshake. He beckoned for English to follow him into the nerve center of his operation.

The big man was greatly feared (or respected). English could not determine the proper adjective for the reactions he was noticing. Employees nervously smiled and nodded as they backed against the wall to let them pass. Those further away hurriedly found side passages to duck down as he approached. Tsumbe paused dramatically before a set of double doors.

"Here is where I can see all that goes on at the Port of Mombasa."

He proudly opened both doors to the control room, watching English's face for the appropriate awestruck reaction. English was indeed impressed as the glow from dozens of monitors lit his face. The entire wall opposite the doors was packed with screens displaying sections of the port. Employees were stationed every few feet and appeared to be intently scrutinizing the security feeds for signs of malfeasance.

After a few moments of looking at various shipping port scenarios on the multitude of screens, Michael's focus shifted to one of the monitors at the far end of the room. English looked in that direction but saw nothing amiss before the hulking man rushed to the other side of the room with all the grace of a charging rhino.

"There," he said, pointing at the third monitor from the bottom. "Bring that up on the big monitor."

A large screen in the center of the display lit up with the image that had caught Tsumbe's attention. English saw two men standing near a cargo container. He suddenly realized one of the men had a pair of bolt cutters. The ne'er-do-well stepped out of the camera's view while his accomplice looked about nervously. Michael keyed the radio and ordered security to respond to the situation. English was impressed with the man's professionalism and efficiency as he provided the responders with pertinent details. After he had finished on the radio, Michael smiled at English.

"We are fortunate in our timing. While we have our share of criminal activity, it is usually very routine."

English smiled back. "It seems quite exciting. Your ability to pick out those two from so many video streams was remarkable."

Michael laughed. "Only remarkable if you have not done this for a long time. I saw the shiny red bolt cutters. If those two worked on the port, their tools would be dirty and greasy if not rusted. Now we get to enjoy the spectacle."

They watched the monitors as the security team closed in on the would-be thieves. After a short scuffle, the men were handcuffed and driven away. English's skeptical side wondered if the arrest was genuine or staged for his benefit. Keeping his suspicions to himself, he worked hard to ensure his face did not betray his thoughts.

Real or not, English was impressed, and he let Michael know it. "Excellent work, my friend. What will happen to those two men?"

"My team will process them, gather evidence like this video and their bolt cutters, and then deliver them to the Mombasa police. What happens afterwards is out of my control," the big man declared as he pantomimed washing his hands of the affair.

"Yes, we all have our parts to play."

English made a note to follow up with the police to see if these two were actually turned in. If they were, it leaned in Tsumbe's favor that he might be a legitimate partner in the fight against corruption. An arrest was not a foolproof guarantee of Michael's intentions; he could be willing to let some of his people rot in jail to win English's trust. It would just add a bit of weight to one side of the scale or the other. An added bonus would be using this opportunity to suss out the police commissioner's motivations.

The rest of the day was indeed uneventful. Michael towed him from one location to another, introducing him to all levels of port management. English was fairly certain he was being paraded around to demonstrate Tsumbe's connections with high-ranking officials. English didn't care how many hands he had to shake. He was here for one reason only. If English found the man pictured in the newspaper and Michael's career benefitted, he considered them even. If not, he would have to hope any goodwill generated here today would be repaid at some point in the future. With this in mind, he did his best to smile, glad-handed everyone he was introduced to, and talked up his "friend" as much as possible.

English began to lose hope that he would find the man he sought as the hours passed.

Michael asked, "Would you like to sit in on the operations meeting?" English was hard-pressed to show enthusiasm, but Michael plowed on. "It would provide an opportunity to understand how the port runs and meet the key players."

How many key players could be left? I have been put on display for half the port's workforce. But he felt obliged to continue until Michael ended their time together.

"Of course. I would be most interested in joining the meeting," English replied. "If I would not be intruding, that is."

"Hakuna matata, my friend. A guest of Michael Tsumbe is no intrusion."

Michael gestured English through the doorway he held ajar. The door opened into a large conference room half-full of people settling in for the meeting. The din of idle chatter intermingled with spoons clinking in mugs filled the air. English and Michael found seats as people continued filtering into the conference room.

Even when the room was filled to capacity, the meeting showed no signs of starting. English looked down at his watch, which showed five minutes past the hour. *Are they waiting for someone? Do they always run late?* he wondered impatiently. Safari prayed the operations meeting would soon get underway as he idly listened to Tsumbe's thoughts on the day's topics. English contributed the occasional "mmhmm" while he scanned the faces in the room. He returned smiles and nods to the people Michael had introduced him to earlier.

All eyes turned to the door near the head of the table as it opened. A man entered, his eyes buried in his phone as he furiously typed out a message. English had to suppress a gasp as he realized this was the man Elijah had circled. The gentleman took his seat at the head of the table, looking up from his phone only long enough to glance around the room and make sure he didn't miss his chair as he lowered himself.

English turned to ask who his mystery man was but found his host standing. When he looked up, Michael smiled down at him and raised his eyebrows provocatively.

"Everyone?" Tsumbe paused while the group settled and turned their attention to him. "I have brought a special guest today. This is my friend, English Safari, the new Deputy Commissioner of KRA's Southern Region." English nodded and slightly waved as the eyes in the room fixed on him. "I brought Deputy Commissioner Safari here today for him to better understand how we run things at the port. I would like him to say a few words if he does not mind."

English internally winced. He had ultimately hoped to find the man from the photo without bringing attention to himself. Having that hope dashed so bluntly by Michael was disappointing. Safari gathered himself, rose, and nodded to his host, who was now sitting. English mentally unfurled one of the canned speeches he had for such occasions.

"First, I would like to thank my host, Michael, for such an informative tour. I observed his operation today, and you are indeed lucky to have such an effective and inspiring leader as your head of security for the Port of Mombasa."

The big man's chest swelled with pride, letting English know he had sufficiently placated his ego. Afterwards, he was able to drop into the rote of his prepared talk, allowing him to observe the listeners, especially the one at the head of the table who rarely looked up from his phone. English hardly noticed the words rolling off his tongue; he had practiced it so often. "We would like to be a help, not a hindrance…spirit of cooperation…true partners for Kenya's future…again, I look forward to our working together. Thank you for your time."

Michael led the room in a round of applause, which seemed to be the only reason the man at the head of the table noticed English had stopped speaking. English nodded and smiled appreciatively all around as he sat.

As the meeting progressed, Michael whispered various facts or gossip about the speakers or the topics they raised. Safari feigned appropriate interest for each comment as he bid his time, waiting for an opportunity to ask about the man he came here to find. Finally, Tsumbe appeared to lose noteworthy tidbits to share, and English jumped at the chance.

"Michael, who is that man at the head of the table?"

The security director smiled and leaned in as if he was going to divulge a particularly juicy morsel.

"Ah, yes. That is Mr. Atieno Nnamani. He is the director of operations for the entire port. Nothing comes or goes into Kenya by boat without his approval. Several shipping companies have gone out of business on just a word from him." The beefy mitt silently simulated snapping his fingers to emphasize the director's power. "I will introduce you after the meeting if you wish."

"I would be most appreciative," English admitted.

The broad smile greeted him again. He was obviously a man who traded in favors and thought he was about to make a large deposit.

As managers droned on about various statistics and reports on the condition of cranes and reach stackers, English began devising how to play his upcoming meeting. *I should probably just meet him.* He would assume no nefarious motives and certainly not imply knowledge of any. English could gather information now that he knew Atieno Nnamani's name and position. English's suspicions about the port director's potential involvement in Elijah's disappearance were tenuous, at best.

Thinking about his friend got his anger flaring. Safari quickly worked to quell those feelings. He would bring undue attention to himself if he let his anger slip or showed the disgust he felt. English's face readily displayed his emotions. That was one of the main reasons his friend Alex loved playing cards with him. "An easier read than a comic strip," was how he phrased it. The lighter memories helped English plaster the smile back on, where it would stay until he returned to his car. It may make him look 'the fool,' but no one ever suspects 'the fool.'

The man sitting opposite English's target spoke after the last presenter.

"Excellent reports, everyone. Are there further comments?"

With that, every head in the room shifted from side to side, almost daring someone to raise their voice and extend the meeting further.

"Very well, with that…" The speaker paused until Nnamani looked up from his phone long enough to nod. "We will adjourn."

Everyone stood to leave, including English's quarry. The throng of people rushing out looked like it might prevent English from meeting Mr. Nnamani. Tsumbe, however, would not be denied his favor banking and used his great bulk to push through the meeting attendees. His meaty clutch pulled English along behind him. Just before the port director left the room entirely through his private entrance, the big man's voice boomed over the room's din.

"Mr. Nnamani. Do you have a moment?"

The director stopped mid-stride and stepped backwards into the room.

"What is it, Mr. Tsumbe?" The man's eyes were still fixed on the phone in his hand. *Nnamani must be reading a novel on the device,* English quipped to himself. He quickly pushed the glasses up his nose before the director took notice of him.

The hulking figure took a deep breath and stood up taller, if that was even possible. Tsumbe's open hand beckoned English forward.

"Mr. Atieno Nnamani, I would like to introduce my esteemed guest, Mr. English Safari, Deputy Commissioner of KRA's Southern Region. Mr. Safari, may I present Mr. Atieno Nnamani, Director of Operations for the Port of Mombasa."

English extended a hand that Nnamani looked at for a moment before shaking.

"Habari, Mr. Nnamani. It is a pleasure to meet you. Michael has been providing me with an overview of your port." Tsumbe defied belief by seeming to puff up even further. The port appears to be a model of efficiency under your leadership," complimented English. Neither man believed that to be true, but it was proper etiquette to say so, at least upon first meeting.

"Karibu sana, Mr. Safari, asante. You give a good speech about cooperation, Mr. Safari. I sincerely hope your ideas about collaboration do not involve causing slowdowns in the operations here at the port."

"We will try our best not to cause any disruption while ensuring the Revenue Authority's objectives are still being met," English assured.

The director studied English's face briefly before finally breaking the handshake.

"In that case, welcome to the Port of Mombasa, Mr. Safari. Please let me know if Mr. Tsumbe fails in any way as your host here."

The director shot a look at Michael, who suddenly appeared a little smaller than just an instant before.

English laughed. "I do not think that will be necessary. Mr. Tsumbe has been an excellent tour guide."

"Bora. Then, if there is nothing further, I have another meeting to attend…"

"No, of course. I am certain we will have many opportunities to work together in the future. It was a pleasure meeting you, Mr. Atieno Nnamani."

"You as well, kwa heri."

"Kwa heri."

The director nodded once at Michael, then quickly left the room via his private entrance.

English looked at his watch long enough to ensure Michael saw him checking the time. Now that he had identified Nnamani, he had no desire to remain at the port. Elijah's mysterious disappearance, not to mention his job, was demanding his presence.

"Unfortunately, I must be getting back to the office as well."

Michael's face was the definition of disappointment. He must have planned to show his trophy off to more colleagues. English doubted he enjoyed his company enough to warrant such an expression.

"No, surely you can spare a little while longer?" Michael pleaded.

"I fear I cannot. The office has been hectic since the reorganization. I dread the amount of work that has accumulated in the time I have been here," English answered truthfully.

"At least you can stay for a cup of tea?" Michael had his most hopeful look displayed.

English had figured some refreshment would be the minimum charge in order to make his exit. Given the late time, he was glad Tsumbe hadn't insisted on dinner. He felt quite relieved.

"Of course, my friend. I am Kenyan. There is always time for tea." Both men smiled broadly.

"Then let us drive to my office, and after our tea, I will release you back to your world of paperwork."

English laughed. "Right, you are. Ten minutes of that, and I am certain I will wish I had never left the port." He suddenly remembered Kelly had mentioned Thomas, who operated the port's X-ray scanner, needed to speak to him.

"Michael, KRA's X-ray scanner is between here and your office, is it not?"

"It is. Why do you ask?"

"I have just remembered one of my X-ray operators needed to speak with me. Might we stop there on the way?"

"Of course, it will give my people time to prepare the tea."

At the X-ray building, Safari hopped out of the car. Michael remained behind to make some calls. English was confident Michael was trying to arrange for as many attendees as possible to join them for tea.

When English entered the room, both X-ray operators jumped to their feet.

"Jambo, habari," English greeted the men. The big boss showing up unannounced had unnerved them. Recognizing their plight, English shook their hands to put them at ease.

"I am on the port being toured around by Michael Tsumbe," English paused when he noticed the two men shooting a quick look at each other. "He is outside as we speak, so I only have a moment. Thomas, Kelly mentioned you had called the office?"

Worry crept onto their faces before Thomas replied.

"Yes, Deputy Commissioner. Elijah had us collect some container X-ray data last week. He stated that if he didn't return on Monday, we were to deliver the X-rays straight to you."

"Was there anything on these scans?" English asked, concerned, looking at the operators over his glasses as he opened the proffered folder.

"Nothing much in these, sir, except there does seem to be a dense rectangular shape in each image."

Looking through the X-ray images, English saw the same strange dense block he had seen in the container scans Elijah had at his home.

The two operators were looking nervously at one another when English looked up.

"Is there something more?"

Thomas stammered so severely he hardly got the words out. "Yes, sir."

"Elijah, er, Mr. Botsole had another container scan. It appeared to have…" Thomas cleared his throat while staring pleadingly at the other operator to jump in and save him, but no such salvation was forthcoming.

"It appeared to have what, Thomas?" English asked curtly. He was sympathetic to Thomas not wanting to be the bearer of bad news, but Tsumbe was outside. The man could enter at any moment, shutting down this conversation.

Thomas swallowed hard and continued in a dry-mouthed whisper. "People, Deputy Commissioner."

Shock and confusion registered on English's face. "People? What do you mean, *people?*"

Thomas steadied himself and somewhat recovered his voice. "Just that, sir. We saw what appeared to be many people inside a container. Mr. Botsole took the image, but we both saw it." The other operator nodded in affirmation.

English's face still showed bewilderment, so Thomas continued.

"They were lying all about the container, sir, even on top of one another, it appeared. Who would ship people in a container?"

"Who, indeed?" English whispered as he looked at the file folder in his hand. "You said Elijah took the image?" Safari nearly cursed when they confirmed

"We did record the container number if that helps, Deputy Commissioner."

Safari perked up. "It most certainly will." Thomas copied the number onto a scrap of paper and handed it to English. Quickly looking at it, he tucked it into his shirt pocket just as Michael's head poked into the doorway.

English leaned in towards his men. "Let us keep this between ourselves," he whispered. Both men nodded in response. "Good work, men. As you can see, Mr. Tsumbe is waiting to take me to tea. We will continue this conversation at a later date."

"Yes, Deputy Commissioner," both men simultaneously replied.

"Sorry to keep you waiting, Michael."

"Hakuna matata, my friend. Was the issue serious? I heard you tell your men to keep it between you three."

English fought hard not to wince. "Nothing too serious," he lied. "The men feel they deserve a raise because they operate such a complex piece of machinery. Quite reasonable, I suppose, but I need to go through the budget before deciding. I want to ensure they do not tell anyone. Otherwise, stories about why everyone in my organization deserves a raise will inundate my office."

Michael chortled. "Good luck with that, my friend. Men like to brag as much as an animal likes to chitter. Once your other men hear about it, they will be like hyenas on the scent of a carcass. They will never give up until they get their fill."

"Too true," English agreed. "Surely, you have dealt with this issue before. What do you do? How do you handle the hyenas?"

Michael turned to face English as far as the steering wheel would allow his girth.

"I deal with the hyenas the same way a lion or a bull elephant would." Michael looked back at the road while he paused dramatically. "I put the fear of God in them." His booming laughter seemed overpowering in the small confines of the vehicle, but it had an infectious quality. "Just like hyenas, the men will slowly sneak back, but it buys some time before they require another scare."

"I will need to work on my roar," English joked.

Tsumbe's laughter once again filled the vehicle. English's mind slowly drifted back to the purpose of his visit and the contents of the file folder he now carried. *What had Elijah uncovered? Human smuggling? Terrorists? More importantly, where is he, and is he ok?* He had not long to ponder before Michael parked outside the security office. He led English to another large conference room holding twenty-five or so people, confirming his suspicions about who the big man had been calling.

The information gathered today was worth the price, English thought as he put his game face back on. A smile and enthusiastic greetings met all of Michael's "friends." He hoped this would be payment enough to close out Tsumbe's favor account.

CHAPTER 5

English heard Kelly answer the phone, and after a moment of pleasantries, she buzzed his office.

"Yes, Kelly?" It had taken English the better part of the week to finally figure out the complex, antiquated phone system. He had called security several times when he meant to speak with her. There was a time not long ago when ringing security would have been more commonplace than talking to your assistant, probably mid-revolution. *Repelling rioters might be more enjoyable than computing the latest tariff figures,* English thought sardonically. Kelly's voice disrupted his musings before he genuinely hoped rioters would stop him from working on the books.

"Deputy Commissioner, I have Mr. Alex Stoney on line one for you."

"Thank you, Kelly. Please put him through."

"Alex, my friend, your timing is perfect. I desperately needed a distraction from these numbers. I believe I am beginning to go a little cross-eyed." So thinking, English pulled off his glasses and rubbed his eyes.

Alex laughed for a moment. "Well, then, I'm glad I called. You know no one is better than me at distracting someone."

English could almost see Alex's devilish grin in his tone.

"I know too well how you excel in your chosen field," English replied as recollections of their mischievous adventures flooded his thoughts. "So often were my university assignments pushed back until the night before they were due."

"Too true, English, but I hope the memories were worth a few sleepless nights."

"More than worth it, my friend, but I seem to remember it being more than a few sleepless nights," English retorted.

Both men laughed heartily at the reminiscences.

"Fair enough," Alex acknowledged. "Are you up for another distraction? I'd like to take you to lunch to celebrate your first successful week as Deputy Commissioner."

"I would very much appreciate that. Where did you have in mind?"

Even before the words had left his mouth, English knew where Alex wanted to go, and the two men spoke in unison.

"Galaxy Chinese."

They shared another laugh.

"I've grown predictable, I see. We could go elsewhere if you'd like. Grab a pizza or a masala, maybe?" Alex offered.

"No, Galaxy is fine. The food is good, and I know how much you like it."

It was true. Galaxy was Alex's favorite restaurant.

He was such a loyal customer that Mr. Ping, the proprietor, would prepare Alex anything he wanted, whether or not it was on the menu. However, English was sure Galaxy's tight security was what endeared the restaurant to Alex's heart.

Alex's being white made him a target even though he was born in Kenya and darkly tanned. Whether it was beggars, merchants, or those with more nefarious motives, they all assumed he was a tourist and had money. Alex was constantly harangued by those desiring to ply money from him either by annoyance or violence. Years of being so plagued had forced him to carefully choose his preferred venues and the roads between them. He regularly changed the routes to prevent being ambushed because of close calls he had in the past. Alex escaped several makeshift roadblocks set up by gangs and corrupt police officers thanks to his souped-up Toyota Landcruiser with oversized bumpers. Although English had used his own four-wheel drive to escape such traps, it would be much less disastrous for him than for a mzungu.

English buzzed Kelly on the intercom. "Kelly, would you call down to have Sammy bring the car around?"

"Right away, Deputy Commissioner."

"Asante," he replied before hanging up.

The thought of crunching numbers while in the vehicle nearly caused English to lose his appetite. Unfortunately, his budget was due, so he gathered his department's papers to work on in the car. Safari opened his briefcase, and Elijah's files stared guiltily back at him. He had made little progress on the inquiry since identifying the port director as the man from the photo with the Vice President. The only other piece of the puzzle he discerned was some of Elijah's container X-rays were missing. Thomas had confirmed as much.

English initially attributed the missing images to the fact that typically only a fraction of containers are scanned, but now knew there was more to it. After checking the system, English found Elijah had input orders for the shipyard to transport all the containers on his list to the scanning area. A physical inspection would have been the next step if the X-rays confirmed his suspicions. Unfortunately, no records of these container scans or physical inspections seemed to exist. Either someone did not perform the assessments, or they wiped the evidence from the computer.

"What have you gotten yourself into, my friend," English whispered aloud. English sat back at his desk and thumbed through the files for a few minutes before he remembered he was to meet Alex for lunch. He shook his head to clear his obsessiveness, dumped all the paperwork into his briefcase, and headed for the stairs. Sammy was waiting by the car and opened the door when English approached.

"Asante, Sammy," English said as he slid across the leather seat.

"You are most welcome, Deputy Commissioner." Sammy's indefatigable grin seemed to fill the space as he closed the door. English smiled. *If only crunching numbers gave me as much joy.* After jogging around to the driver's seat, Sammy addressed him while looking in the rear-view mirror.

"Where to, sir?"

"Galaxy Chinese, Sammy. It's on the corner of..."

The enthusiastic driver interjected, "Sammy knows the Galaxy's location. Asante. He will have you there in no time."

"Excellent." Sammy grinned even wider at his boss's praise before launching into traffic. English sat back and began working on the revenue figures, but he seemed to make little progress before Sammy announced they had arrived.

English knocked twice on the Galaxy's steel door, and the restaurant's rectangular peephole slid open. A pair of eyes stared out at him.

"Yes? What do you want?"

"English Safari here to have lunch." The eyes belonged to Matumbe, the Galaxy's hulking guard, who looked down to check his list. English found this excruciatingly frustrating. He had eaten here dozens of times, but Matumbe always put him through this ritual. "Alex Stoney is expecting me," he added.

English heard the papers stop shuffling and the great bolts unlatching before the door swung open. Matumbe blocked the door with his bulk to ensure no one tried to tailgate English through. Not since speakeasies during prohibition had there been this much caution. No other restaurants in Mombasa had this type of security. On the other hand, the Galaxy had never been robbed, so who could question Mr. Ping's methods? Besides, Alex liked the safety these precautions offered.

English found his friend at his usual table with his back to a corner of the restaurant. Alex looked up from the paper he was reading and let a genuine smile flow onto his face when he saw Safari approaching. When English smiled back, Alex rushed over to embrace him.

"Good to see you, my friend. It's been too long."

"Indeed it has. I hope I have not kept you waiting."

By the depth Alex had read through the paper, English suspected the invitation to lunch had originated within the restaurant. He slyly wondered what Alex would have done had he suggested an alternate location.

"Any news?" English inclined his head towards the paper as they sat down.

"News…not that it's news, but it's bloody dangerous to be a mzungu in Kenya." Stoney slapped the paper down in front of English, pointing his drink at the headline.

"Tsavo National Park closed by Vice President," he read aloud. "How is this 'mzungu' related?"

"How is it…" Alex trailed off in disbelief. "Do you ever watch the news?" He continued before English could mount a defense centering on how busy he had been. "Lord Marcus Anson's been killed." When English's face still registered blank, Alex sighed, exasperated. He took a few deep breaths before continuing. "Lord Anson owns the tsavorite mines. His family donated the land for Tsavo National Park on the condition they keep the mineral rights. They are saying his murder was either connected to a workers' strike gone wrong or the Waliangulu tribe whose hunting rights were curtailed." English skimmed the article while Alex pondered the situation.

Alex leaned in as he lowered his voice. "Neither scenario makes sense to me. The Waliangulu tribe, they've no quarrel with Lord Anson. It was the government that shut down their hunting. And, workers' strike," Alex pshawed. "I've been to the tsavorite mines. Lord Anson's employees may not have loved him, but they were well paid. That usually buys at least some loyalty."

Safari smiled at his friend. "Now I see what has you

so worked up."

"What, you mean besides this horrid state of affairs?" Alex asked incredulously.

"Yes. You are worried those adoring employees of yours do not love you as much as you think they do," English taunted.

Alex playfully contorted his face into a mix of fake outrage and shock. Both men looked up at Matumbe, who had sidled up to their table to eavesdrop and was now chuckling at Alex's stammering denials. The mzungu addressed the eavesdropper in a faux-angry tone. "Don't you have a door to guard?" Matumbe raised his hands apologetically before moving back to the front of the restaurant.

Alex put the paper down on the table and dismissed it with a wave. "Enough of the news. I invited you here to see how you are and to congratulate you formally on the promotion."

Both men raised their drinks. "Thank you, my friend." After a deep draught of his beloved Tangawizi, English placed the ice-cold glass on the table and thoughtfully watched the condensation drip down its side.

"*Although*, I am no longer certain I should have taken the position," English admitted. He used his pointer finger to trace a pattern in the droplets on his glass while debating how much of the "Elijah situation" he should let his friend in on. *This is stacking up to be very dangerous.* Not only was ignorance bliss, but sometimes it was your only protection. Before Alex could pry any information from English, Mr. Ping came up to the table to greet his best customer.

"Mr. Alex, how are you?" Mr. Ping clasped Alex with a warm two-handed handshake while directing a nod towards English.

"Mr. Safari."

English nodded back.

"Ping, how are you?" Alex asked as he let go of the proprietor's hands.

"Business is very good," Ping happily replied in his heavy accent, indicating the full restaurant behind him with the back of his hand. "Thank you."

Alex raised his glass in a toast to the restaurateur. "To your continued success. I don't know what I'd do without you, Ping."

English chimed in under his breath, "probably starve." Alex gave his friend a wry look in response.

Ping smiled. "Thank you, Mr. Alex. If you have a moment, Mr. Wu would like to say hello and show you how the duck is progressing."

Alex looked to English to silently ask if he minded. English raised his hands nonchalantly to indicate it was okay. Alex got up, put his arm around Ping's shoulders, and walked toward the kitchen. Safari watched them until they disappeared, then looked around the restaurant for something to entertain his thoughts. *Ping was right.* Business appeared to be good; nearly every table was full. Most of the crowd looked to be on business lunch, clad in suits. One table seemed more like a date as the man shamelessly doted on his female companion. On the opposite side of the restaurant, Matumbe stood stoically, arms crossed, fixating on the steel door. *What is he staring at,* English wondered. He could not discern anything from this distance and quickly lost interest.

English was rapidly becoming bored as he tried not to gawk too long at any one table. He desperately wanted to go through Elijah's files again, but he dared not in so public a space. Instead, he turned to the only available source of distraction, Alex's newspaper.

The story Alex had been ranting about was indeed unsettling. By closing Tsavo Park, the government must suspect those responsible for the murder were still a danger to the public. At least English *hoped* that was their motive. A darker thought leapt to his mind. *They might not want witnesses. Maybe that is why they closed the park.* If Lord Marcus Anson was the Vice President's long-time friend and supporter, as the article suggested, he might have ordered troops to the park to quell the suspects.

English reflected on the last time he had been to Tsavo Park. Some friends from university had been visiting Kenya and wanted to see the big five African animals. While Kenya had other wildlife parks, Tsavo was the most convenient place for English to provide that experience.

Alex and Mr. Ping emerged from the kitchen laughing loudly. English looked up from the article when he heard them. He casually flipped the newspaper over, placing it back on the table. Alex bid goodbye to Mr. Ping and rejoined English, who nodded perfunctorily to the owner. Looking down, Safari noticed the article had an accompanying picture and nearly jumped out of his skin. It was the white man Elijah had circled in the photograph. English grabbed the paper and stared at the man whose identity had eluded him these past days. When Alex began to speak, English held up his hand, "Give me a moment."

Safari cautiously looked around the restaurant to ensure no one was paying any attention in their direction. He retrieved his briefcase and pulled the newspaper article from Elijah's files. English glanced around again, causing Alex to look about nervously. Alex had never seen his friend act so paranoid. Confident he was not the subject of undue notice, English laid the photographs side-by-side. He was now positive. "It is him…" English whispered. Alex looked at both photos upside down before leaning in and whispering back to Safari.

"What's going on, mate?"

English paused a moment while looking at his schoolmate's face. Alex's quizzical look implored English to explain why he was acting so strangely. English half-smiled at his friend. He trusted no one above Alex Stoney. He was also the closest thing to family he had left and wanted no harm to come to him. Safari also knew Alex would never let this go until he found out what was behind the secrecy. If English had the ability to lie convincingly to his friend, he would do so to keep him from getting involved, but Alex could always read him too well. *I guess the cat is out of the bag,* he thought defeatedly.

English leaned in further and whispered, "You must first understand no one knows what I am about to share with you." Alex nodded gravely. English's tone was serious. "Elijah has been missing for more than a week."

"What?" Alex hissed.

English anxiously looked around, but whatever interest Alex's outburst drew quickly dissipated.

"Keep it down."

Alex covered his mouth, aghast, as he assessed the room. "Sorry," he whispered. "What do you mean Elijah's missing?"

"Just that," English replied. "Friday night, one week ago, Elijah told Aailyah he was conducting a special assignment for me."

"And?"

"And, I had given no such assignment."

"Have you tried calling his cell?" Alex asked.

English shot a look of utter disbelief at his friend.

Alex gestured apologetically. "Of course, sorry, stupid question. Just trying to process what you're telling me here."

"We were all issued new cellphones in my department. Elijah's cell, like my own, has been replaced. They were activated over the weekend Elijah disappeared. Unfortunately, I found his new phone in his home office."

"I hate even to bring this up, but…" English inclined his head and twitched his fingers to tell Alex to continue. "Is it possible that given his past…" Alex hemmed and hawed for a second before gingerly continuing. "Perhaps our friend has abandoned the straight and narrow path you placed him on and returned to a, shall we say, more familiar and potentially lucrative road?"

"My first thought as well," English admitted, "but after investigating further, I began to wish it was that simple. When Elijah did not show up for work, I went to his house and found he had not been home all weekend. I was perplexed when Aailyah mentioned Elijah was on an assignment for me."

"Ooh, how's she doing?"

"Concerned, but you know Aailyah, always looking on the bright side."

"That's true."

"I led her to believe all the chaos resulting from the reorganization caused me to forget about the assignment. I asked to peruse Elijah's files to jog my memory. Aailyah agreed, but my fear grew when her cheerful facade showed signs that she was worried."

"Yes," Alex agreed, "for her to show anything, it must be truly troubling her." English nodded, then looked around quickly before continuing.

"Flipping through the files in Elijah's desk led me to believe he was investigating something nefarious and dangerous. This newspaper clipping was in there as well." English pointed to the paper he had been comparing with Alex's mzungu story.

"What have we got here?" Alex examined the picture and the circled figures. "Our illustrious Vice President," he practically snorted in derision. "Lord Marcus Anson, or, should I say, the late Lord Marcus Anson. And, is that the Director of Operations for the port?" English nodded his affirmation while silently kicking himself for not showing Alex the photo immediately. Of course, he would know all the important people.

Alex tapped the image of the port director. "I only met him once. He feels as if he's too important to deal with the likes of me. All construction matters go through one of his underlings."

English agreed, "Yes, I just met him myself and got a similar feeling about how he viewed me."

"Did you ask him what he did to Elijah?"

English smiled. Alex might be only half-jesting. He was bold enough to ask the director such a question. If complicit in Elijah's disappearance, the director would simply deny involvement. If not, it would alienate the man forever. Worse still, it would alert the director to the investigation and put a massive target on his own back.

"Of course, you didn't. Always the subtle one, eh

English? Probably the right move with this level of players. Anything else in his files?"

"Yes. Elijah had several shipping manifests and corresponding container X-rays for most of them. There was also an article about the Navy receiving accommodation for minimizing losses to Somali pirates. I do not know if Elijah felt the pirate article was connected to this investigation or if he had slipped it into the folder to save it for later. There were no notes detailing Elijah's thoughts. That is not like him. Either he had his notes on him when he disappeared or was extremely concerned his notes would endanger anyone who read them…" English paused and looked intently at his friend. "That is why I have told no one until this moment. You must keep this quiet, Alex." When he started to protest, English silenced him by pointing and staring intently at his friend until he saw acceptance.

"So, Deputy Commissioner, what did you learn from the manifest and X-rays?"

"Actually, I have been quite stuck in my investigation. Whenever something smelled fishy like this, but I could not put my finger on what was wrong, I would have Elijah give me his opinion. Since you are aware of the situation now, would you mind taking a look? I need a second pair of eyes that I can trust to review the evidence."

"Of course," Alex agreed. "I'll do all I can to help. Elijah's a good man. Consider it done. What have you gleaned from your review?"

"Let me hold back my thoughts until after you have had a chance to go over the evidence. An unbiased analysis would be best."

"Ah, right. Well, let's have them then." English

discreetly transferred Elijah's case files from his briefcase into Alex's well-worn leather messenger bag.

"Great. Call me when you have had a chance to look them over, and we will meet to discuss your thoughts. Asante, brother. After being frustrated for a week, it feels good to have made some progress again." English rose to leave, but Alex grabbed his arm to stop him.

"Where are you going?" Alex asked.

"Back to my office."

"Don't you think that will look a bit odd? I ordered a special meal for the pair of us. If we leave before it's even served, won't that arouse unwanted suspicions? I trust Ping and even Matumbe, but who knows who these other people are in the restaurant? A few shillings is all it takes for people to remember seeing something."

Safari sat back in his chair.

"Of course. In my excitement, I had forgotten why we were here."

Just then, Mr. Ping approached the table; one of his waiters followed behind, carrying a perfectly browned Peking duck. Both diners faked appropriate enthusiasm. The server stood at the ready to carve the duck as they ate, so they talked about more mundane topics. Once they had their fill, the friends bid their goodbyes with a promise to speak soon. English departed while Alex stayed behind to pay and have his regular post-meal chat with Mr. Ping.

CHAPTER 6

English was so consumed by the new development in Elijah's case that he had forgotten to call Sammy before exiting the restaurant. Squinting his eyes against the sunlight did little; he had not realized how dark the restaurant had been until stepping into the midday sun. He used his hand to shade his eyes as he scanned for his car and found it parked under a nearby tree in short order. English was impressed by how Sammy always managed to find a shady place to park, no matter how rare a local tree might be at their given destination.

Safari hurried over to the car but discovered Sammy missing. Although he had no expectation for his driver to always remain with the vehicle, he admittedly found his absence frustrating. As English reluctantly pulled his cell phone out to call Sammy, he spotted the small driver talking to a man across the street.

English hopped over the small pile of refuse collected in the gutter. He then deftly wove his way through the throngs of traffic commonplace in all areas of Mombasa city proper. Sammy caught sight of

English approaching and began stammering out an apology.

"I'm sorry, Deputy Commissioner. I must not have heard your call."

English laughed. "Hakuna matata, Sammy. There was no call. I was about to do so when I noticed you across the way and decided to collect you in person."

The driver pulled out his phone to verify. Sammy visibly relaxed after checking his call log. English found it amusing that Sammy had felt the need to confirm his boss had not rung him.

English raised his chin in greeting to the man who had been talking to Sammy. English thought it best to minimize the interaction unless Sammy introduced them. How the two men had been speaking indicated some familiarity, and English respected his employees' privacy. The stranger had other thoughts as he returned English's greeting with a nod and a laugh.

"Same old Sammy," his acquaintance admonished. "He never wants to make a mistake; that's what made him the best driver." As English extended a handshake, the man stopped him by interjecting, "So…you are the one who stole my Sammy." The accusatory man made a show of looking Safari up and down.

English looked quizzically at Sammy. The driver had only just recovered from his last embarrassment before slipping into this new one. Sammy shot the man a look that might be seen from a parent to a child, warning them to be on their best behavior. The target of Sammy's glare was cowed into civility and raised his hands in acquiescence.

Sammy introduced the two men.

"Deputy Commissioner English Safari, may I

introduce Mr. Apollo Butundu, my *former* employer.

The two men shook hands.

"Habari." English nodded definitively and released his grip, but Apollo held firm.

"I have been most curious to meet the man who poached my best driver. He speaks very highly of you." Sammy blushed at both the compliment and the revelation that he spoke to his former boss about the deputy commissioner. "Not only was he the best taxi driver in Mombasa but also the best Safari guide in the business. One of the main reasons I'm successful is the praise lauded on my company by tourist groups who Sammy had guided. It is only a matter of time before those reviews start to tarnish."

When Apollo released his grip, English responded. "I can only imagine how devastating it is to lose such a valuable employee. He never mentioned the safari guide aspect of his previous employment, only his taxi driving. It seems he gave up one form of safari-driving to drive a Safari around. A bit convoluted, but serendipitous for me."

Apollo smiled at English's hint of humour. "Serendipitous indeed. Unless I manage to steal him back, and *you* are the one relegated to a lesser driver."

English looked over at Sammy. "I would like to believe I would support Sammy if he felt another job provided him a better opportunity."

"Ah, well played, *Commissioner* Safari. Make it appear that I am the callous employer with no concern for our Sammy, but he knows the truth. Now…"

Before Apollo could continue, Sammy interrupted. "Mr. Butundu, you have given Deputy Commissioner Safari enough grief. As I told you, I would consider performing weekend guides when Tsavo Park reopens and will train some of your other drivers so your business does not suffer. I believe that is more than fair." Apollo nodded, looking slightly ashamed. "Now, if you don't mind, I am certain the deputy commissioner has important business to attend to."

"Of course, forgive me," Apollo said as he bowed slightly. English wasn't sure, but the man seemed sincere. It struck English that this Apollo greatly cared what Sammy thought about him. "As you said, losing such a valuable employee is greatly upsetting. Have a good day, Mr. Safari."

"And you as well, Mr. Butundu." English walked a small distance away to give Sammy a moment to say his farewells. Sammy nodded to English when he rejoined him, and the two made their way back to the car.

Before Sammy merged into traffic, he turned to face English in the back seat. "Sorry about Mr. Butundu, Deputy Commissioner. He tends to be a bit possessive when it comes to me. I came to work for him as a young teenager. Apollo and his wife were very kind to me and treated me like a son. After many years, I felt the need to leave the nest. Regrettably, he took it more personally than I had anticipated."

"Hakuna matata, Sammy. I understand Mr. Butundu better than you know. Have you heard that Mr. Elijah Botsole has been missing from work?"

"Yes, sir. I overheard his name from you and Miss Kelly, and I know from the day of your meeting with the police commissioner that his absence was unexpected."

"To say the least. Elijah has long been my number-one employee and one of my best friends. Although it is not the same situation as yours, his disappearing act has been extremely disruptive to me and more than a little worrying, truth be told. All this, and it has been barely over a week. I would find it devastating if I thought his absence permanent."

Sammy eased the vehicle into the sea of cars before addressing English again. "Since my first day driving you, I've been curious about what happened to Mr. Elijah. May I inquire as to where he was?"

Safari half-smiled to himself. English felt naïve for believing Sammy would be oblivious to what was happening behind him as he focused on the road. He was pretty confident Sammy was trustworthy, but he still made a mental note to be careful of what he said on the phone while in the car. Sammy divulging information outside English's inner circle, albeit unintentionally, could be dangerous.

"Unfortunately, Sammy, I still do not know where my friend is. You remember Mrs. Aailyah Botsole?" Sammy nodded. "She is Elijah's wife and was under the impression he was on a special mission for me. Yet, I had given him no such assignment. At first, I believed it plausible he was on an active investigation and was unable to contact us because of the phone switch. As time has stretched on, I fear something more nefarious has transpired to my friend."

Sammy paused a moment. "I am sorry to hear that, sir. Everyone speaks very highly of Mr. Botsole. I hope he turns up soon."

"Asante, so do I." With that, English turned to look discontentedly out the window. As he idly watched the crowds of people wending their way between the makeshift shops and the traffic, he found himself hoping against hope he would see his friend amongst them. The ring of his cell phone woke English from his reverie. The caller ID showed his office number.

"Habari, Kelly."

"Habari, Deputy Commissioner. I just wanted to remind you that the delegation from the U.S. will be here at two o'clock to discuss the status of the radiation detection system installation at the port."

English glanced at his watch—*less than twenty-five minutes*. He allowed himself a small sigh. Even though his people would eventually run the system, he had *very* little to do with the project until the construction was complete. This was just a courtesy visit, which would generally be a pleasant distraction. It felt more like a burden, taking up crucial time English could spend investigating Elijah's disappearance.

"You know me too well, Kelly. It had indeed slipped my mind. Would you have the staff prepare tea and snacks for our guests? I will be there shortly."

"Of course, Deputy Commissioner. Will you require anything else?"

"No, asante. Kwa heri, Kelly."

"Kwa heri, Deputy Commissioner."

English hung up the phone and checked outside the window for familiar landmarks.

"Well, Sammy, I am in need of your magic again. We have about twenty minutes until my meeting with the delegates from America back at the office."

Sammy smiled at him in the mirror.

"Hakuna matata, sir. Sammy will have you there before you know it." The car accelerated and began weaving expertly through impossibly small gaps in the traffic. Safari had seen enough of the man's driving to know if there was a way to make it back in time, he would find it. With his arrival time out of his hands, English sat back and contemplated the possibility that

Elijah had uncovered a criminal conspiracy of the highest levels. What that could mean for his friend's fate did not bode well.

Before English knew it, Sammy parked the car behind KRA headquarters. He checked his watch— *seventeen minutes.* English chuckled. "You have once again saved me, Sammy." He slapped the grinning driver on the shoulder in a friendly manner as he got out of the car. He rushed to the building, took the stairs two at a time, and hurried down the hall to his office.

Kelly was on the phone, so her only available method to chastise him was to roll her eyes in disbelief, which she did effectively. English mouthed "sorry" as he passed her.

Kelly continued her conversation. "Yes, asante, the delegation has permission to enter. Have our guests wait up front, and I will send someone down to escort them. Asante, kwa heri."

Before English closed the door, his intercom was already buzzing. He backed out of the room and looked over at his assistant.

"Cutting it quite close, aren't we, Deputy Commissioner?" Kelly teasingly rebuked him.

"I know, I know. Would it help if I told you my meeting was *extremely* important?"

"Your lunch with Mr. Alex? Is that the *meeting* you are referring to?" Kelly pursed her lips in disbelief.

Safari cursed his misfortune. Of course, Kelly had surmised he was lunching with his friend. Although it started as an ordinary lunch, it became a consequential event and he could not explain that to her at this time. He did not want to risk her safety by bringing her in on Elijah's disappearance.

"Will you just believe me when I say it *was* imperative and leave it at that?"

Kelly continued looking doubtful at English but "mm-hmmed" her agreement in such a way that she implied "for now."

"Asante sana. Please show the Americans in when they get up here. We need not bother with the whole intercom business."

Kelly gave a wide-eyed look of disapproval. She added another "mm-hmm," indicating she would, even though it was under protest for not following protocol.

Safari looked up from his desk with a smile when he heard the song "Jambo Bwana" being sung down the hall. John Collette simply loved that song. English could not recall a visit from John where he was not singing that touristy tune. Safari was humming along when Kelly opened the door to his office and led the Americans through.

John entered first. He was a smallish man with dark brown hair wearing black wire-frame glasses. While on the thin side, it was evident John was not a physically active fellow. He was one of the funniest men English had ever met, who also happened to tell some of the dirtiest jokes English could imagine. It was impossible for Safari to reconcile this man with the picture Alex painted as the 'brutal overlord' who would destroy people in meetings.

Following behind John were two men English knew well. First was Eric, a big man who looked like he was of German descent. Like John, Eric also had a great sense of humor. While John was the project lead, Eric acted as the team's technical expert. Whenever a question arose regarding nuclear, civil, or computer engineering, they looked to Eric. As far as English could tell, he always had the answer. After Eric followed Phil, a man roughly the same size as John. Phil had such a generic look that English pictured police sketch artists starting with Phil's face and modifying it to match witness descriptions. He, too, was a jokester. Safari suspected having a sense of humor was a requirement to be on John's team. A big, Scandinavian-looking fellow with pale blond hair brought up the rear. English had never met this newcomer, who seemed to have a greenish complexion and was sweating profusely.

John excitedly shook Safari's hand. "Jambo, English. How are you, my friend?" The man's enthusiasm was contagious, and Safari found himself grinning wildly back at him.

"Jambo, John. I am well. And yourself?"

"Good, good. A bit jet-lagged, but what can you expect? You remember Eric and Phil?"

"Of course, habari?" English shook both men's hands.

"And the new guy here is Spencer. He's a project manager here to discuss some contract stuff."

"Hello." The big man weakly raised a hand in a wave.

"Hello." English waved back.

John spoke up again. "Spencer's not feeling too well. May he avail himself of your facilities?"

"Oh, of course." English squeezed past Spencer to address the guard who had escorted the delegation to his office.

"Michael, would you escort Mr. Spencer here to the water closet? He's feeling under the weather."

"Of course, sir." The guard turned to address Spencer. "Please, sir, follow me." Spencer nodded in thanks and lumbered out of the room to follow his savior down the hall. English moved behind his desk and indicated the chairs across from him.

"Please have a seat." English looked towards his doorway. "I hope your friend is all right. He was positively green."

Phil and Eric side-eyed one another. English was sure something was going on but didn't have to wait long before John practically snorted.

"Hah, *friend*," he sneered. "It couldn't happen to a nicer guy, let me tell you." The other two men were nodding their agreement. English's face was one of confusion, so John elaborated. "The guy's incompetent. He's related to some muckety-muck, so they dropped him on me. The guy's a complete ass. He knows no one can do anything to him, so he's abusive and takes advantage of everyone. It's good to see him get some comeuppance for once."

That was the harshest English had ever heard John speak. Maybe he *could* turn on the 'brutal overlord' mode when he desired, as Alex claimed. English chuckled.

"I am sorry, my friend. A discordant team member can make any job unpleasant. I have had my share over the years."

"I bet. Get this; the man doesn't even like Tangawizi."

English feigned a seriously offended face followed by a wicked grin. "The sacrilege. Maybe we can find him some warthog anus or some bush meat. That seems to turn even the strongest westerner's stomach; I cannot imagine how it might affect someone in Mr. Spencer's condition." All four shared a laugh. "Shall we have some tea while we wait?" When the men nodded, English activated the intercom. "Kelly, would you have the tea brought up?

"Yes, Deputy Commissioner."

John perked up. "That's right. I forgot to congratulate you on your promotion. Congratulations, my friend, you truly deserve it."

"Asante sana. I can hardly believe when you first came here, I was a field agent and have been promoted twice since we first met," English mused.

John smiled. "Either your career is going great, or our project is taking *way* too long."

English laughed. "Perhaps a bit of both." The tea arrived at the door.

"A bit of both, indeed. This project's been both a boon and a bust for me. Every delay hurts my career, but when it's finished, I won't be able to visit your beautiful country, pester you, drink your tea, and eat all your biscuits." So saying, John snaked his hand out to grab a biscuit as the tea cart passed him on its way to the corner of the room. Everyone laughed as John raised his eyebrows devilishly and popped the biscuit in his mouth.

"You are never a pest, my friend. Rather, you are a welcome respite from the tedium that comes with my promotion." English dejectedly indicated the stack in his inbox. "The paperwork is…endless."

"Well, if no other common ground existed between our countries or our positions, we can at least commiserate over the joys inherent in bureaucracies." All four men nodded and laughed. Just then, Spencer shuffled into the room, looking ashen and wholly drained, sending the men further into fits of laughter. They had no qualms about making fun of each other when something eaten disagreed with one of them.

Spencer did not look like he was taking it well, but English did not trust a man who disliked Tangawizi, so he had no problem joining their good-natured ribbing at his expense.

The men idly chatted while enjoying the tea and biscuits. All but Spencer, that is. He sat leaning against a wall, sweating through his shirt, all his concentration being applied to keeping control of his bowels. English felt sorry for him no matter what John said about the man. Many people, including locals, have fallen victim to the unhygienic conditions created by the poor infrastructure and scarcity of clean water. One of English's hopes is that if his department stamps out some of the corruption, more revenue will be available to improve everyone's living conditions in Kenya. Still, the big man's pitiful response to a bout of the runs was a bit humorous.

English turned his attention back to John. "You were saying the project was experiencing some delays?" Alex had told him the same thing at lunch but hadn't expounded on the details.

"Yeah, it's the damnedest thing. Either I'm the unluckiest person in the world, or someone's sabotaging the site."

"Oh? Why would you suspect that?"

"Well, at the beginning of the project, someone was stealing equipment from the job sites. There was always a power outage during the thefts, so port security saw nothing and had no video evidence. Either these burglars were causing the power outages or were extremely fortuitous in their timing. After many back and forths, we agreed to pay for security guards. The thefts stopped, but then accidents started occurring. Since then, two trucks and a crane have crashed into our equipment. It's costing us hundreds of thousands in equipment costs plus about the same in labor to re-do the work." John could see English was puzzled about his last statement, so he went into an explanation. "For some reason, our contracting department uses cost-plus contracts instead of fixed-price contracts." John shook his head in disbelief at his own words. "No matter how much the project costs, we pay it plus a fee. It's easier for our procurement people up front, but it places all of the risk on us. I can't stand our process, but it is what it is. As it sits, I can only see two parties who might benefit from these delays. That's our U.S. contractor or the local firm, Constructicon."

English leaned his elbows on the desk and clasped his fingers. Using his thumbs to support his chin, he momentarily pondered John's implications.

"I see your concern. My father used to tell me growing up, 'Never attribute to malice what may just as easily be explained by incompetence.' I wonder if that applies here. Unfortunately, many people are hired in Kenya solely because of nepotism, especially for high-paying jobs such as those provided by the port. I believe this is the chief reason our port has so many accidents. Did you know there are several deaths at the port each week attributed to workplace accidents?" English found it hard to fathom even as he stated the statistic aloud.

"Oh, my lord," John gasped. "That is unbelievable. How does the government allow the port to stay open?"

"Money," English stated flatly. "Is that not always the case? The port is the country's number one source of income by ten times its closest competitor. I do not know your U.S. contractor, but I have known the owner of Constructicon for many years, and I would vouch for his character. His company's reputation is everything to him. Besides, he was complaining to me recently about all the troubles on this project. I doubt it would be so upsetting if it were his doing."

"I suppose that's true. You say you've known Mr. Stoney a long time?"

"Indeed, Alex Stoney and I went to university in England," English confirmed. "Both being from Kenya, the university thought placing us together in the dormitory was a good idea." Safari chuckled as he recalled that first day. "They could not know what different worlds the two of us came from. I was on a full scholarship. Alex was from one of the wealthiest families in Kenya." English smiled and lowered his voice. "Even so, I suspect Alex's parents had to grease a few palms to get him admitted." The men laughed.

John interjected, "I can see that. He struck me as a man who liked to party in his younger days."

Safari chuckled again, remembering back to some unshared memory. "Indeed he was. Against all odds, we became fast friends. He imparted some bad habits on me, and I some good upon him. Although, to be fair, he would argue those roles were reversed. Still, after all these years, I trust no one above Alex. I am certain he is not intentionally damaging the equipment to extort additional funds from you."

"That's good to know. It's not like I could do much about it if he were. I would have a hard time proving sabotage, not to mention recouping any losses, in the U.S., let alone here in Kenya. Isn't that right, Spencer?"

The queasy man nodded weakly in agreement, but

even that effort sent him over the edge, and he stumbled from the room again toward the water closet.

John watched him go, then shook his head slowly in disgust. "For a big guy, you'd think he could man up a bit." He shook his head again as Eric and Phil chuckled at their coworker's predicament.

Because Spencer had left the door open, Safari heard the phone ring in his antechamber and Kelly's voice when she picked it up. "Kenya Revenue Authority, Southern Region, Deputy Commissioner Safari's office. How may I help you?" Kelly paused as she listened to the caller. "No, I am sorry; the deputy commissioner is in a meeting. May I take a message?" There was another pause before Kelly spoke again, this time more forcefully. "No! As I said, he is in a meeting and cannot come to the phone right now. I am happy to take a message."

Kelly gasped, piquing a mixture of surprise, concern, and curiosity in English. He looked in her direction even though the position of her desk kept her out of his line of sight. All three of his visitors turned in curiosity as well.

Kelly screamed out. "What?! Oh my God. English!"

That got Safari moving. Not once since he had taken his new position had Kelly addressed him as other than deputy commissioner or sir. Even that level of informality was exceedingly rare. He bolted to her desk, leaving three stunned Americans in his wake.

"Kelly, what is it?"

She held the phone pressed against her chest. "Oh, sir, it's the assistant police commissioner. He says they have found one of our officers...*murdered*."

English's heart sank, and he found he had difficulty

swallowing. *Please, not Elijah!* He reached for the phone, and Kelly handed it to him slowly through her state of shock.

Safari's voice failed when he first tried to speak, and he cleared his throat before attempting again.

"This is Deputy Commissioner Safari. With whom am I speaking?"

"This is Joseph Onyango, assistant to Police Commissioner Abasi Chongoi. As I was telling your girl, we have found a body. One of our men thinks he recognizes him as one of your officers. We have found some evidence to support such a claim as well. The police commissioner would like you or someone from your office to come down and identify him if you can."

English tried to remain steady, forcing himself to think it must be a mistake. However, he could not help but make the leap that this was the call he had been dreading. As soon as the thought had formed in his mind, it fixed itself firmly in his consciousness and was not going anywhere. *Elijah was dead.* Once he had internally voiced the thought, his calm façade cracked. His face drained, and he swallowed hard before answering. When Kelly saw his reaction to the call, she, too, knew what it likely meant. Tears rushed to her eyes, and she hurried from the room.

With a cracking voice, English finally spoke. "Where do I need to be?"

"Do you know Kismayu Road?"

"I do."

"OK, just past the container freight services yard, there is a dirt road. Follow that towards the water, and you will see our crime scene. Just tell the guard you're there to see the police commissioner or me, and they will let you pass."

"May I collect your cell number in case there are difficulties?" English scribbled the man's number on a notepad along with the directions he was given. "I will be there shortly."

Safari hung up the phone and returned to his office.

"I am sorry, my friends, but an emergency has come up."

John was already standing when he entered the room. "We heard. Is there anything we can do?" English looked at all four men. Each face, even Spencer's, was showing genuine concern. He was startled that he hadn't noticed Spencer returning to the office. *When did he squeeze past me?* It emphasized how out of sorts the news had put him.

English smiled a weak smile. "No, asante, but I fear I must end our visit early."

"Of course, no worries, English. We'll be here all week if you need anything."

English shook John's hand. "Asante. Feel free to finish your tea and to use my office as long as you need." He grabbed his cell phone off his desk, gave a quick wave to the four Americans, and headed for the stairs.

CHAPTER 7

As he raced down the stairs, English found his thoughts wholly unfocused. His mind flashed from scenario to scenario to try and explain what the police had told him. Nothing made sense. When he reached the ground floor, Safari took out his keys and hurried towards his Landcruiser. Sammy saw his boss heading towards his car and ran to intercept.

"Sir, do you need me to drive you somewhere?"

The young man's voice slowly penetrated the fog that had clouded English's mind. He looked at the ever-present smile and felt a tinge better. After a deep sigh, he answered.

"No, Sammy, I think I will drive myself. The police just called. They believe they found one of our men...dead."

"Oh no, sir. It's not your friend, Mr. Elijah, is it?"

English stopped in his tracks. "I do not know. The police asked if I could come and try to identify the body."

"Oh, sir, you must let me drive you. If it is your

friend, you will be in no condition to drive yourself."

By the time English saw the wisdom in Sammy's words, the young man had already taken his briefcase and somehow directed him to his official vehicle. English slumped into the backseat and handed Sammy the scrap of paper where he had scribbled the directions. The driver read the note, looked up, and mentally traced the route in his head. Then, he ran to the front and started the car. Out of respect for the situation, both men were silent. Sammy focused on the traffic while English stared out the window, seeing nothing but vague shapes that vanished before his eyes could focus on them.

English remained in his dazed state until the car lurched as it hit one of the deep ruts on the dirt road. He looked around to get his bearings. They weren't far now. If he remembered correctly, just ahead is the pyramid-shaped boulder. The police commissioner's assistant said it was down the road from there. English was correct. The top of the pyramid had just come into view. Sammy drove past it, and English saw the police vehicles a few moments later. Sammy parked as close as possible and then ran around to open the door, but English was already exiting the car before he got there.

"Would you like me to go with you, sir?"

English smiled a close-mouthed smile. "Asante, no. I think as few of us as possible should see this."

Sammy nodded, "Yes, sir. I will be here if you need me."

English nodded back and began trudging towards the police barrier. Even though he felt like he was walking slowly, the blockade arrived too quickly for his comfort. He swallowed hard but felt as if the contents of his stomach would shortly be coming up. A policeman standing near the makeshift barrier nodded expectantly at English.

English forcefully cleared his throat to ensure his voice was stronger than he felt at the moment. "Deputy Commissioner Safari here as requested by Police Commissioner Abasi Chongoi." The policeman looked him up and down before waving him through.

English worked his way between police cars and stopped short when he saw the cloth-covered body on the ground. He took a few deep breaths to calm himself before letting his eyes fully take in the scene before him. Two policemen stood at semi-attention on either side of the body while several more lounged casually, leaning on their cars in the distance. Their nonchalant attitude raised his ire significantly. Boredom had clearly set in for those men as they struggled to stay awake. Safari let his eyes move past them before he got too angry. He stopped scanning when he saw the police commissioner staring intently at him. A man, possibly his assistant, was speaking emphatically to him, but the commissioner's eyes never looked away. English assumed Abasi was sizing him up, but he didn't care. He looked away from Abasi and let his eyes once again rest on the body lying on the ground.

English slightly jumped when he felt a hand on his shoulder.

"Are you all right, English?"

English turned to face the police commissioner. He nodded slowly before his eyes returned to the white sheet.

"It just feels a bit surreal, is all."

"Have you never seen a body before?" the

commissioner asked.

Safari's mind flashed back to when he had found his parents before he could stamp out the memory. Now was not the time to think about such things; it would compound his feelings, doing him no good. "I am Kenyan, Commissioner," he answered stoically. "Death follows us through life as surely as the predator follows the gazelle."

"Of course. You seem out of sorts."

"I dread knowing who lies below the sheet. I fear I may know already. My number one man has been missing for over a week without leaving word for myself or his wife."

"Why didn't you report him missing?"

Safari tore his focus from the body to aim a stern expression at Abasi. "I do not know you yet." His tone added the unsaid "nor do I trust you."

"I see…" the police commissioner let his eyes follow English's gaze back towards the body as he searched for the best path forward. Putting his arm on Safari's shoulder, he pulled the forlorn man a short distance from the others, where the body was also out of sight.

"It is no secret this is my first murder case as police commissioner. As I am certain it is for you in your new position, all eyes are on me in this matter." English nodded his understanding. "I need to prepare you for what you're about to see. The man we found is likely your number two. We found this in his back trouser pocket." The police commissioner pulled a folded paper from an evidence bag. "Do you know what this is?"

The image on the paper was faded from being wet, but it was a container scan printout. "May I?" English asked as he held out his hand to hold the image.

"Carefully. The paper is quite fragile at this point."

English nodded and gingerly took the paper from the commissioner. Part of the container number had disintegrated, but English knew this was one of Elijah's missing scans from the remaining digits. His heart sank even further. He cleared his throat as he thought about how much he should share with the new police commissioner. He looked at Chongoi's face and got the impression that he wanted to uphold the law, but English decided that he best play it safe. After all, Elijah might very well be dead twenty yards away because of what he found in this container. There was simply no way of telling who was involved without further investigation.

"It is an X-ray scan of a container from the port," English confidently stated.

"That is why I thought he might be one of yours. Your team operates the scanner, correct?"

English nodded. "We have the only container scanner in the region."

"When one of my men thought he had seen the victim around the port, the image you're holding seemed enough corroboration to call your office for help in his identification." English agreed with the police commissioner's logic. "Anything else you can glean from the image?" Chongoi asked.

English pushed his glasses back up, then focused closely on the paper. "See here. Part of the container number is visible." English held the printout with one hand as he pointed with the other. "But the image…" he squinted at the container contents, "is very faded."

"If you had to guess?" pressed Abasi.

English knew what the image showed but was

unsure how much he should disclose. Safari looked him up and down quickly. *Still impeccably dressed.* The man was *very* prepared for their first meeting. It was likely Abasi could tell what was on the image or, more worrisome, *knew* the contents of the container and was testing English. Telling the truth was the only path forward here. Either he was helping a good man solve a murder or assuaging an evil man that Safari was naive.

"I hate to say it," English mustered, "but it looks like there are *many* people inside the container."

The police commissioner rubbed his chin in contemplation. "That is what I see also." He looked thoughtfully at English. "In your expert opinion, what does that imply?"

Safari's mouth twisted to the side as he pondered for a moment. "There are a few possibilities. People are being smuggled into or out of the country. This seems unlikely as we have such open borders and virtually no consistency in identification standards in this country. Even the most wanted individuals could come and go as they please."

Abasi nodded in agreement with this point and indicated English should continue.

"Also, people would not voluntarily subject themselves to the horrific conditions of being transported in a shipping container." English bobbed his head back and forth as he weighed the possibilities. "If they were nefarious people, criminals or terrorists, for example, I suppose that is conceivable. They would have to be *terribly* desperate."

"The most likely scenario, in my opinion, would be human trafficking. Unfortunately, both slavery and sex slave trading occur, as I am sure you are aware. Of course, I cannot say for certain, but I would venture that is what this image portends."

Abasi took the photo and returned it to the evidence bag. "Yes, that was my guess as well. Was your man investigating such a case?"

"Truthfully, I do not know," English admitted. "Elijah had excellent hunches and the autonomy to follow where they led."

"I see...I don't believe we can go any further at this point. I think it may be time to try and identify the body if you're ready."

English took a deep breath and nodded at the commissioner.

"All right then. To prepare you: we think this man was shot in the back and dumped in the water. We're guessing shortly thereafter, a croc got his legs." English stifled a gasp, and Abasi paused to let the shocked man collect himself. English motioned for Abasi to push on. "A fisherman found his body entangled in the mangrove roots along the water. We moved him onto land a short while ago. The medical examiner estimates his body sat in the water for a week or so, as best he can tell. The exposure to the water left him...*damaged,* I guess would be the polite word for it."

Looking a bit pale, English shifted his weight from one foot to the other as dread began to build again within him. Thinking about the case had distracted him, but now, all he could conjure up was Elijah's decomposing form.

"I only described the body's condition so vividly in order to lessen the shock when we get over there." English, unsure of his voice, nodded his understanding.

Though the walk was only about twenty yards, it

seemed like time had slowed. English felt the weight of the situation compound with each step he took towards the covered remains. When they finally arrived, Commissioner Chongoi nodded at an officer standing near the body. The officer folded down the sheet, exposing Elijah's head and shoulders. English cursed to himself and knelt by the body to take a closer look. Although there was some bloating and other decomposition, it was undeniably his dear friend. The gruesome image destroyed English's last vestige of hope that Elijah was on a secret mission and would return.

English looked up at the police commissioner and nodded once. "It is him. It is Elijah Botsole, my friend." The last was said in a near whisper.

"I am sorry for your loss. We'll give you a minute to say your goodbyes." English nodded his thanks, and the two policemen walked a short distance off.

English looked down at the swollen face of his friend and whispered. "Oh, Elijah. What did you get yourself into here? I looked at your files but do not have your gift of connecting the dots. I wish you had told me what trail you were following, my friend. How ever am I to tell your Aailyah? You have put me in a most difficult position. One in which I never expected to be placed."

Safari looked up and let out a deep breath before looking back at Elijah. "Kwa heri, my friend. May the angels guide you to heaven. I hope there is Tangawizi there."

English smiled a slight smile and patted his friend's chest in closure. He stopped short when he felt a small lump beneath his hand. Being frisked many times in his life, Elijah noticed no one ever checked him just above his stomach. While his criminal days were in the past, he still believed there might be an occasion or two where he would have to hide an object from a corrupt official or other less savory individuals. So thinking, Elijah had Aailyah sew small pockets on the inside of his shirts, and English suddenly believed he had found something in one of those secret pockets.

Safari looked over at the police commissioner, who appeared deep in conversation with the young officer guarding Elijah's body. He quickly looked around to ensure no one was watching him. Most of the police had been here for hours, and the initial rush of being called to a murder investigation had worn off. They stood around looking bored, wishing they were elsewhere. Thinking it was now or never, English fished into the pocket and pulled out a small object. Without looking at it, he slipped the discovery into his pants pocket as he stood.

English walked as calmly as he could manage over to the police commissioner and offered his hand. The man's iron grip somehow managed to convey sympathy. "Thank you, Commissioner Chongoi. Unless you need anything further from me, I think I will take my leave." The commissioner's grip held tight, slightly worrying English that he had been seen pocketing potential evidence.

"Just a couple of quick questions…Did your Mr. Botsole have a family?"

"Yes. A wife and two young children. I still do not know how I will tell them," English lamented.

"That was my next question. I thought the news might come easier from a friend of the family. I will still need to ask his wife a few questions. Will you let her know I will be coming around?" English nodded somberly. "Can you also provide their address?"

"Certainly."

The police commissioner released his hand as he pulled a small notebook from his pocket. After Abasi finished jotting down the address, he closed the book and put it away. English had to suppress the urge to breathe a sigh of relief as he realized he would not be interrogated about his discovery.

"If we have further questions or any developments occur, I will contact your office. And, Mr. Safari, if you think of anything that can help the case, I expect you will do the same."

"Of course, Commissioner Chongoi. I want the culprit who did this brought to justice." Even as English said these words, he doubted justice would be found through the police. "Kwa heri, Commissioner."

"Kwa heri. You will be hearing from me."

English turned and walked quickly to where Sammy was waiting.

"Was it him, sir?" Sammy asked as he angled the police barricade to allow English to fit through the opening.

"It was." Safari shook his head in disbelief. Even though he had suspected something terrible had befallen Elijah, none of the scenarios he imagined were this horrendous. "Take me back to the office, Sammy. I have a lot of people to deliver bad news to today."

"I'm sorry, sir. It's very hard to lose those closest to us." The driver's face showed genuine empathy. Safari realized the young man must have never fully recovered from the loss of his parents at such a young age. English placed a kind hand on Sammy's shoulder.

"Yes, indeed it is. Asante." The pair plodded to the car, where English waved off Sammy's efforts to get the door.   As he got in, he noticed the police commissioner watching him leave. He wondered if the commissioner was somehow involved in Elijah's fate but decided to put it from his mind. Now was the time for grief. Justice, if there could be any in Kenya, could wait until tomorrow to be sought.

English stared out the window until they were a considerable distance from the police before pulling the pilfered evidence out of his pocket. It was a ring— a pale green ring that appeared to be carved from a single large gemstone. He turned it over in his hands slowly. A simple pattern was engraved on the outside with no discernable markings on the interior. Was this modest band the cause of Elijah's demise? It didn't seem likely. With its unpolished finish, he could not imagine it had great financial worth. *Maybe it was not related at all.* Elijah might have found it lying on the ground and tucked it away for safekeeping because he liked the look of it.

English slipped his fingers under his glasses to rub the bridge of his nose in frustration. *Elijah was murdered.* It felt surreal. Anger began to fuel a desire to avenge his friend. He looked at the ring again before shoving it back into his pocket. Gazing out the window again, he fondly remembered all the adventures he and Elijah had shared.   They were determined to make a difference for their country and had started to see results. A more significant impact was the one they had on each other.   They had become brothers. English felt that devastating loss and tears began to well in his eyes.

English's leaden legs barely cleared the steps as he trudged up the stairs to his office. All his energy had drained when he saw Elijah's remains lying there. It felt like a piece of him had died as well. Kelly looked up when he entered the antechamber and gasped when she noticed his red-rimmed eyes.

"Oh, English," she cried out and ran to embrace him with tears streaming down her face. Kelly buried her head into his chest, and they stood consoling each other for a long while. She pulled back when she felt ready, wiping the tears from her cheeks.

"What happened to him?" Kelly asked as she began straightening her dress

English wondered how much to tell her. She had been with him for nearly as long as Elijah. Besides Alex, there was no one he trusted more than Kelly. One look at her distraught face told him he should minimize the details. "The police believe he was shot in the back and fell into Kilindini Harbor. Someone just found his body today."

"Shot in the back?" Kelly's eyes flashed anger, something English had never witnessed in all the years he knew her. Then her expression suddenly changed to one of realization. "Was it work-related?"

"Therein lies the rub. I do not know; it may be completely unrelated to work, but I suspect it is. We need to be extra cautious until I figure out who killed Elijah. As I see it, there are only a few scenarios that could have led to Elijah's murder. First, he was simply in the wrong place at the wrong time. Another possibility is that the corrupt system we are fighting against is fighting back. Many people are unhappy that our team has replaced the previous regime. Perhaps someone is willing to kill to keep the status quo. While both of these scenarios could be true, in all likelihood, it was probably the specific case he had been working on that led to his death. Last Friday, Elijah told his wife he would be out of contact because he was going on a secret mission. A mission which I knew nothing about but have begun looking into. No matter which of these is true or if some other business is to blame, our guard must be up. We must assume everyone we have cause to deal with is not our friend. Agreed?"

Kelly nodded. "Yes, Deputy Commissioner. Should I send out an email to the entire team about Elijah?"

"No, you should take the rest of the day off and go home."

Kelly started to protest, prepared to cite everything that needed to be done, but English cut her off.

"Kelly, all of it can wait until tomorrow. I will send out an email to the team and call the commissioner. She will want to know right away. Afterwards, I will also leave; rest assured. I need to go to Elijah's house, but have no idea how to break the tragic news to Aailyah. She may never forgive me if this turns out to be work-related."

English had braced himself for further protest from Kelly, but none came. Instead, she nodded in agreement while averting her eyes, then retrieved her purse from behind her desk. After sliding her bag's straps over her shoulder, she wiped more tears from her eyes and grabbed several extra tissues. Kelly gave English another sad look and headed out the door. English could hear her muffled crying until the elevator doors closed.

English stared up at the ceiling while breathing out sharply. *That was exceedingly hard.* How was he ever to tell Aaliyah? He took another deep breath, letting it puff out his cheeks before noisily exhaling again. *One step at a time, English*, he thought. First, he would call the commissioner; she would need to know immediately.

English retreated into his office and slumped into his chair, totally defeated. He tossed his glasses onto his appointment book and massaged his temples. English wished he had listened to Elijah and hidden a bottle or two of something strong in his office. He could *really* use a drink right now. Sometimes, being such a stickler for the rules came back to bite him.

English exhaled deeply once more before slipping his glasses back on. He glanced at his watch. It was late, but Commissioner Sambu was likely still at her office; she tended to work long hours.

English stifled a yawn as he tiredly dialed the commissioner's number. He sighed slightly as her assistant answered the phone. He had held out some small hope that the commissioner had gone home for the night and he could put off this call until the morning.

"Good evening, Kenya Revenue Authority, Commissioner Sambu's office, Maria speaking. How may I help you?"

"Hello, Maria, Deputy Commissioner Safari for Commissioner Sambu."

"Habari, Deputy Commissioner. Is Kelly well? You're making your own calls now?"

"I am afraid it is quite urgent, Maria." He did not wish to alienate the commissioner's assistant but could not muster a more generous demeanor.

"Of course, sorry, sir. I'll put you right through."

A moment later, the commissioner was on the phone.

"English, what is it?"

Even though the commissioner frequently used his

first name, he never felt comfortable reciprocating. "Commissioner, I am greatly saddened to tell you my second in command, Elijah Botsole, has been found, *murdered.*"

The commissioner audibly gasped. "Oh, English, I am so sorry. I know how close the two of you were."

"Thank you, Commissioner. He was a dear friend and a good man."

"He had a wife and two young children, did he not?"

"Yes, Commissioner."

"How are they faring?" she asked with genuine concern filling her voice.

Though the commissioner could not see him, English shrugged and shook his head as he imagined Aaliyah's reaction once he informed her. "I have not been to their house yet. I have only just come from the crime scene and will be heading to her home after we get off the phone."

"So, she does not know yet?"

"No. The police commissioner thought it might be easier coming from someone she knows."

Commissioner Sambu nearly snorted. "Easier for him, he means."

"That is certainly true. I dread delivering this news but want to be there for Aaliyah when she hears it."

"You are a good man, English. Please convey my condolences."

"Of course, Commissioner."

"Was his murder work-related?"

"It appears to be the case. Elijah had excellent instincts. I think he was onto something big. Unfortunately, he kept what he was working on a secret. There was a container scan on him when he died. The image showed people hidden in the container, suggesting human trafficking. Because of this, the police commissioner suspects Elijah's death to be work-related and will be pursuing that line of inquiry."

"Someone has murdered one of our own. Don't think for a second they would hesitate to add another body to their count. You be exceptionally careful, English," the commissioner ordered. "Do you understand me?"

"Yes, Commissioner, I will be cautious. Regardless of the risk, I will not let the killer get away with murdering my friend."

"Nor was I suggesting we let them, English, just that we be smart about how we proceed. Would anyone have more details about what Elijah was working on?"

"Not to my knowledge, Commissioner. Elijah trusted no one above me and still kept me in the dark. His usual meticulous records regarding what he was chasing down are suspiciously absent. Besides that container scan I mentioned, Elijah had a file folder of various container scans and shipping manifests. I am trying to piece together what I can from the evidence in that folder. Also, you should know the American delegation was in my office when I received the call from the police to identify a body. No one knows at KRA about Elijah's death except for Kelly and Sammy. I will email the team after we get off the phone. My hope is that someone has evidence in their possession and will come forward. On the other hand, my concern is they would genuinely fear sharing in Elijah's fate and will likely never come forward. I imagine they will quickly *'forget'* what they know. The small clues

Elijah left behind may be the only help I receive towards this investigation."

"Unfortunately, your assumption is probably correct. Is there anything I can do to help you, English?"

"Possibly. Do you know anyone that can...," English hesitated, "*discreetly* find out what type of man the police commissioner is?"

"Hmm...there may be a few trees I can shake. Why? Do you suspect he is involved?"

"No. Not as of yet. I would like to know if he is a person to be trusted or to be avoided."

"You met with him, correct?"

"I did, Commissioner."

"What was your impression?"

"Commissioner Chongoi was a stark contrast to his predecessor, to be sure. He is a meticulous man who takes great care in appearances, from his pressed uniform down to the arrangement of his office. Which, by the way, held a vast array of legal books. When we spoke, he made a point of putting me 'in my place,' which was uncalled for, but on the positive side, he appeared to be interested in upholding the law. Overall, I left the commissioner's office feeling somewhat optimistic. Is it enough to overcome the Mombasa Police Department's reputation? Time will tell. Another red flag is that Chongoi is quite young."

"I see. Let's hold out some hope he will be an ally. Never forget that most consider you young for your position. Our government has pockets of virtue, even when it gives the impression otherwise."

"I have not given up hope yet, Commissioner. Although Elijah's death has sorely tested it."

"As it will for all of us, I'm certain. Let's see what I

can dig up on your police commissioner. Is there anything else I can do?"

"Not at this time, Commissioner."

"In that case, please convey my deepest sympathies to Elijah's wife."

"I will, Commissioner, asante."

"Take heart, English. Adversity is our true test. If we pass, we will be that much stronger for it. I know such words are lacking for times like these, but sometimes the thinnest ledge can support our weight while we look for sturdier ground."

"Yes, asante sana, Commissioner. Now, if there is nothing further, I must inform Elijah's wife before she hears the news from someone else."

"Of course, English, and, again, I am very sorry for your loss. True friends are infinitely precious in this life."

"Asante, Commissioner, kwa heri."

"Kwa heri, English."

English hung up the phone, placed his glasses on his desk, then closed his eyes and leaned back in his chair. He again wondered how he would ever be able to tell Aaliyah. His father's words came rushing into his head. *A difficult problem is like pulling weeds. It becomes no easier the longer it has to grow. As it grows, its roots take hold and steal resources from everything around it. Then, you will be forced to expend much greater effort to deal with the problem than when it first came to your attention.* Silently acknowledging his father's wisdom, English slipped on his glasses and headed for the door.

English was so wistful he hardly noticed the traffic. Operating on auto-pilot, he was almost surprised to find himself pulling up in front of Elijah's home. He turned off the car and rested his forehead on the steering wheel. He hoped one more moment would give him the words and the strength to tell Aaliyah. Nothing came to mind, but his resolve stiffened, and he exited the cruiser. Only as he went to shut the car door did he see Aaliyah watching him from the porch. When English's sorrow-weary eyes met hers, she knew. He saw her optimistic mask shatter, taking her strength with it. She collapsed to her knees and cried out in anguish.

English raced to the porch and threw his arms around her. They stayed there for several minutes as she sobbed. His extensive vocabulary failed him, so he remained silent. No words seemed as eloquent or effective as his silence was proving.

When her tears were exhausted, she leaned back to nod at English, letting him know it was okay to stand. He stood and offered her help up. She used the back of her hands to wipe the tears and mascara from her face, then dried them on her dress before letting him lead her into the house.

English went to put the kettle on after seeing her to a chair in the parlor. When he returned, speaking still seemed inappropriate, so he offered his hand again. He tried to share his strength with her but felt he was gaining more than he provided until the kettle's piercing whistle forced him to his feet. He set the tea to steeping and returned with the tray.

When it was ready, English poured her a cup and added milk and sugar as she liked. Aaliyah did not drink but seemed to take comfort from the cup's warmth between her hands and the wisps of steam that caressed her face. She inhaled deeply, bringing the scent of the freshly brewed tea deep within her. English had seen her do it before. In the past, he thought she was eliciting some childhood memory as a smile would touch her lips. No smile came today, but she appeared stronger when she sat the cup back on the tray.

English waited a few moments more before offering his sympathies. "Aaliyah, I am so sorry. You know I would give anything to be delivering news of any other nature." Aaliyah kept her eyes focused on a point on the floor a few feet in front of her and angled away from English. Even though she could not meet his eyes, she nodded in agreement. "Elijah was more of a brother to me than if we had shared parents."

English immediately regretted that statement as Aaliyah burst into tears again. He offered his hand to her, and though her eyes were still averted, she latched on with an iron grip. After getting herself under control, she finally turned her eyes to him and offered a slight smile. Aaliyah gave his hand a quick squeeze in thanks. Then, she went to work fixing her appearance, attempting to wipe away tears and straighten her hair and dress.

She looked at her makeup-stained hands and let out a quick laugh of despair.

"Look at me. What a silly little girl I'm being."

English scoffed. "Crying in this situation is not silly, Aaliyah. It seems a very reasonable response."

Aaliyah tsked. "Not when I've known for so long he wouldn't be returning. When you came by, inquiring after him, I knew right then something had happened to my Elijah, but I allowed hope to bury that feeling. Each day that went by without word lessened the likelihood of his return, yet I still held off accepting that he was gone."

English wanted desperately to tell her it had been

right to hold out hope, but he had internally chastised himself for doing the same.

Aaliyah shook her head, took a deep breath, and let it audibly escape her lips. "What happened to him? Was it work-related?"

English hesitated, unsure if he should fully describe what had befallen her husband.

"English Safari!" she snapped. "Don't you dare *filter* your story! I'm a big girl who's already done her crying. I *need* to know what happened to my husband. Do I not deserve the truth?"

"Of course you do," English agreed. "I am still struggling with this myself. Besides finding my parents, this has been the singularly most difficult situation I have ever experienced. I have no words. Please, forgive me."

Aaliyah nodded sympathetically.

"The police called my office this afternoon telling us they had found a body that one of their men believed to be a KRA officer." Aaliyah had a sharp intake of breath but indicated he should continue. "They asked if I would come to the scene and try to identify him. At this point, I knew it had to be Elijah, but I hoped I was wrong." English shook his head slowly but continued speaking when he saw Aaliyah biting her nails in apprehension.

"Sammy drove me there. It was near the harbor, just past the pyramid boulder. Police were everywhere. They showed me his body; it was Elijah. Someone had found him in the water. They still need to do an autopsy, but they believe he was…shot in the back. The police also think it may be work-related because Elijah had an X-ray scan of a container folded up in his pocket. The police commissioner showed it to me. It appeared to indicate people being smuggled inside that container."

Aaliyah gasped. "So Elijah died trying to save people?"

"It looks that way. The image was faded from being in the water, but the scan showed quite a few people lying throughout the container." English, suddenly remembering, dug in his pocket and pulled the ring out.

"I almost forgot. Elijah had this tucked into one of his secret pockets. I took it, thinking it must be important if he had hidden it. Was this his, or would he have gotten it for you?"

Aaliyah raised an eyebrow in disbelief at his question as she reached for it. When she slipped the ring over her finger, it looked like two of her slender fingers could fit inside its diameter. English shook his head. *Of course, it is too large to be a woman's ring,* he thought, but chalked it up to not examining the ring very closely. The shock of it all was keeping him from thinking clearly.

"It's definitely not Elijah's," Aaliyah confirmed. "Is it a clue as to who did this to him?"

"I believe so. I plan to follow the few clues I have uncovered to find those responsible. If, however, you would like me to turn this ring and Elijah's case files over to the police, I will. He was your husband. I completely understand if you want the authorities to handle his case. Unfortunately, I do not know the new police commissioner well enough to judge his intentions."

Aaliyah smiled a small smile as a tear slowly ran down her cheek. "I believe *Elijah* would trust no one other than you to find his murderer. I think I will let him choose his champion one last time."

English, honored, placed his hand over his heart in thanks.

Aaliyah looked intently at the ring. "I think this ring is made of tsavorite. It looks ancient." She drew his attention to the side of the ring. "See here," she pointed, "even though the carvings have been worn smooth, they look as if they were rough originally. Local craftsmen might have purposefully 'aged' it, though. You can never be certain because replicas are big money-makers. Maybe an expert could tell you more."

"Thank you. I will find a trustworthy expert to examine the ring. We have more immediate concerns, however. The police plan to question you soon. Since they suspected his death was work-related, let them know Elijah told you he was working on a case and would be away for a few days. I came by when he turned up missing, but neither of us knew what he was working on. If you wish to keep them out of this, I suggest not telling them about this ring or the files I copied."

Aaliyah exhaled a deep breath as she nodded in understanding.

"Again, if you decide at any point you want the police fully informed, I will completely understand." Aaliyah patted his arm dismissively so he would quit repeating his concern.

"Now, English, let me pour myself a glass of wine, and you can tell me some stories about Elijah's adventures or, should I say *misadventures*, with you by his side."

English smiled. He knew just the story to tell her. When she sat back down and took a sip, he began to set the stage.

"Now you must understand. I have for many years trusted Elijah's hunches implicitly." Aaliyah smiled knowingly as English had used this clause to disavow any liability in the past. This was the first of many stories, laughs, and tears they would share before English finally took his leave much later that night.

CHAPTER 8

English once again let his brain's auto-pilot lead him home as the empty roads gave him a moment of peace to run through the evidence related to Elijah's murder. He felt there must be more to this than human smuggling. Although it was a terrible crime, he could not understand why Elijah did not inform him about it unless those involved were extremely powerful. No, even then, he would have brought the case to English.

Were those articles part of the same investigation? How could the Navy receiving an accommodation for their efforts against pirates be related? That story being related might make sense if it were becoming easier for pirates rather than harder. English stretched his neck back and forth to try and remove some of the kinks. "Elijah, what were you thinking?" Evoking his name brought those grizzly images from the crime scene to his consciousness. English found he could no longer concentrate on the case after that evil image invaded his mind. He hoped to banish such horrible visions with some beers and sleep when he arrived home.

Safari tried flipping the lights on as he entered, but the room stayed dark. *The power must be out again,* English thought, *maybe one of the rolling brownouts the city had implemented to compensate for the lack of power-generating capacity in the region.* Most people became quite agitated during a power outage, but not English. Except for the chance of food spoiling, he rather enjoyed the outages at night. Never were Mombasa night skies more beautiful than during a blackout. English dropped his bag onto a chair and headed into the rear garden to enjoy the view.

English opened the refrigerator located on the patio and reached for a Tusker. As he felt around for the magnetized bottle opener he kept on the fridge, he heard some glass clink behind him. Instead of the opener, he found the cricket bat displayed on the wall and turned to face whoever was on his property.

Another sound of glass hitting his patio sent goosebumps to his skin, but he kept advancing. The sound had morphed. If he had to guess, he would say a bottle was rolling slowly towards him. His every nerve was on fire in anticipation. A faint groan just ahead nearly had him jumping out of his skin. Someone was definitely in his garden. *Was it an assassin waiting to put an end to his investigation?*

Another groan came from a few feet before him and low to the ground. Whoever the person was knew he would come back here and was lying in wait. He must be unable to see English in the dark, or he would not be making so much noise. English raised the bat in preparation for a strike. The power was restored at that moment, and the fridge, whose door he had never bothered shutting, lit him up from behind.

"Christ!" A figure shouted as it scrambled out of a

lounge chair. A combination of crawling and running carried the figure out of English's range.

"Who are you?!" English yelled in a deep, menacing voice.

"English?" A voice asked from behind the palm tree.

"Yes, now show yourself," English ordered.

"Oh, Christ. You scared the piss out of me."

"Alex?" English asked, recognizing the voice.

"Yeah, it's me. What were you doing? Since when do you brain people you find in your garden?"

"When they are in my garden in the dark at this late hour."

"Hmm. Good point, I suppose," Alex laughed.

"What are you doing here? You scared me half to death."

Alex grunted as he got up from his crouching position. He held his side as he limped over to English.

Safari chuckled. "Did you hurt yourself hiding behind my tree?"

Alex looked down at his hand and shook his head as he dropped his arm back down. "No, mate. Someone else hurt me. That's why I was back here. To give you a warning."

"Warning? Wait, are you all right?"

"Hakuna matata, brother." Even in the low light, English could see Alex's broad smile. "Not the worst I've ever gotten." English righted the chair and helped lower Alex into it. The man winced and sucked air through his teeth as he sat. "Not the best I've felt either." Another smile assured English that Alex would mend, and he walked back to the fridge to get his Tusker.

"You want one?"

"Are they cold?"

"Yes, the power must not have been out for very long."

"Do they have alcohol?" Alex asked sarcastically.

English laughed. He should have known. *When did Alex ever turn down a drink?* "Past experience tells me yes, they do."

Alex smiled. "In that case, sure."

English shook his head as he returned with the brews. "You know, it is not my fault my parents raised me with manners, yet you always answer me sardonically when I use them."

"True, but it's your fault for still using them." Alex grabbed the beer and aimed the long neck at Safari as if he had scored some deep point in a well-planned debate.

English cocked his head to the side. He decided he really could not argue with that. Instead, he realized he hadn't opened Alex's Tusker and went back to retrieve the opener. He grabbed it, flicked on the exterior light, then returned to open the beer. He took it from Alex, popped the top off, and handed it back to the supine man. English grimaced when he got close enough to see Alex's bruised face.

"Ouch. What happened? You said you came to give me a warning?" A tone of empathy permeated Safari's questions.

"Truth be told, I'm not sure if you need a warning or not."

"Oh?"

Alex tried to sit up, then thought better of it. "Yeah, so I was asking around about these shipping containers of yours. One of my guys had heard someone talking at a club about a big deal going through the port. He thought it might be connected and said he had sometimes seen the guy at lunch at one of the restaurants off Mwembe Tayari Road. I went around and started asking questions. Questions that seriously pissed someone off, I think. I mean, it *could* have been because I'm a mzungu. That has happened before, but this seemed different. I think they were going to kill me. Had some of my boys not been eating lunch nearby, and had they not passed when I was almost finished…" Alex cocked his head to the side while grimacing to indicate what he believed would have happened.

English thought for a moment. "I see…" he stood up and took a deep swill of his beer. "The police found Elijah today." His somber tone implied to Alex in what condition they found him. He sat up, which brought renewed pain to his rib cage.

"Oh, English, I'm so sorry. Elijah was a good guy and a good friend. What happened to him?" Alex took a sip and then held the cold bottle against his bruised eye socket. He winced until the cool glass dulled the pain but kept his good eye trained on English as he awaited his answer.

English took another long pull on his bottle before speaking. The adrenaline of finding an intruder in his garden was wearing off, and physical and emotional exhaustion was taking its place. He sat down heavily on the foot end of Alex's lounge chair, bringing another wince and swift intake of air from his friend.

English tapped Alex's shin in apology. "Sorry, rafiki. I suddenly felt spent."

Alex waved off the apology; even such a simple movement seemed to bring more distress to the injured man's face.

"They found Elijah in the harbor. The Police Commissioner told me it looked like he had been shot in the back and dumped in. A fisherman found his body entangled in the mangrove roots along the bank. A croc had gotten to his legs…" Alex looked queasy as he imagined the scene English described.

"Was it related to this case?"

"I think so. The Police Commissioner showed me a faded container scan they found on Elijah."

"Could you…"

"Yes," English interrupted, anticipating Alex's question. "Being in the water deteriorated the image, but it was clear enough to show there were people inside the container."

"People?" Alex asked, confused.

"Yes, lots of them. They were lying all about the container. Thomas, one of my X-ray operators, informed me Elijah had taken a scan that showed people strewn about the inside of a container. I suppose this was that scan."

"So, what are you thinking? Slave trafficking?" Alex furrowed his brow as he tried to devise other reasonable explanations for why people would be shipped via container.

"Normally, I would say that was likely…"

"And when it's not normal?" Alex asked.

English shrugged his shoulders. "When it is not normal, I usually consult with Elijah…" English paused to take a sip. "I am still taking a cue from him, as it were. If it were simply a case of slave trading, Elijah would have come to me. Since he did not, I must assume the situation is more complex than what is presented before us. That reminds me…" English put down his bottle and patted his pockets until he found the ring. He held it up in the direction of the porch light.

"Elijah had this secreted away in one of his hidden pockets." He eyed it closely one more time before handing it over to Alex. The injured man turned the ring over several times as he inspected it, looking fastidiously at the carvings. He even tried it on before holding it up for English to take it back.

"So, how does this ring tie into the case?"

"I do not know…yet. Aailyah was certain it was not Elijah's." Safari looked at it once more before tucking it back into his pocket. Almost as an afterthought, he added, "She did think it was made of tsavorite…"

Alex sat up quickly, forcing him to release a groan and clutch his side. After a few gulps of air and a chuckle at his own stupidity, he grabbed Safari's arm. "That's our connection, don't you see?" English shook his head to admit he did not. "The ring is tsavorite. Elijah had Lord Anson circled in those photos. Lord Anson was recently killed. And what did Lord Anson own?"

Both men spoke in unison, English in a whisper to himself, Alex loud and proud. "The tsavorite mines."

English thought through the possibilities, devising different scenarios and weighing their likelihood.

"I think you are right, rafiki," English said pointedly. "They are connected." Alex smugly sat up higher. "But what does it mean?"

Alex opened his mouth to answer before realizing he had no idea and snapped it shut. He carefully lowered himself back down to his reclining position. English stood up to pace as he talked through the different options.

"It seems to me that I have reached a fork in the

road of this investigation. On one path lies Tsavo Park. The link between the Tsavo Mines and this case is unclear, but there are no coincidences. Certainly, one exists. I fear I would not recognize the connection unless it were brazenly transparent."

"That's why you have me." Alex was grinning widely at the thought of a daring adventure.

"You, my friend, are practically an invalid. I doubt you would survive the roads to Tsavo, let alone the terrain inside the park."

Alex scoffed. The slight movement caused some renewed pain in his ribs. He grimaced as he carefully probed his side. English took that as a reluctant agreement and pressed on.

"The park is closed right now due to Lord Anson's death. I wonder if the park has other entrances beyond the south and east gates…" English mused aloud. He made a mental note to do some internet research on Tsavo. He suddenly wished he had paid more attention during his visits there in the past.

"The other path leads to the port," English continued. "I can discreetly check if any of the containers Elijah flagged are still in the stacks. Although we are reasonably certain that human smuggling is involved in one container, the other X-rays only show a weird, dense anomaly. I doubt I can replicate Elijah's targeting pattern without some hint as to why he initially determined to screen those particular containers. If I stepped up random inspection rates, it would *definitely* raise red flags. It might even endanger more of my officers."

"I say start with what you know best," Alex said seriously before coyly adding. "That's why I play the good-looking card so often." English looked at Alex incredulously. Alex looked back with a devilish grin and raised his beer in a salute. "Besides, it will raise fewer red flags with the police if they see you going about your usual business."

"Why would the police care what I do? I am not a suspect," English declared.

"Oh, no?" Alex asked knowingly. English shook his head while raising his hands to question where he was going with this. "If you're not a suspect, ndugu, then why, pray tell, is there a policeman outside your house in one of their," Alex made dismissive air quotes, "*unmarked* cars?"

"What? A policeman is watching my home?" Safari's voice drifted into a whisper.

"Come on, mate. Don't tell me you didn't see him."

English admitted that he did not. "I was too distraught to notice anything when I got home." Alex nodded his understanding. "I did not even see your vehicle, let alone some clandestine officer."

"First, you didn't see my cruiser because I parked around back and hopped the wall."

Now, it was English's turn to be dubious. He made a point of looking past his friend at his ten-foot garden wall. A wall capped with shards of broken glass like most homes in his neighborhood.

Alex held up his hands to acknowledge being caught in a fib. "Fine, I didn't *hop*," he said snarkily, "the wall. I climbed through my car's sunroof onto the wall, then lowered myself slash fell into your garden." Alex continued before English had time to give him grief. "*Secondly*, he wasn't very clandestine. A bobby is sitting in front of your neighbor's house but clearly watching yours. If he had moved even one or two more houses down the lane, I wouldn't have noticed him, but as it is…"

"Is this your way of telling me to keep my eyes open?" English asked tiredly.

"That and you're a suspect, or more dangerously, a threat in the eyes of the police commissioner," Alex stated firmly.

English sat heavily in the lounge chair next to Alex, pondering what that meant. "So, do you think the commissioner believes me a suspect, or is he involved in whatever Elijah was investigating?"

Alex shrugged. "I don't know, but I do know only the police commissioner could authorize using the official unmarked police car."

English had to admit Alex's argument had merit. They would have used their private vehicle if the surveillance were not authorized. He sat quietly, thinking at length about his next step as he sipped his Tusker. Eventually, he noticed Alex's breathing had settled into the rhythmic sounds of deep sleep.

English looked over at his friend's bruised face. He had taken quite a beating. He thought how fortunate he had been to make such fast friends in this life. Elijah had died trying to keep English out of harm's way, and now Alex lay battered in the garden because he tried to help. He looked up at the night sky and saw only stars, not a cloud in sight. *Good, the weather should hold.* He could leave Alex to sleep on the lounger until he woke of his own accord. He quietly gathered up the empty Tusker bottles and went inside.

Setting the bottles down on the counter, English checked his watch. It was late. Even though he felt exhausted, he was so on edge that he doubted his ability to sleep. He pulled Elijah's ring from his pocket and gave it a once over, running his thumb across its carvings. *I need to do something.* Since he had not yet researched Tsavo, he decided to go to the port. "No time like the present, English," he said to himself. He stashed the ring under the corner floorboard where he had created a hidden storage area. Tired of his new glasses slipping, he swapped them for his old pair, scooped up his keys and Elijah's list of container numbers, and headed out the door.

CHAPTER 9

As Safari climbed into his Landcruiser, he spied the unmarked car Alex had warned him about. The man was indeed obvious. English chastised himself. It was past time to be extra vigilant, no matter his emotional state. The conspicuous nature of the surveillance was worrisome. *Is that incompetence, or did Commissioner Chongoi tell him to be intentionally noticeable to make a point?*

Safari pulled out quickly and sped off in the opposite direction of the parked policeman. Hopefully, he could lose the tail before it started. He took several side roads even though they were unpaved. Seeing no signs he was being followed, he worked his way back to the main road leading to the city side of the port. No matter the time of day, the gates on the other side would be backed up with trucks trying to deliver their cargo. Besides the inescapable traffic delays, the large concentration of trucks meant a police presence. Ostensibly, they were there to break up the frequent clashes between the drivers as they vied for position in the queue or post-accident. The steep hill leading down to the port, combined with poorly maintained trucks, ensured nightly incidents. English had also heard it was a convenient location for corrupt police to demand bribes to allow the drivers to continue on their way. With or without traffic causing slowdowns at that gate, the police presence would require a different entry point.

Safari flashed his badge to the guard in the booth on the lesser-used side of the port. English tried to maintain a calm façade as the guard compared his port pass photo to his face. *Just another day at the office*, he thought to himself but swallowed hard when his subconscious added, *except for the fact that it was the middle of the night.* The guard looked into the backseat before returning the pass and slowly waving him on his way. English began to feel relief as the guard booth shrank in his rearview mirror. He was not sure why he had panicked and worked to shake off the rest of his newfound anxiety. The guard, probably hired because of some family connection, was likely a guard in name only.

The port's main KRA office had newer computers and a fast ethernet connection to the Port Authority's system. Problematically, that office was located in the same building as Port Security, while the X-ray office (with its slower computers) was a separate facility. Even though KRA could not afford to staff their offices twenty-four seven, he was positive security would be manned. After a short drive, English was unlocking the X-ray scanning office. *Stealth, at this juncture, was far more important than speed*, he kept reminding himself as he powered on the antiquated computer.

Safari distracted himself by looking at the container

scans posted on the walls until he heard the system's strange, growl-like sound, indicating it was fully loaded. English logged in under the username RAF Kenya. It was one of many fictitious accounts he and Elijah created when they were junior officers to minimize the chance their investigations could be traced back to them.

English typed in the container number from the missing scan Elijah had on him when he died. He pawed painfully at his cheeks, his mouth agape at the device's slowness. He chuckled at the memory of their introduction to the system when this computer was new. They had been amazed at its blistering speed compared to manually retrieving the records from the hand-bound logs.

The record finally scrolled onto the screen, and English quickly checked it. *The container was still at the port.* A note indicated a hold had been placed on it. Much of the required information, most notably who had ordered the hold, was missing. Suspicions suitably raised, English jotted down the container's location in the stacks and went on to the next container. After a painful process of anticipatory waiting followed by disappointment, English discovered only the first container was still on the port.

With only one container left, it truly was now or never. English walked to the tool locker and pulled out KRA's well-worn bolt cutters. He shut the computer down and quickly looked around to ensure everything was in place. After determining nothing was amiss, he flicked the lights off and headed out. He eyed his cruiser lustfully but knew a private vehicle weaving between the container stacks would draw too much attention at this hour. The port system computer indicated his container was near bulk cargo Shed 13, so he headed in that direction in a light jog.

English had forgotten how creepy the port could be at night. He wound his way through containers and broken-down port equipment—their skeletal remains like some rusted beasts of the Jurassic period. Docked ships and cranes belched diesel smoke into the air as the sounds of their rough engines did the dirty work of world commerce.

As English reached cargo Shed 12, he noticed the port began to change. The towering floodlights that periodically dotted the landscape were suspiciously burnt out or powered off. The roadways were missing large chunks of paver stones, and the containers were stacked in a much less orderly and haphazard manner. Safari had known this area of the port was where the less-than-legal activities took place, but to see it so blatantly abandoned to the nefarious was disheartening, to say the least.

Suddenly, rowdy voices approaching had Safari pressing himself tightly against a rusty container. As he peered around the corner, he immediately knew he was right to be cautious. While he couldn't make out their words over the various port noises, their seedy appearances showed these were not standard port workers. Whether they were hardened criminals or just hooligans who snuck onto the port for a bit of fun, he could not venture a guess. He needed to steer clear of them in either case and ducked quietly in the opposite direction.

English narrowly avoided two other groups as he wove his way towards the Shed 13 stack area. One group of men was walking along the crane tracks. The other was huddled around a barrel fire, passing a bottle between them as they raucously laughed at the story one of their number was telling.

After what felt like an eternity at his cautious, snail's pace, English finally reached the Shed 13 stacks. The area looked increasingly perilous and darker. Even the skies seemed to be conspiring against him as clouds rolled in front of the moon. The darkness would have proven a valuable ally if he merely wished to pass undetected. However, in order to read the container numbers, he would need the light. Safari desperately wished he had thought to bring a torch as he looked at the currently useless bolt cutters in his hand. His heart was racing as he leaned his back against a container. He could not be sure if the jog or the fear of being in the field at night was affecting him. He begrudgingly admitted it had been far too long since the last time he had done either.

English drew several calming breaths as he scanned the night sky. Clouds appeared to cover the sky in all directions, as no stars were visible anywhere. He conceded defeat as he realized he would either need to make his way back to the office to retrieve a torch or come back tomorrow. Every day reduced the likelihood Elijah's container would stay at the port. Safari dejectedly started back to the office when he remembered his phone. KRA had only just upgraded them to smartphones from the flip phones they had used for many years. English shook his head at how far his organization was behind the average Kenyan regarding technology. He excitedly took the phone from his pocket and scrolled through the apps. After a moment of scanning the unfamiliar territory, he found the flashlight button and turned it on and off. It slightly night-blinded him, but his emotions soared as his mission could continue.

Safari slipped between the stacks, using his hands to feel along the containers and steady himself when he worked his way over the piles of garbage accumulated there. Shipping containers had specific marking requirements, so he flashed his phone's light at the upper right corner of the door as he searched for his number. In the daytime, he could have quickly scanned sides, fronts, or backs to eliminate containers in every direction, but these working conditions made it slow-going.

About twenty minutes into his search, he found his target. It was at the end of a long row of containers with only one container on top of it. He had not thought about what he would have done if it had been one of the upper containers or under a heavy stack and thanked his luck. English hated operating without proper preparation, but the situation was what it was, and he had to act quickly. He held the bolt cutters in one hand and used his phone's light to line up the cutters with the lock. *There's no lock,* he thought, surprised. He pulled on the container's door handle, wincing at the metal's loud squeal.

Disappointment shot through English when he opened the door to find the container empty. *Another dead-end,* he realized as he huffed disgruntledly. Still, to be thorough, he needed to check all the way to the back of the container to ensure there was no false panel short of the total length. It was a favorite technique of smugglers since it was cheap and had a high success rate for fooling physical inspections. It was tremendously difficult to tell how far the insides of a container went back when it was packed or if you did not use a tape measure. Most inspectors did not carry one, confident in their ability to eyeball the distance, even after being shown that supposition to be wrong during tests.

A foul odor greeted English as he entered, and he scrunched up his nose at the pungent smell. He lifted his phone light but doubted he would find anything. Those involved with this case were always one step ahead of him, and frustration was beginning to boil his blood. His foot squished into something, and he swung the light down to determine what it was. He could see it was blood from his full height, but he squatted down and dabbed his handkerchief in it to verify. As he panned his light across the container, he saw most of the wooden floor was soaked in the sticky gore. He took several photos and carefully folded his handkerchief for evidence. It was not enough proof to convict anyone, but it should be sufficient to open an official investigation.

English walked to the back of the container, looking for more evidence. Blood was everywhere. The people in the X-ray scan were not part of the slave trade. Clearly, they had been executed. *Who would do this and why?* Fortunately, Elijah had left some clues regarding his suspects. Nothing but the blood stood out as evidence throughout the rest of the length of the container. English kicked the back wall in a few places to assuage himself that it was the actual wall. Then he hurried to exit what had been a group coffin until recently. Switching the phone's light off, he used his shoulder to force the rusted door closed.

"Deputy Commissioner," English recognized the booming voice before he turned to see Michael Tsumbe's hulking frame. "What are you doing out here at this hour, rafiki?"

The man shone his security flashlight in English's face. English held his hand to shade his eyes as they darted back and forth, looking for an escape route. A few meters in front of Tsumbe was a narrow opening between two containers, just wide enough to squeeze through. The big man, almost seeming to sense English's thoughts, took several steps forward, blocking his only escape.

"Michael, habari? I had a tip that someone was smuggling contraband here, but it appears to have been a false lead. This container is empty. Perhaps I was being led on a wild goose chase." English hoped his air of nonchalance was more convincing than it felt.

Tsumbe finally took his light off Safari's face to illuminate the container behind him. English blinked hard a few times to clear the spots in his vision. Hoping to buy himself some time to get out of the situation, English asked, "What are you doing here?" Before belatedly adding, "At this hour?"

The big man's resounding laughter filled the night sky as he lowered his torch. He lumbered in English's direction while speaking. "My job, Deputy Commissioner."

Panic drove Safari's heart into his throat. *So, Tsumbe was in on it.* His grip on the bolt cutters tightened. He wasn't confident he could take the big man in a fight even using them as a weapon. There was no gun in sight—*perhaps I have a chance*, he ventured. Again, Tsumbe appeared to be psychic as his eyes panned down to the cutters in the commissioner's hands.

The big man laughed again. "It's all thanks to your friend."

"My friend?"

"Yes, your friend, Alex Stoney. He is the reason I am here at this ungodly hour."

Safari's heart dropped, and he nearly lost his grip on the cutters. *Alex betrayed me?* He had trusted Alex above all others. *How could I have been so wrong?*

Tsumbe continued, seemingly ignorant of Safari's state of mind. "Alex has complained so much I finally have taken matters into my own hands." English slowly shook his head in disbelief. "I know," Tsumbe agreed. "I could not believe his persistence either. Those Americans pay him more money every time there is a delay in the project. Why should it bother him so much when someone vandalizes his construction works?"

A puzzled look sprung to English's face. "His construction works?"

"Yes, Deputy Commissioner. The radiation detection system he is installing keeps getting damaged at night. I was certain you were informed of the situation."

Awareness spread quickly. *Alex had not betrayed me,* but he still had to deal with Tsumbe. English realized Michael was still talking.

"I've been watching for three nights now, and nothing. Radiation is the least of my worries," Tsumbe said dismissively. "I only agreed to support the project because they are installing additional cameras and optical character readers for container numbers."

Still not trusting, English took a casual step in the big man's direction. Tsumbe loved to hear himself talk. If English could get close enough, perhaps he could brain him with the bolt cutters and abscond before he recovered.

"As I said, three nights with nothing. No sign of

anyone being remotely interested in Stoney's project, but what do I see? My dear rafiki, Deputy Commissioner English Safari, running through my port with a pair of bolt cutters." English's only response was another slow step and a tighter grip on the cutters.

"My men lost you around Shed 12, but I figured you must be heading to this area if you needed the cover of night to do your work." Michael looked around warily, and English took the chance to close the gap even further. After a few deep breaths, he decided he would strike. English had fought and injured men in the course of his job, but never anyone he knew as well as Tsumbe. A blow from these cutters could easily kill the man, but English used the thought of Elijah's body to firm his resolve and got ready to swing.

"Well, rafiki, if you've finished your work, I suggest we leave this area. Even I feel ill at ease near Shed 13 after dark. Can I give you a lift, or is there something else to inspect?"

Safari's eyes looked up in thought. It did not sound like Tsumbe was here to interfere with him but rather did arrive to help. Perhaps he could test him. He still had the bolt cutters if it came to it.

"Michael, I found a great deal of blood in the container behind me. The X-ray scan of this container had images of many people inside. It appears they were all murdered."

The behemoth stood up straighter to look over Safari's head at the container and sighed heavily. He almost seemed to deflate.

"Murdered," Michael repeated the word quietly. "Things have been different around here lately," he confided. "I knew it was too good to be true.

Common crime has been down… *significantly*. I tried to attribute it to my proficiency, but even I didn't believe I could be so effective. I feared something big was happening on the port."

"I agree. My deputy, Elijah, disappeared last week. They found his body yesterday. I think he was murdered because one of his investigations led him to this container."

English was aghast. Not only did he not involve Michael as port security, but he almost caved the man's skull in over a fallacious hunch.

Again, Tsumbe seemed as if he read Safari's mind. "I know why you did not involve me. Perhaps we can develop more trust in the future, but I do understand. Had I not fully vetted you, Deputy Commissioner, seeing you running around with bolt cutters on my port might have given me pause." English only considered what would occur if he had been caught by nefarious actors, not legitimate security forces. Michael continued. "As it is, your character is unassailable, so I knew you had some legitimate concern and followed to offer you my services."

"Forgive me, Michael. I should have come directly to you, but I suspected someone on the port might be involved and do not know you as well as I should. Some of the things you have said led me to believe…" English struggled with how to say Tsumbe seemed corrupt without sounding downright offensive.

Michael waved his giant mitt dismissively with a chuckle. "We all play a part. I've chosen a role that is effective for me to get my job done. So now I say hakuna matat…" A loud crack sounded, and Michael cut off speaking with a lurch.

Tsumbe looked down and seemed off-balance

when he looked back up at English. "Run!" he emphatically implored in a hoarse whisper as blood followed the word. Confusion spread across Safari's face, and Michael whipped around, displaying the bullet wound in his back for a moment before he accelerated with a growl. English was stunned at the blistering speed the big man demonstrated. The perpetrator who had shot Michael fired two more rounds that barely fazed Tsumbe before his hulking frame slammed into the gunman, crushing him against a container. The shooter's fearful scream died before both men collapsed in a broken heap.

English stepped forward. His instinct was to ignore Tsumbe's last word and help the man who had just saved him, but he heard angry voices approaching. English quickly squeezed into the gap between the containers he had identified as an escape route from the security director just moments ago.

He cautiously peered out when he reached the end of the containers and, seeing no one, tore out in a sprint. Some man up ahead, apparently a guard of sorts, yelled and jumped up from where he had been sitting. The guard fumbled with his old rifle, and English took full advantage. He swung the bolt cutters without slowing and felt some satisfaction as the tool's metal connected with a sickening crunch. By the time the guard dropped to the ground, English had run a good distance past him.

Safari heard shouts behind him and turned to see six or so men in pursuit. He dodged between some containers to avoid gunfire but smashed his phone in the process. English hoped his pictures were salvageable, but right now, he needed to ensure he survived. He would worry about his phone and the small amount of evidence it contained later.

The men following English were younger than he was, and he sensed them closing in on him. He knew if he tried to outrun them in a flat run, they would catch up or shoot him in the back like they had Elijah and Tsumbe. So thinking, English darted between the rusted and damaged containers stacked about the area surrounding Shed 13. He ducked and weaved at every chance until he saw an opportunity. A container up ahead had its door half open, and he raced toward it, diving through the opening. He landed hard on the splintered wood floor, evoking pain in his hands and knees. English gritted his teeth to keep from crying out. He rolled to the side of the container and crawled to the darkest corner, where he hoped he could wait out the night.

English tried to silence his breathing when he heard footsteps approaching. The voices of several men talking outside his hiding place were audible, but he could not make out their words. He said a silent prayer that they, having lost his trail, would give up and return to wherever they had been before the alert sounded. His heart quickened when he heard a man shout, followed by fingers snapping. He stood up when he saw a light flash through the container door. English rushed forward when the torch shone on his face, but the door slammed shut before he got there. The latching mechanism groaned into place as he slammed his shoulder futilely against the door.

A man shouted to ensure English heard him. "A fine fat fish we have caught here." Raucous laughter responded, followed by a sound English assumed to be the men slapping hands in victory. Then he overheard a man speaking Swahili, perhaps on the phone, since he could detect no responses. English attempted to discern what was being said, but his claustrophobia made the walls close in, and panic overwhelmed his other senses. He forced his thoughts to focus on the situation at hand. The walls were not going to kill him. These men were.

Safari frantically dug his phone out of his pocket. He pressed some buttons hopefully, but the shattered device did not respond. Someone outside was speaking again. English listened intently this time.

"The boss will be here in ten minutes. He said you all did well. Look sharp, and we'll all have some drinking money tonight!" A cheer and laughter followed.

Ten minutes to get out of here. English began pressing on the container's walls. If a spot was rusted enough, perhaps he could push it out or use the cutters to open a section large enough to squeeze through. He worked quickly, but the entire container was solid. "Ugh!" he groaned before kicking the wall in a few spots out of frustration. His banging elicited more laughter from the men outside. English reluctantly accepted he was stuck and probably about to be murdered.

English decided he would not go without a fight. He grabbed the bolt cutters tight in his hand. When the door opened, he was going to smash the face of everyone he could. If he were lucky, he would get the "boss." At least Elijah's death, and his own, might impact their operations to a small degree. English almost laughed. They would just put someone else in the "boss's" position. Criminals were like monkeys. Just as you shoo one away, another takes his place.

Several minutes ticked by, and English struggled to keep the ever-closer walls at bay. One of the men outside shouted, and something slammed against the container door. Several shots rang out, followed by more shouting and other loud sounds. *Are they fighting?* If English had to guess, he would say they were, and it was violent. This infighting may mean fewer people to confront when they open the door. English would still be in for the fight of his life, but his odds just went up.

Safari heard the sound of the door's latching mechanism and girded himself for an attack. He gripped the cutters tight and prepared to charge. The rusty door barely opened.

"Deputy Commissioner Safari?" a hushed voice urgently whispered.

English did not recognize the voice, but there was a familiarity to it. He stood up slightly and whispered a cautious reply. "Yes?"

"You are a fortunate man," the voice outside responded in a relieved tone. The door opened further, catching English unaware as a torch shone in his eyes. His plan to charge evaporated.

"Hurry up! Let's get out of here before whoever they were waiting on appears."

English hesitated a moment longer, then bolted for the exit. The unimpeded night sky pushed away the panic the enclosure had heaped upon him. The men guarding English were strewn about the ground, seemingly lifeless. He looked up to see who his rescuer was and saw Police Commissioner Abasi Chongoi's grim face.

"Commissioner Chongoi?" Safari's tone held so many questions.

"Luckily, I had you followed since you pocketed evidence at your man's murder site."

"You saw that?" English winced.

Abasi nodded. "I figured I would find more information by having you tailed than if I confronted you directly."

Safari was impressed. *Abasi was certainly no fool.* English looked around at the disabled guards, *nor was he someone to trifle with.*

"If we get out of this, I want a full accounting of what you know." English nodded assuringly. If this did not earn the police commissioner a measure of trust, nothing would. Abasi hid behind the container door, swearing. "We've stayed too long. They've arrived."

English snuck a quick glance where Abasi had been looking and saw a motorcade arriving. Several guard trucks surrounding a luxury sedan were pulling around towards the container.

"Can you swim?"

"Yes," English answered, not particularly liking where this was going.

"Good, we should split up. That way, at least one of us might get away."

Abasi shone his torch on English's arm, highlighting the blood that covered it, and swore again. "You can't go in the water with that; the crocs will be all over you. You run that way," he indicated the direction opposite the cars, "and I'll head for the water. If they see me, maybe you'll get lucky, and no one will follow you. We need to talk if we both survive this."

English nodded his agreement, then grabbed the commissioner's arm. "Asante sana, Abasi." The man looked down at Safari's hand and nodded once.

"Ready?" English took a deep breath and nodded. "Let's go!"

Both men sprinted in opposite directions—Abasi

towards the water, English back to the container stacks. Shouts of alarm and gunshots followed Abasi. Abasi had been right. Since they only expected one prisoner, there was no pursuit behind English. He hesitated when he reached the nearest stack of containers and looked to see if he could determine who was in the car. The darkened window only lowered slightly to convey orders to a nearby henchman. English redirected his eyes to where Abasi was running and saw him dive from the pier. The police commissioner had a significant lead over his pursuers, but they fired rapidly into the water when they reached his launching point. Hearing no shouts of excitement gave English hope that Abasi had escaped. He watched a moment longer before running off in the direction of his car.

As he approached the X-ray office, Safari slowed to scour the area for a trap. When he was reasonably assured no one lay in wait, he ran over to his Landcruiser and jumped in. He threw the bolt cutters he still held onto the floor in front of the passenger seat. A wave of relief flooded over him as the full realization of his *almost* fate sank in.

Snap out of it, English. You are not out of the woods yet, he chastised himself.

He tore out of the parking lot and raced towards the exit gate. As he had hoped, the gate's drop arm was up. Usually, the guards overrode the system to keep it that way since it meant less work for them. He stepped harder on the accelerator and practically flew past the guard shack. The guard ran out yelling but went back in nearly as fast. The apathetic man was probably more upset that he was woken up than if any crime had just been committed.

English kept his foot down on the accelerator, blaring his horn or weaving to avoid the pedestrians who meandered about the roads each night. Walking the streets in the dark was much easier than on uneven land, but it inevitably led to pedestrians being killed. Hit and runs were common in Kenya, and English desperately did not wish to add to the statistics, so he slowed marginally.

English knew he could not go home but needed to warn people and get to Tsavo Park. Until tonight, this criminal syndicate likely did not know who he was. After his encounter at the port, it would not be long before they did. Tsumbe had told him he was seen on the security cameras. He was out of time—it was most certainly solve this case or die trying at this juncture. He could go into hiding and lie low, but that would not help those around him. Nor would he be doing right by Elijah *or Tsumbe, for that matter.* No, he would see this through and make those responsible for his friend's death face justice, such as it is in Kenya.

Having a sudden thought, English tore down a side road. He knew where to find a phone at this hour, nightclub row. It would likely be in full swing, and someone would take a few shillings to let him borrow their phone to make some calls. The Miami Club appeared full to capacity, so English whipped around back to park.

English hopped out of his cruiser and quickly surveyed the landscape. He saw a group of women gathered to the side of the club's entrance. They were obviously waiting to solicit foreigners, and English made a beeline directly for them. The girls saw him approaching with intent and straightened up, doing their best to put their wares on display. A tall woman wearing a sequined hot pink mini dress stepped forward with a big smile.

"Jambo, sugar. You see something you like?"

English did his best to return the smile. "You are all quite lovely…" the girls began batting their eyes and twirling their hair even more emphatically. "Unfortunately," he continued, "I am in quite a dire situation. I broke my phone and desperately need to make a few calls."

English held up his mangled phone in the hopes of eliciting some sympathy. It seemed to have the opposite effect as the girls reverted to their previous postures and conversations. Some audibly sighed while others lit cigarettes and began scanning newcomers for potential customers.

"I can pay," he hastily added. A few of the girls turned back in his direction as he fished his wallet out of his pocket. The tall woman who initially greeted him touched his arm to stop him.

"That's OK, sugar. You can borrow my phone," she said, taking the latest version of the iPhone from her bra. She held it in English's direction but pulled it back slightly as she asked, "Now, I can trust you won't run off with this, right, sugar?"

English smiled. "Yes, ma'am."

Now, it was the woman's turn to smile. "Ma'am, I kinda like that. The name's Sarah," she said, handing him the phone.

"Mine is English," he replied while taking the phone. "Asante, Sarah," he raised the phone appreciatively as he thanked her. Turning slightly, he dialed Alex's number. It rang several times before a voice groggily answered.

"Hello?"

"Humperdinck," English said in a monotone voice.

Dead silence answered him at first. "Understood." The phone disconnected.

"Humperdinck?" Sarah asked in disbelief. "You are in dire straits for a phone and call someone to say 'Humperdinck'?"

English smiled at Sarah as he struggled to summon Kelly's phone number from memory. "It is a code word."

Sarah perked up.

"Ooh, a code word. Are you some sort of secret agent?"

English smiled again. "No, ma'am, just warning a friend. We went to university together, and one Professor we called Humperdinck always seemed to stumble upon our hijinks inadvertently or intentionally (we never knew which), so we began using his name as a warning when we did not wish to say more."

Sarah seemed impressed. "A university man, eh? Are you sure you don't need some company?"

"Unfortunately, Sarah, I am quite pressed for time. Besides, I believe you may be more woman than I could handle."

Sarah smiled naughtily. "You have no idea, sugar."

English finally worked out Kelly's number and called her.

A sleep-filled voice answered after a few rings. "Hello?"

"Kelly, it is English."

"Deputy Commissioner, is something the matter?"

"Yes, Kelly. A lot has happened, and I am worried there will be trouble. I need you to stay with your family until you hear from me again. Do you understand?"

Kelly voiced her understanding, although her tone emanated panic.

"Kelly, my phone is broken. I need Sammy's number."

"Just a second." English heard the phone switch to speaker as Kelly scrolled through some menus.

"Are you ready?"

English sandwiched Sarah's phone between his ear and shoulder and pulled a pen from his pocket.

"Go ahead."

English wrote the numbers on his hand as Kelly rattled them off.

"Asante, Kelly. Now, you must leave immediately and do not take your phone with you. If you do not hear from me, I believe both Police Commissioner Abasi Chongoi and Commissioner Sambu can be trusted."

"Oh, English, surely…"

Safari cut her off. "I am serious, Kelly. You must leave at once."

His tone left her no option but to agree.

"Asante, Kelly. Kwa heri." English heard the despair in her voice but had no time to console her. He needed information and quick. He hung up the phone and started dialing Sammy's number.

"One last call," he promised Sarah.

"Oh, you're fine, sugar. It sounds like you need all the help you can get."

Safari nodded his exasperated agreement. He really did need some help.

The phone rang once before Sammy's energetic voice answered.

"Hello?"

"Hello, Sammy, it is English."

"Yes, sir," the cheerful voice replied.

"Sammy, I am going to ask you some questions. Do not answer specifics, just yes or no, please. Do you understand?"

"Yes."

"Do you remember where I met your former employer?"

"Yes."

"Good. I need information about the primary location where you worked for him. Can you meet me now at the place I met your former employer and give me that information?"

"Yes."

"Excellent. Sammy, do not bring your work phone with you. Understand?"

"Yes."

"See you shortly, then."

"Yes." Sammy hung up, and English handed the phone back to Sarah.

"Asante sana, Sarah. Are you certain you will not accept something for your inconvenience?"

"No, you're fine, sugar. Those calls seemed quite serious. I just hope a nice man like yourself hasn't gotten himself in over his head."

"Me too, but I fear reality has dashed that hope."

"Nothing's that dire, sugar," Sarah said as she touched his shoulder. "You'll pull through. You'll see."

English patted her hand with a smile. "Asante, Sarah, I needed to hear that." The woman smiled back before English turned and jogged over to his Landcruiser. He tore out of the parking lot and raced towards the Galaxy restaurant, dodging pedestrians as they seemed to materialize purposefully before his headlights.

Safari estimated it took less than ten minutes to get to their meeting place. Unbelievably, when he arrived, Sammy was already waiting, leaning against the side of a beat-up Landcruiser.

"Sir," the diminutive man said as he pushed himself off the car, his ever-present smile firmly affixed despite the late hour.

"Sammy, asante sana for coming."

"Of course, sir. Sammy's available day or night. What is it you need to know?"

"I want to know if there are any ways to get onto Tsavo Park beyond the main entrances."

"Of course, sir, Sammy knows all the ways into and out of Tsavo. Where is it you need to go in the park?"

"I genuinely do not know. Several clues are pointing me to Tsavo. Elijah had an ancient tsavorite ring on him when he was murdered, and Lord Anson, who owned the tsavorite mines, was also murdered. I suppose the most likely place to begin is the mines."

"Okay, sir. Just a moment." The young man crawled into the driver's side and shuffled through some papers on the far side of his vehicle. He emerged holding a map and unfolded it on the hood.

"Here, sir," Sammy began while still flattening the well-used paper, "is a map of Tsavo."

English ran his eyes over the map as the young man used a small flashlight to illuminate the parchment. He scrutinized all the notations and symbols someone, presumably Sammy, had marked about the entire map.

"You have three main entrances, here, here, and … here." The driver pointed at each with a pen as he spoke. Sammy looked at English to verify he had been properly oriented before continuing.

"Now, this area here," Sammy outlined a hashed, circular shape on the map, "are the tsavorite mines."

"Why did you mark it like that?"

"Well, sir, the big equipment scares the animals away, and the mines aren't suitable for tourists, so I mostly avoided that area."

"Have you ever been there?"

"Oh, yes, sir. I have often gone to watch the workers there while waiting on clients. There is a fourth main entrance used primarily by the mines over here." Sammy's voice strained as he stretched to the far side of the map. "But I assume you wish to be more ... discreet than that," a questioning tone entered his voice as he spoke.

English nodded his concurrence.

"Then the route I would suggest would be..." Sammy paused as he studied his notes. "Right here." The young driver used the pen to reinforce a small set of brackets drawn on the map. "Before the land was donated to be a park, this was the dirt road that served the mines. It has been unused for many years, and there are places where the lack of maintenance is abundantly clear, but it is still passable with four-wheel drive."

"Do you think this road will be unguarded?"

"Most definitely, sir. There are few who even know of its existence, and those of us who know don't advertise its location so that it does not get worn down faster."

"Excellent, asante sana, Sammy. May I take this?" English started pulling the map, but Sammy placed a hand on it.

"Hold on, sir. If you wish to remain unnoticed, I would also recommend this route." The young man once again pointed at the map with his pen. "The highway would take you directly past this main entrance. However, if you turn off the road here," he said, pointing at a small offshoot, "you will drive through Marekani Town, and at the far side of town, another road drops you out past the main entrance right here." The driver traced another small road until it met back up with the route English had intended to drive.

"Good advice, asante. It is probably best to avoid detection if possible. Now, I must be off," English said firmly as he checked the time. "Getting onto Tsavo and back off before sunrise will be tight. Sammy, you need to avoid going to work for a few days. I hope I have not brought any danger to your door, but if anyone questions you about me, please tell them what you know. Too many people have been hurt over this case already. Asante sana," English thanked the driver as he lifted the map off the car's hood. "Kwa heri, Sammy."

Again, the diminutive man stopped Safari. "I'm sorry, sir, but if you truly wish to get onto Tsavo, you'll need Sammy to take you there." English began to protest, but Sammy waved him off. "You'll never find the entrance. Even in the daylight, the vegetation would prevent all but the most observant from detecting it. At night, it would be all but impossible."

"No, Sammy, I must go alone. It is simply too dangerous. Several people have been killed already."

"Do not worry, sir. Sammy knows it is dangerous." English hesitated, so the driver pushed his case. "Sammy can take care of himself, sir; he is very resourceful, as you have seen." English pondered for a moment. The man was not wrong. He was indeed resourceful. "Besides, sir, as I said, you would never find the entrance without Sammy and would have made the drive for nothing."

Finally, English raised his hands in acquiescence. "All right, Sammy, you win. But you must promise me you will use every caution."

"Of course, sir. Now, if you'll get in, Sammy must take some protective measures."

Safari eyed the older Landcruiser suspiciously before looking at his own, much newer model. "Sammy, we can take mine..."

Sammy shook his hand and head dismissively. "No, no, no, sir. *This* is the vehicle you want for such a mission." The man patted the car affectionately before rounding the back and opening the hatch. English followed to see if he could offer assistance to speed up their departure.

Sammy reached his hand inside a small hole over the wheel well and released a latch, which allowed him to lift the cargo hold's false bottom to reveal a plethora of supplies. English was impressed. Right off the bat, he saw tools, emergency supplies, and a rifle neatly organized in the hidden compartment.

Sammy held the rifle out to English. "Here, sir, if you wouldn't mind."

Safari took the weapon, albeit reluctantly. "I hope we will not have a need for this."

"As does Sammy, sir, but Sammy would rather have it and not need it than the reverse."

English had to admit he wished he had a gun back at the port. Tsumbe might still be alive had he been prepared like Sammy.

The young driver pulled a screwdriver from his toolkit and unwrapped a stack of license plates that were bound together in an old towel. English pursed his lips slightly but said nothing. Sammy answered the unspoken question anyway as he swapped plates.

"It would do us little good to be stealthy now only to be tracked down by license plate on the off chance it is seen or photographed."

Sammy was indeed cautious. Perhaps it was best he would be accompanying him, English thought. His anger over Elijah's death and frustration with the case had made him reckless. Sammy affixed the plate and then wrapped and stored the unused ones back in their hiding place. The driver looked over the other supplies and grabbed binoculars and a torch before lowering the false floor back in place.

"Let's go, sir." Sammy hurried around to jump into the driver's seat. English, still carrying the rifle, hustled to the passenger's side.

"Are you quite sure about this, Sammy?" Safari asked, apprehensive about involving anyone else in this deadly matter. "Two, possibly three, men I know have been killed because of this investigation."

The small man paused for only a moment. "Most definitely, sir. If we allow these men to intimidate us, then your friend Elijah and the others will have died in vain.

The two men locked eyes, and English nodded resolutely when he saw the steely determination in the usually happy-go-lucky face. Sammy returned the gesture before firing up the Landcruiser. Safari was caught off-guard by the engine's roar and the vehicle's rapid acceleration. It was clear Sammy had made more modifications to the run-down-looking vehicle than just hidden compartments.

Sammy smiled over at English when he stiffened

up. "I told you, sir, *this* is the vehicle you want for such a mission." When English nervously nodded in agreement and returned the smile as best he could, Sammy's smile grew even broader before turning into a burst of pleased laughter.

Once their vehicle had left Mombasa city limits, English's adrenaline high wore off, and he struggled to stay awake. He looked over at Sammy. The driver appeared perfectly alert for this time of night. Safari trusted Sammy's driving completely. He had proven himself many times over. So thinking, English rested his eyes briefly while he went over the events of the past few weeks in his head.

CHAPTER 10

The next thing English knew, a hand on his shoulder was jostling him awake. "We're here, sir."

"Hmm?" was all he managed to reply.

"Marekani Town, sir. I thought you would like to see the back route in case you have need to return."

"What? Oh, yes, asante, Sammy." English rubbed his eyes under his glasses to help himself wake up more fully.

Had Sammy not awoken him, the cruiser's violent lurching would have done so in short order. The 'road' (if it could be called a road) had devolved into a deeply rutted and potholed dirt path after they had turned off the highway. Had English driven himself, he likely would have turned back, assuming he had made a wrong turn somewhere. Sammy, however, confidently pressed on, relying on his cruiser's four-wheel drive and souped-up engine to get him through this unintended obstacle course.

It quickly became apparent to English why this lesser-used route would not be guarded, but it was slow going. The pace raised his sense of urgency, and the violent jerking rapidly added to his desire to exit the vehicle. Just when he thought he might need to ask Sammy to stop the car for a minute, the driver slowed to a crawl. They turned down a side road and soon rejoined the blissfully smooth paved surface. Sammy only drove a short distance before slowing the cruiser again.

"This is it, sir," the young man whispered as he pointed slightly to the right with his head while turning the vehicle.

English saw what he thought might be a set of tire tracks, barely visible in the tall grass. Even with Sammy revealing the location, English was doubtful he would find it a second time. Although it didn't look like a road, Safari immediately noticed this path had fewer ruts and potholes than the official 'road' they had just used to traverse Marekani Town.

Nature had erased all signs of civilization within just a moment of driving. Tall grass and brush nearly engulfed them on both sides. English felt a modicum of his claustrophobia kicking in but focused his eyes on the path ahead to avoid seeing the encroaching vegetation. This tactic worked for a few minutes until Sammy stopped the cruiser about ten meters from a solid wall of green. The driver put the car in neutral and applied the parking brake.

As he made to get out of the vehicle, he turned to Safari. "Would you mind giving me a hand, sir? It goes much faster with two people."

English nodded uncertainly but exited the car and followed Sammy to the greenery blocking their way. The young man gave a few violent tugs on some vines on the right-hand side of the path. To Safari's surprise, the entire wall seemed to move.

"You must feel around this side, sir. The drivers who know and use this gate always tie it closed. The vines grow about it, but it's worth the inconvenience to keep its existence known to only a few of us." Even facing away from the headlights, English could see Sammy's broad smile beaming with pride at his secret knowledge.

English plunged his hands through the vines until he touched the gate's metal with his fingertips. He slid his hands upwards, feeling for anything man-made that might seem to be barring the gate closed. Sammy had begun pulling and cutting vines that entangled both sides of the portal. English looked back to his hands when he felt them catch on something. A bit of probing determined that a thick wire was twisted around the gate to hold it closed. He untwisted it until the two halves separated and pulled it free. Safari gave the gate a tug to test if it was moveable, but the remaining vines held it fast. English showed the wire to Sammy and backed away to provide the driver with room to work. Sammy quickly made his way up the fence, cutting vines along the gate's opening. Once satisfied that no more vines obstructed its path, Sammy began tugging it open. English rushed forward to help pull the vine-laden gate open wide enough for the cruiser to pass through.

After driving through, Sammy hopped out to close the gate behind them. When he returned to the driver's seat, Sammy looked over at English.

"Now you see why I had to come with you, sir?" English nodded. "It is a very well-kept secret. Even the park rangers don't know about it, or else they would likely seal it shut."

English thought about it. Like Sammy claimed, probably only a handful of people knew about this entrance. Tsavo was fenced long before anyone in Kenya used engineering drawings for construction projects. Everyone involved in its installation was likely dead. If not, they would be very elderly and probably have better stories to discuss than old fencing projects they worked on in their youth. Safari was curious how Sammy learned about this secret entrance, but that story could wait for less dangerous times if they ever arrived again.

A few moments later, Sammy shifted the cruiser into four-wheel drive. "The road gets a bit rough up here, sir," he explained. Soon after, the cruiser began lurching side-to-side as Sammy tried to navigate between the deepest potholes, but some were simply unavoidable. Thankfully, the sudden heaves interrupted the rhythmic swaying, or English felt he might drift off to sleep again. To help him stay awake, English scanned the bushes for the reflective eyes that were appearing more frequently the further they drove. Safari could not identify a body to go with most of the glowing orbs and found it quite unsettling after a time. To avoid thinking about the sheer volume of animals watching their vehicle pass, he turned his eyes towards the night sky. Out here, away from the ever-present city lights, the stars exploded. This was the same sky that made him enjoy the rolling blackouts in Mombasa, and he was comforted by the thought. Sammy's voice soon brought him out of his reverie.

"*Here* is where it gets a bit tricky, sir."

English sat up and looked over the hood at a deep gorge in the path that a fast-flowing stream had carved. Sammy shifted to four-low and confidently plunged into the water. The cruiser's souped-up engine roared in protest but powered through to the far side with only a few slips along the way. After cresting the ridge, Sammy rubbed the dashboard lovingly as he smiled at English.

"She's very reliable, sir. She's never failed to get Sammy where he wanted to go." English smiled back at Sammy's appreciation for his vehicle. The cruiser's rough exterior hid a transportation gem worthy of adulation.

Perhaps because the gorge they had just crossed limited the vehicles or just the mysterious ways of nature, their path smoothed dramatically. The ride was now more uniform than many of the city roads in Mombasa.

Between the clear night sky, the smooth path, and his faith in Sammy's driving, English felt somewhat at peace for the first time in weeks. It was a calm he had not known since before Elijah went missing. He enjoyed the tranquility until it was disturbed by Sammy decelerating. The driver slid forward in his seat and stared intently over the dash. English followed Sammy's gaze and noticed a glow on the horizon.

"That's not normal, sir," Sammy emphasized the light source by jutting his chin in the direction of the glow.

"Fire?" English guessed as to what could be so bright.

"I do not think so, sir. It's too white and too steady to be a fire." The young man cut the vehicle's lights. "I think it best that whoever, or whatever, is making the light not see ours coming over the ridge."

"Agreed. Perhaps we should park and proceed on foot."

Sammy nodded and slowed the car to a stop. He reached into the back and handed the binoculars to English while pulling the rifle to himself. Sammy gave English a look that he interpreted as better safe than sorry. After what happened at the port to Tsumbe, English knew it to be a wise choice and exited the vehicle. Both men closed their doors as silently as possible.

Together, they crept slowly towards the summit. Tension was building so great in English that he felt he might crush the binoculars but could not relax his grip. His mind raced as to what could lie beyond the ridge. English knew he would find out soon enough, so he refocused on the path ahead. It would not do for either of them to trip and alert whoever was there to their presence. English intuitively lowered himself incrementally as they approached the apex. From the corner of his eye, he noticed Sammy doing the same. The pair crawled as they crested the ridge. The light that greeted them was so bright they were forced to squint as their eyes adjusted.

The valley was flooded with activity. The mine entrance was to the left, and mining operations were underway. What drew English's attention, however, was a giant temporary structure a short distance away. The whole tent-like building was lit up, powered by a myriad of generators surrounding the facility. Whatever was being done down there clearly required a lot of power. Men periodically entered and exited in some sort of containment suits. Even with Sammy's field glasses, English could not make out enough detail to guess what was occurring before his eyes. He handed the binoculars over to Sammy.

"Is that normal operations for the mine?" English's

whisper reflected his confusion.

Sammy scanned the area, making several adjustments as he tried to focus on the building.

"No, sir. I've never seen such activity before. The building is new, too. Besides, the mine is supposedly closed due to the Waliangulu tribe's hostilities."

English took the binoculars back and scanned the area again.

"That is what the public has been told. It is evident, however, that was not true as the mine is open and very active."

To be able to make an educated guess about the structure's purpose, he would need to get closer. The only details English could make out from this distance, beyond those he had already noted, were several large trucks parked alongside some costly vehicles near the tent. Frustrated, English lowered the binoculars and took in the terrain. A tree about halfway down the hill cropped out from a small ridgeline. Nothing else visible offered any semblance of a safe vantage point. He decided working his way down to it was his only hope of discovering anything useful without endangering himself or Sammy.

"Sammy, do you see that tree over there?" Sammy's eyes followed where English pointed.

"Yes, sir." The driver answered with a hint of a question in his voice.

"I am going down there to see if I can get a better view."

Before acknowledging, Sammy paused long enough to let English know he thought it a bad idea.

"Understood, sir. Do you wish for me to go with or stay here?"

"I think it best if you stay here in case someone sees

me and I am captured *or worse*. In that event, you must get word to Police Commissioner Abasi Chongoi, if he still lives, and Alex Stoney. You can trust both of them; *hopefully,* someone can get to the bottom of this."

"Of course, sir. But, be careful, and that someone will be you."

English nodded once and took a deep breath to center himself. He crouched down and began making his way to his chosen lookout point. The ground was a mix of loose gravel and some sort of barbed ground growth, which made for a tortuously slow descent. Several slips caused by the gravel resulted in cut hands as he was forced to catch himself. This investigation was undoubtedly taking its toll on him. Both his mind and body felt battered. Images of Elijah's mangled body flashed in his memory, guilting him to quit whining, even if he only did it internally.

English eventually made it to the tree and looked around cautiously. Once he was sure he was alone, he took out the binoculars and looked closer at the tent and the surroundings below. A few armed guards walked around, but not many more specifics were visible. The sounds of machinery faintly emanated from the tent. Safari tilted his head slightly so his right ear was directed towards the sounds. Unfortunately, it was not distinct enough to identify anything audibly, either. He began to feel frustrated again. He was confident the key to solving this case was in that tent, but by the looks of those guards, there was no way to discern what was in there without being killed.

Safari hunkered down for what looked like a long stakeout before realizing dawn was rapidly approaching. His vantage point would be worrisomely visible in the daylight. He could only see his quarry because of the powerful work lights strewn about the tent's perimeter. Dawn would even the playing field.

Hanging his head in resignation, English stood to leave when a flurry of activity near the tent's opening caught his eye. He focused the binoculars optimistically on that area. Workers rushed to the tent's entrance and held the flaps back, allowing several people in their contamination suits to exit. The workers proceeded to check the men with some instruments. They must have signaled the okay as the men began removing the suits.

Full of hope, English concentrated the field glasses on the group and saw an older man emerge from the protective gear. He was struck almost immediately by a familiarity with the individual. The other person had his back to English, but he was positive he had seen the man facing in his direction before. Safari scoured his memories as he watched him share a laugh with the other men.

English's memory suddenly fired, bringing familiarity to recognition when the target of his observation reached out to shake the other man's hand with a smile. He was one of the men in the picture of the port ceremony Elijah had in his files. It was none other than the 'late' Lord Marcus Anson. English could not contain his shock. The government claimed the Waliangulu tribe had killed Lord Anson and closed Tsavo Park because of it. *What could be so valuable to cause all these powerful players to conspire with the government?*

Another person clad in one of the protective suits emerged from the tent carrying a silver briefcase, which he laid on a table. They pulled a glass jar from the case, and the man who had shaken hands with Lord Anson stepped forward. He grabbed a device from the table and held it to the jar for several minutes. The device must have finished whatever it was doing, for a cheer went up, and the men all began congratulating one another.

The man using the device slightly turned as he spoke with Lord Anson. English was taken further aback as he recognized this man as well. It was Spencer, the sickly member of John Collette's party, who the rest of the team did not particularly like. As he looked for a way to get closer for a better view or to hear some of the conversations, English was startled by Sammy's voice behind him.

"Do not move, sir."

Safari responded in a harsh whisper. "Sammy, keep your voice down."

Again, the driver responded, this time with more urgency. "Do not move, sir."

Exasperated, English stood from his crouching position and turned to face the young man. He was shocked to find Sammy pointing the rifle in his direction.

"Sammy, for God's sake. What are you doing?"

"I told you not to move, sir," was all Sammy said before firing.

English flinched before looking down at his chest, expecting to see blood gushing from an open wound. Instead, he was nearly bowled over as a heavy object struck him from above. When he recovered, he saw at his feet a large leopard, blood pouring from a bullet wound in its neck.

Shock tore through English's body again, quickly replaced by gratitude. The young man had probably just saved his life. Shouts and alarms cancelled any chance of him thanking Sammy. Instead, the pair scrambled back towards the Landcruiser. Before they had reached the ridgeline, the guards began firing randomly up the hill. English chanced a look behind and saw Lord Anson and the American bolting from the tent entrance towards the luxury cars.

English was only a second behind Sammy as both men jumped into their seats. Sammy turned the key, and the cruiser roared to life. He slammed it into gear and tore out in the direction they had come. English and Sammy were quiet as they took turns checking the mirrors for signs of pursuit. After a few minutes, English broke the silence.

"Thank you, Sammy. I did not see that big cat. I would have been finished if it were not for you. I am forever grateful."

The driver nodded in acknowledgement. "Yes, sir. He looked as if he were about to pounce, or else I would not have fired. It is a shame. He was a beautiful animal. But you do pay my salary, so..." Sammy trailed off into one of his enormous smiles, which elicited a chuckle from English.

"Indeed. Remind me to look into a raise for you when things settle down."

Impossibly, Sammy's smile seemed to widen further. "Do not worry, sir. Sammy will remind you."

After another shared laugh, both men fell silent. English was trying to decide what his next move should be while Sammy's total concentration was focused on the path the cruiser was careening down. He only slowed when they crossed the treacherous gorge, but the cruiser managed it handily before Sammy was again gunning the accelerator.

Sammy finally broke the silence again. "Where to, once we leave the park, sir?"

English had been asking himself the same question with no adequate answer coming to mind. He looked out the window to where the sun was rising, turning the sky a mixture of pink and orange.

"I need to go somewhere safe to think about these new revelations, how it is all connected, and what my next move will be. From what we observed back there, the only certain fact we know is the government is lying about why they closed Tsavo. Since the government is involved and appears to be silencing people who find out, we need to go somewhere the government has no real presence. The slums are a possibility, but I can see a lot of danger between here and Nairobi if they are looking for us."

"Somewhere the government is not, hmm…" the driver said, thinking out loud. "What about Malindi?"

"Malindi," English nodded approvingly. "That is a good thought."

English considered the driver's suggestion. The Italian Mafia had taken over Malindi decades earlier as an inroad to various African markets. They also used it as a vacation spot or hideout for their members as needed. The government had long ago decided they had enough problems without taking on the Mafia. They did police their own to what the government considered an acceptable level, which was a plus.

"Once again, Sammy, you have proven your worth. Let us head towards Malindi. We can regroup and perhaps find our path forward."

"Yes, sir," Sammy replied as he stepped harder on the accelerator. When he saw Safari put his hand on the dash to steady himself, he spoke again. "Sorry, sir, but if we are to beat any pursuit to the front gates of Tsavo, Sammy is going to need to drive quite fast."

"Do what you need, Sammy.   I trust your judgment."

Even as he said the words, English was forced to grip tightly to the handle as Sammy violently swerved to avoid an animal stopped on the path.

"That was a close one." The driver smiled as he leaned forward to better view the terrain ahead. Before long, Sammy stomped hard on the brakes and sent English to open the secret gate. English closed the gate after the cruiser passed and then raced to the car. Even before the door closed, Sammy was accelerating again.

The landscape flew by as the dawn light grew quickly. The Landcruiser's speedometer maxed out at 180 kilometers per hour, and in short order, Sammy had it pegged. The landscape on each side was a blur in the low light, but the road was well-lit after Sammy switched on the safari floodlights. Sammy spoke in a distracted manner as he scoured the road ahead.

"If we are fortunate, sir, they will not realize we had our own exit and will only block the main ones. However, we may be in a sticky wicket if they are clever enough to block the highway."

English had not thought that far ahead. Getting to Tsavo was where his plan ended. He was grateful for Sammy's help and would likely have died from a leopard attack if he had not been there. He did not want the young man to suffer consequences for his loyalty to him. So thinking, English looked woefully at Sammy's rifle before pulling it to the front seat to keep at the ready. Seeing the move, Sammy pressed harder on the accelerator, hoping to draw more power out of the already maxed-out engine.

"The moment of truth is here," the driver wistfully muttered as he flipped the lights off and slowed the cruiser as they approached the Tsavo Park main entrance.

It had taken less time than English had expected. He gripped the rifle tightly and swallowed hard to force his heart back down out of his throat. Their cruiser crested a slight rise in the road, and the lights from the park's main entrance were now easily seen ahead. Both men said silent prayers while they sped towards them.

As they drew near the entrance, English and Sammy grew cautiously optimistic. No sign of guards or roadblocks was visible, and the driver gave Safari one of his broad smiles. Now, all they had to do was make it a short distance past the entrance turn-off, and they would likely be home-free. English loosened his vice-like grip on the rifle, allowing some color to return to his fingers.

They were close enough now that English could see the front gates, and he leaned over to see around Sammy. Relief hit him. "Closed." The tension left him as he sat back heavily in his seat.

Sammy kept a constant speed until they reached the point where Tsavo's entrance lights illuminated the road. Then, they heard a sound that brought back dread—a solitary gunshot pealed in the distance. English's grip immediately tightened on the gun, and Sammy's foot slammed the gas pedal back to the floor. More shots rang out, and both men ducked as best as they could as several bullets connected with the cruiser. Panic peaked when the rear window exploded, causing Sammy to swerve wildly before regaining control of the vehicle. Once they crested a small hill, Sammy flipped the lights back on and wiped the sweat from his forehead with the back of his hand. English twisted around to examine the window and look for signs of pursuit.

"Are you all right, Sammy?"

Even after their close call, a small smile crept onto his face. "Yes, sir, although I fear my lady did not fare as well." The man's smile momentarily turned to a frown as he rubbed the dashboard consolingly.

"Sorry about that. I promise when this is all done, I will pay to fix her."

"Hakuna matata, sir. Sammy will fix her."

"Once we get these bastards, we will see to fixing her," insisted English.

Sammy swerved into the other lane to give a group of camels walking down the road a wide berth. Even so, the animals, spooked by the cruiser's speed, bolted in all directions.

"Let us hope we get to safety first, sir, and then we can worry about fixing her up."

"Agreed. Do you think we are in the clear?" English asked as he swiveled in his seat to look behind them.

Sammy checked the rearview and both side mirrors. "It is hard to say, sir. They were behind closed gates, which bought us some time, and not many vehicles can keep up with Sammy's lady here." The driver patted the steering wheel in a mixture of love and pride.

English smiled at the young driver. This is why he joined the government. A young man starting with nothing is motivated to improve his situation and makes something of himself through hard work and determination. It would not surprise English if, in a few short years, Sammy had a fleet of vehicles under his own company. He only wished the government would afford people like Sammy the opportunity to try without corrupt officials or criminals taking away that dream.

English looked behind them again and, seeing no pursuit, suddenly heard his father's voice usher a warning in his subconscious.

"My father used to tell me, 'Never forget, you may outrun a man or a car, but you will never outrun a radio.' He told me this to dampen any desires I might have had to be a criminal, but I fear the lesson may apply here. If I were our friends from Tsavo, I would have called ahead to block the turn-off to Mombasa. Since that storm destroyed the direct road to Malindi there is no other route available. Mombasa is where they must assume we are going. Although I doubt they know who we are unless they have seen us far better than I expect they have."

Sammy leaned forward as if he could coax more speed from his cruiser. "Yes, perhaps they believe we are poachers who merely stumbled upon their operation. That is what I would assume in their situation, sir."

"Agreed, but it is doubtful they would let any witness live if they have gone to all the trouble they have to keep this quiet." Sammy solemnly nodded before English continued. "Do you know another route past the turn-off to Malindi?"

The driver thought for a moment before blurting out his answer. "The cement factory!"

English tried to recall a cement factory, and only one place fit that description near here.

"Do you mean the crocodile farm?"

"Yes, sir. Before it was the crocodile farm and feeder of today, it was the largest cement factory in Kenya. The family who owned it had donated the land when they returned to England."

Safari had taken some friends there when they visited many years ago to watch the crocodiles being fed. All he remembered of the place was the large pit above which workers dangled chickens to get the crocs to jump for the tourists. He was not sure how this area would help their current situation.

"There must be more to the crocodile farm than I am aware of for it to be useful to us."

Sammy nodded emphatically. "Oh, yes, sir, much more. It has many roads in and out that were once used by the trucks to bypass the busy intersection area as they delivered cement to Nairobi, Mombasa, and even Malindi. The roads on site are likely in severe disrepair but should still be quite passable if we can find the entrance on this side."

"*If* we can find the entrance?"

"Yes, sir, sorry, sir. Sammy has only seen the gate from the other side. Sometimes, while waiting for my tourist groups, I would explore while they fed the crocs, and once, I came upon one of the other entrances. Afterwards, I spoke to one of the croc handlers, who told me where that gate led and of the other entrances. I never had the chance to find any of the others."

English chuckled. "You have nothing to be sorry for, Sammy. You are once again saving our bacon, as they say in England. Without you, I would never have made it tonight."

The driver smiled broadly at the praise. "Look for any turnoffs ahead on the left, sir. I am unsure of the distance between the main entrance of the croc farm and the entrance on this side, but I believe it must be in the next few kilometers."

"Do you have a spotlight?"

Sammy smiled, "Of course, sir, Sammy is always prepared. It is in the back."

English crawled into the back seat and rummaged in the hatch area until he found the spotlight. He awkwardly clambered back into the passenger seat and settled himself before plugging the light into the cruiser's twelve-volt. With a flip of the switch, Safari illuminated the side of the road as if it were mid-day.

"Keep in mind, sir, the path is likely overgrown. It would just appear less overgrown than its surroundings."

"Understood." *Well, this should be conspicuous,* English sarcastically thought as he squinted at the all-too-alike foliage.

Several kilometers into the search, Safari had to rub his eyes to reduce the strain his eyes were feeling from focusing so intently. He was beginning to doubt he could discern any path when a slight clearing of the brush caught his eye.

"Stop!" he cried out, and Sammy stomped on the brakes, causing the cruiser to skid to a halt. "Backup, backup!"

The driver shifted into reverse and tore backwards down the road until English signaled him to slow.

Pointing at an area with the spotlight, English asked, "What do you think?"

"Very promising, sir. Good eye."

The cruiser turned down English's 'path,' and Sammy leaned all the way forward to ensure he saw everything they might be driving over. The cruiser's thick steel jungle bumper made quick work of the saplings struggling to take hold on the path. A large tree root had lifted the ground ahead, confirming for English and Sammy they were indeed on a concrete road. Sammy drove to the side to avoid the exposed rebar that nature had so easily broken. He stopped the cruiser several times and got out to inspect the ground to determine which direction the road veered. Each time Sammy exited the vehicle, English heard howls of protest and warning from the various creatures that made this stretch of jungle home.

They kept creeping along this way, periodically checking the ground and avoiding obstacles Sammy did not feel like pitting his 'lady' against. Their snail's pace made English question if they had made the right call getting off the highway. Just as he thought to tell Sammy it might be wise to turn around, the driver slowed to a stop.

"It looks like we have found it, sir." Both men looked out at the rusted chain-link gate illuminated by their headlights.

"I will open the gate." Sammy nodded in response as English exited the cruiser.

The gate was easily over four meters high and heavily corroded. Fortunately, it was less overgrown than Tsavo's gate, and English quickly found the latch. Unfortunately, he also found a heavy chain and padlock on it. A massive vervet monkey perched atop the fence eyed him suspiciously as he rattled the chain futilely. He returned to the vehicle to ask Sammy if he had anything he could use to break the lock.

"I could drive through it, sir."

"No, Sammy. I would rather not give a path for the stray croc to get into nearby villages if I can avoid it."

"Good point, sir. Let us see what Sammy has in the back."

The diminutive man jumped out of the driver's seat and opened the hatch. He lifted the false floor and propped it up. Sammy dismissively touched several tools before grabbing a hammer and a long, flat-tip screwdriver.

"I do not see anything else that might be useful, sir. The pliers and other tools would snap before they damaged a chain like that."

English briefly lamented his missing bolt cutters before answering. "Agreed, we can try the hammer and perhaps your tire iron?"

"Yes, sir. That would be better." Sammy returned the screwdriver and unlocked the tire iron from its holder.

English returned to the gate and, with the help of a few whacks from the hammer, managed to force the tire iron into the lock's shackle. A few strong slams on the iron saw the lock separated and a slice in his right hand, which began bleeding profusely.

Safari cursed himself for not taking precautions against such an injury, then elevated his hand and proceeded to open the gate with his left. English waited till Sammy drove through, then closed the gate, stopping to gather the tools as he did. English grabbed a rag from the cruiser's cargo, wrapped his wound tightly, and returned the hammer and tire iron to their respective spots before closing it again. English returned to the passenger's seat but paused to tuck the end of the makeshift bandage inside the wrap, hoping it would not unravel.

English hopped into his seat, using his left hand to open and close the door.

"Are you all right, sir?" Sammy asked with concern laced in his voice.

"Hakuna matata, Sammy. I have had much worse." In truth, he had been slammed into containers, locked inside one awaiting torture or death, shot at, and nearly eaten by a leopard in just the last day alone. He was feeling quite fortunate that this was the worst of it.

"I am afraid I am not very familiar with the grounds this deep within the cement factory property, sir. I believe we will arrive at the central loading facility if I head east. From there, heading northeast should bring us beyond the Mombasa turnoff and onto the road to Malindi."

"Sounds reasonable to me, Sammy. I just hope we can avoid any run-ins with the staff."

"We should, sir. Most who work here attend the croc feeding pits and the main gate area. This path will likely take us far from any chance of an interaction."

"That is good. Even if a confrontation was fairly benign, the condition of your cruiser might raise some eyebrows. If anyone were to (though unlikely) call the police, our stealthy path would be exposed. Let us pray we have a spell of good luck for a change."

"Yes, sir. The current streak must come to an end eventually." Sammy's big smile was infectious, and both men were laughing before long.

Either the staff regularly maintained the pavement or the fence helped keep the jungle at bay as it was primarily foliage-free. Sammy picked up speed as he grew more confident that the roads held no surprises. This felt exhilarating after the brutally slow pace forced upon them by the jungle outside the gates.

The good feelings were short-lived as Sammy was again required to slam on the brakes. When the cruiser came to a complete stop, both men stared incredulously at the enormous Cape buffalo casually looking back at them.

English shook his head. "This truly is

unbelievable—a nyati on the road. Everywhere we turn, an obstacle appears. I would have given up on this case long ago if they had not killed Elijah. As it is…" English let his thought drift off as he grabbed the rifle and exited to scare the creature away.

Safari jumped around and yelled, but the great beast merely kept an eye on him as it lazily chewed its cud. Sammy tried revving the engine, but this blockade seemed acclimatized to vehicles, or perhaps it was deaf, for it had little discernable reaction to all the commotion the two men were making.

English pointed the rifle menacingly at the creature. "Oh, you are lucky we are trying to keep our mission clandestine," he said aloud before laughing at himself. "Now I am threatening wild animals. It has been quite a week."

English picked up a stick and poked the buffalo with it. Its only response was a snort and a couple of ear flicks. Safari turned back to Sammy, who gave an exasperated shoulder shrug in response to his querying look. Frustrated, he tossed the stick into the ravine along the side of the road. It landed near the snout of an enormous croc stealthily resting in the water. It snapped angrily at the disturbance, which sent a violent chain reaction in other crocs that had, until now, been undetected.

Seeing all those snapping teeth motivated the lumbering roadblock, and it bolted away. English nearly leapt with joy as he hustled back to the passenger seat. Sammy looked down into the ravine.

"I am thrilled it was not one of those monsters who had parked itself on the road."

"Do not give the universe any ideas, Sammy," English said wearily.

"Yes, sir," the driver said before gunning it down the road again.

After a few minutes of calm driving, English's adrenaline levels began dropping back to normal. In conjunction, the pain in his newly sliced hand began to rise proportionately. The throbbing made him want to clench his fist, but he knew it would likely cause the profusely bleeding wound to flow more. To take his mind away from the injury, English tried to sort the facts of the case as he knew them.

The most significant wrinkle in his working theory that Elijah's murder was related to Tsavo Park is the involvement of the Americans. He did not know the new team member he saw at Tsavo, but he had known John for years. He simply could not believe the man he knew would sanction murder. On top of that, the American government would have to authorize such a thing. It just struck him as not plausible.

English also found it impossible that it was not connected. Elijah had the tsavorite ring on him when he died. Then, there was the sudden appearance of the miraculously alive Lord Anson. Why would they fake his death and close all of Tsavo if not for an illicit purpose?

The third mystery was the material that excited Lord Anson and the American. The men had the yellow-hued substance in small glass jars. Gold would have been his first guess had he just seen the material. The glass jars, however, made him doubt that likelihood. Perhaps he could research it more if he had access to a computer.

Thinking about all the dangers he had just faced, English suddenly wanted to reiterate his gratitude to Sammy for all his help. He turned to face the driver.

"I want to thank you, Sammy, for all your help. You have placed yourself in great danger to bring justice for a man, my dear friend, whom you did not know. Without your skills, I would have never made it to the tsavorite mines, let alone survived."

Sammy started protesting his praise with an aw-shucks face, but English cut him off before he began.

"It is true, Sammy. You are a courageous and resourceful young man. You have earned my eternal gratitude and respect."

Sammy looked away from Safari. A look that showed both pride and discomfort at his boss's praise plastered on his face.

"Thank you, sir. That means a great deal coming from you."

They sat for quite a while after that in a slightly awkward silence typical of men forced to share their emotions.

English finally broke the quiet with a question. "Sammy, what are your thoughts on what those men were doing at Tsavo?"

Sammy looked momentarily inquisitive as he mulled what he knew about the situation before answering.

"Well, sir, we know a few things for certain. First, whatever they are mining is incredibly valuable. Otherwise, none of this would be happening." English nodded his agreement. "We also know some very influential people are involved if they are able to close Tsavo Park and fake Lord Anson's death." Sammy thought for a second before continuing. "Lord Anson may have done that himself to get the park closed, and it was a normal, predictable government reaction, but it seems excessive and unlikely since it disrupts tourist shillings. I would also think whatever the operation is, it is illegal. Why else go through such trouble and have such firepower on site if it was not?"

English interjected his agreement. "Precisely, Sammy. All of that is true and not even considering the possibility that Elijah's and Port Security Director Tsumbe's murders are connected."

"Indeed, sir. It would be only logical to think they are connected. It seems impossible to believe someone would risk one, let alone two, high-profile murders in so short a timespan in such a brazen fashion. If either murder was made to look like an accident, I might believe they were unrelated. It seems whoever carried out these killings had no fear of prosecution. Even the police would worry about assassinating someone above a certain social status. Either the killers are *very* well-connected, or an extremely unfortunate set of coincidences has occurred."

English interjected again, his voice a low growl. "I have found there is rarely such a thing as a coincidence."

"Agreed, sir. What we witnessed at Tsavo is likely the source of the troubles."

Safari took off his glasses as he thought aloud. "The question now is, who would have the authority, let alone the integrity, and, quite frankly, the firepower to go onto Tsavo and investigate properly? Police Commissioner Chongoi could make an argument for authority if we could link the murders to Tsavo. His forces would be hopelessly outgunned, and, as you said, these animals do not worry about killing even high-profile individuals. This would have to be a military operation. Who to speak with and how to convince them to perform such an operation is beyond my ken. When we get to Malindi, I will inform the director of what we know and, if possible, Police Commissioner Chongoi. I fear after that, we may have to lay low until we figure a path forward."

Sammy pointed ahead using his chin. "It appears we have reached the exit." English let his eyes follow and saw a small drive ending in another vine-covered gate. Both men exited the vehicle and began pulling and cutting vegetation until they felt the barrier could be moved. Safari reluctantly lifted the tire iron in preparation to break another lock. Instead, relief flooded his mind as Sammy began opening the gate.

"It looks like they forgot about this one when they were securing the grounds." English smiled as he used his good hand to help Sammy force the gate open wide enough for their cruiser. Sammy ran back and drove his badly damaged cruiser through the opening. English pulled the gate shut and joined the young man in the vehicle. A short, bumpy ride saw them able to enter the highway.

The sun finished off any vestiges of darkness remaining as the two men sped towards Malindi, encapsulated in utter silence. English was happy enough to see the night sky disappear, which angered him further about this entire situation. He had always loved Mombasa nights. The clear starlit skies, the cool breezes, and the sounds of nature had always felt like home. Now, he could only associate Mombasa nights with the evil being done by these animals.

He had always known criminals operated in darkness. English's new stark reality of Elijah's death, seeing Michael Tsumbe's murder, and now being chased and shot at by those at Tsavo shattered any lingering romantic notions about nighttime in Mombasa. The darkness offered protection, which allowed the evil in men's hearts to come out to play. It seemed that only during the day was there a chance for men to let their better angels rule their hearts. Never had Safari felt so hopeless nor so pessimistic about Kenya's future. More anger settled into English for these men who not only murdered his friend and destroyed his love of Mombasa nights, but they also eliminated his sanguine expectations for his country's destiny.

A hint of a smile touched English's lips as he remembered Elijah telling him he was mad for holding such notions, but Elijah also had begun to believe. The smile was short-lived as the happy visage of Elijah from that memory truculently morphed into one of his bloated carcass lying motionless. Safari knew he needed to bring these men to justice, or he would never remember Elijah as he was, and he knew Mombasa nights would never again bring him joy.

The following two hours, English spent silently evaluating his list of allies, which, unfortunately, was sparse if he was being generous with himself. There was KRA Commissioner Sambu, Police Commissioner Chongoi (if he still lived), his friend Alex Stoney, and a few friends serving in the Navy. Though these were influential people in their own right, they were woefully inadequate against the forces that appeared to be coalescing as he peeled back another layer of the conspiracy Elijah had uncovered. English, himself, headed an enormous branch of KRA here in Mombasa but was only sure of Kelly's and Sammy's loyalty. Last night Sammy's dedication and courage were unquestionably proven. Indeed, without Sammy, English would have joined Elijah in his fate. His allies might be few in number, but each of them was of such boundless character that, with a bit of luck, they might just best the cabal responsible for the murder of his friend.

CHAPTER 11

Sammy slowed the cruiser as they neared the outskirts of Old Malindi proper.

"Best to not draw attention to ourselves," the young driver explained.

English looked around at the bullet-ridden vehicle with shattered windows and gave a small chuckle. "Yes, just two men returning after a bit of a hunting accident."

Sammy shrugged off his boss's concern. "Not to worry, sir. Many vehicles outside the larger cities are in much worse condition than Sammy's baby." The driver consolingly patted the dashboard of his beloved cruiser.

The young man's face turned serious as he slowed further and pulled the vehicle to the side of the road. "That is new." He added a chin point down the road to draw English's eyes towards the drop bar visible across the street in the distance.

"I have not been to Malindi for some time, but I *definitely* do not remember being required to cross a checkpoint to enter. The question, Sammy, is, has that been set up for us? I find it nearly impossible to believe our enemies had figured out we would head to Malindi when we only decided that a short while ago. Then again, the last few days have redefined the word *impossible* for me. I think we must get closer and take a better look. Would you agree?" The driver nodded that he did. "In that case, let us proceed. Just be ready to get us out of here if things go badly."

The driver shifted the cruiser into gear and let the vehicle crawl forward. His eyes scanned the road ahead as he whispered, "Sammy is always ready." He pulled the cruiser back onto the roadway and drove towards the red and white drop arm that hung across it.

Sammy slowed again once they were close enough to see the situation clearly to give English time to decide whether to proceed or not. There were only two people visible at the checkpoint. One was a tall, thin African man whose position placed him as the operator of the manual drop arm. The other was a white man standing between the drop arm and a high-end Mercedes sedan positioned to block vehicles attempting to bypass the checkpoint.

Safari took this as a good sign. "It looks like the Italians are controlling access to Malindi. I believe this is the best scenario we could face at this juncture."

"I agree, sir. From what I know, the Italians would not get involved with something as overt as what we saw at Tsavo."

"That would indeed be a significant deviation from their historical modus operandi. Besides, there are only two of them. These are the best odds we have faced all night. I vote to risk it. What say you, Sammy?"

"Sammy votes yes as well, sir. Entering Malindi is one of our safer options. Sammy loves driving, but it would also be good to stretch my legs, and baby, here, will need some petrol before long."

"That settles it. We enter Malindi, get petrol and food, and perhaps devise a plan more ambitious than living through the night. Pray we fare better in Malindi than we have elsewhere." English shook his head, partly in disbelief at how crazy his life had become since Elijah went missing and partly to clear the worrisome thoughts that went against the words he had just uttered.

"Do not worry, sir. Sammy has a good feeling about Malindi." The smiling driver's positivity was inherently infectious. Safari found himself subtly smiling as they stopped before the drop arm.

Sammy rolled down his window as the Italian strolled over. English's nerves were rattled when the man looked towards the rear of the cruiser and headed there instead of approaching the open window. Both men watched in the rear-view mirror as the guard took note of the damage, even taking a picture before coming back to interrogate them. Safari renewed his appreciation of Sammy's prudent decision to swap his plates before this venture.

"Troubles?" The stocky man asked Sammy, his thick accent confirming English's theory that the guard was Italian.

Sammy flashed his big smile while denying it with several shakes of his hand. "Jambo, hakuna matata. Another driver thought I had stolen his business, is all. He did not take it well." Sammy chuckled, and the sentry grunted in acknowledgment.

"You here for business or pleasure?"

"Just stopping for a spot of lunch, some petrol, and to stretch our legs for a bit."

"In that case, make sure you visit L'osteria di Malindi and tell them Ginu sent you. It's my cousin's place. He'll set you up real nice."

Ginu looked as if he were about to turn away, but English's curiosity got the better of him. "Why the security? Neither of us remembers such measures from the last time we were here." The Italian looked carefully at Safari for the first time, and his face lit up in recognition, immediately making English regret opening his mouth. Even Sammy's face looked pained.

The guard brought his cell phone up and began scrolling with his thumb as he answered. "We had some troubles at the port a few weeks ago. Some things don't mix with our tourist industry, and we can't have that now, can we?" Both passengers nodded and muttered nos to agree with Ginu. Ginu stopped scrolling when he seemed to find what he was searching for. He held the phone up and looked between it and English several times. "Are you sure you're here on pleasure, Deputy Commissioner?"

Safari could kick himself. So much for being discreet. "Quite certain. Just some food and petrol. I would be in my official vehicle if I were here on *official* business."

"I would guess there's more to this story than I am being told." Ginu paused but continued when neither Sammy nor English moved to fill in any details. "Suit yourself. We in Malindi understand playing your cards close to your vest. I am willing to grant you access to Malindi. Just be sure if you return in an *official* capacity, you remember our hospitality." The big man had tilted his head downward to give English an intense look.

"Of course. I will consider your kindness in any future endeavors."

Safari hated making this promise, but favors were the currency through which much of the world operated.

"Good to hear. Enjoy yourself, Deputy Commissioner. Do try L'osteria di Malindi. You won't regret it." With that and a double tap on the cruiser, Ginu nodded to the arm operator and backed away from the vehicle. Sammy sped forward as soon as the arm provided clearance.

"Remind me to keep my mouth shut, Sammy." The driver smiled as he simulated wiping sweat from his brow and added a "phew." English chuckled. "I must be delirious from exhaustion. I refuse to believe I would have made that mistake if my wits were fully intact."

"Certainly, that is the case, sir. Perhaps while you are in this state of mind, we should discuss my pay raise." Both men laughed as they drove towards L'osteria di Malindi. Ginu was not wrong in recommending it. The restaurant did indeed have an excellent reputation.

The pair found L'osteria di Malindi. It was an impressive building with Mediterranean architectural influences. Though it was a restaurant now, it was evident L'osteria was once the villa of a very wealthy Italian. Not only was it a grand home, but it was centrally located in downtown Old Malindi Proper. That right was likely reserved for only the most well-connected individuals.

It was still early for lunch on the African coast, so plenty of parking was available at the famous eatery. Several customers' vehicles could be seen in the lot across from L'osteria, and English surmised it would be full in another hour or so. Safari was famished but instructed Sammy to keep driving. The young driver's stomach growled in protest, but he did as he was bid.

"I believe it best if we get the beast here," English patted the dashboard appreciatively, "some petrol before we fuel ourselves. Now that we know I foolishly let myself be identified, there is a genuine possibility for a hasty retreat. If that possibility comes to fruition, I would hate for us to be scuttled by an empty tank."

"Very wise, sir. I admit my belly has been doing most of the thinking since Ginu mentioned L'osteria." Both men chuckled as English held his abdomen and nodded in agreement. "Sammy is pleased to see your newfound appreciation for his baby." The driver smiled wide as his hands caressed the steering wheel.

"She deserves every accolade. I am not certain my cruiser would have made it past some of our obstacles last night, let alone taken the beating she has received since."

Sammy nodded his concurrence as they pulled into a filling station.

English checked his wallet. He tended to carry large amounts of paper money because he had fallen victim to a bank card machine theft some years earlier. A machine near the Nakumatt had a skimmer inserted, and he, along with hundreds of others, had their accounts compromised. Since then, he has withdrawn money directly from the bank and only used his card at places he trusted well. Most Kenyans quickly converted to the technology where all purchases are made via mobile, but English felt that was just another unnecessary risk. Besides, he only had a work mobile and thought it inappropriate to install such applications on it. Unfortunately, with all that had occurred recently, it had been some time since his last visit to the bank. His funds were somewhat depleted. Some quick calculations led him to believe he had just enough to cover the petrol, lunch, and, if they were cheap enough, a pair of pay-as-you-go phones. He would not risk using his card unless it were *absolutely* necessary to avoid alerting anyone to their location.

Both men opened their doors and exited the cruiser—Sammy with the verve of a young man who is accustomed to passing many hours in the car. English eyed the driver with envy as his body protested the simple act of standing up. The time spent as a passenger seemed to have given every inch of him the realization of how badly he had been maltreated these past few days. When he and Elijah had started at KRA, they would conduct lengthy stakeouts, give chase, and occasionally be forced to get physical to bring criminals to justice. He did not remember ever feeling the aftermath of his endeavors this badly before. Safari idly wondered if age was beginning to weigh into the equation. He checked the pump number, stretched his stiff back, and headed to the station to pay.

English nodded to the attendant, who watched Sammy suspiciously from behind the counter. He couldn't blame the clerk. Their cruiser was rough-looking, was missing a rear window, and was riddled with bullet holes. Safari had to admit that if he saw them pull up looking as they did, he would also be eyeing them sideways. He ignored the teller and headed towards the case holding the pay-as-you-go phones.

The selection left much to be desired. Only empty

hooks greeted English from where cheap smartphones would usually be. The only options were basic flip phones or expensive smartphones (locked behind plexiglass). Considering his budget constraints, Safari grabbed two flip phones and proceeded to the cash register. He had to work to get the attendant to pull his eyes from Sammy filling the battered cruiser's tank.

"Hello, samahani bwana." The man finally looked at English as he held up the two phones. "Do you know if these work well?"

"Ndiyo, they're good. Not fancy, but you can call and text on them, and they come with sixty minutes. You can buy more here or call the number on the back and punch in your credit card number. It's cheaper if you purchase up front."

"Asante, sixty minutes should suffice. I will take both of these and the petrol on pump three."

The attendant's face relaxed now that someone was paying for the petrol Sammy was pumping. "Would you like me to help set up those phones? I've become quite proficient."

"Tafadhali, it would save me much frustration. I am afraid technology does not like me very much." Both men smiled as English passed the phones to the now-helpful attendant.

Indeed, the man was proficient. He had unboxed the phones, installed the batteries, and connected the SIM cards in no time. "Would you like me to call one of the phones from the other so the numbers are in the directory?" Safari nodded, and the man began punching the numbers from one of the phones into the other before handing it back. English answered it as it rang.

"Hello."

"Hello," the attendant answered on the other phone.

Safari was pleased both phones worked, and he did not have to figure out how to set them up.

"Asante sana, this is the first thing that has gone well today. Perhaps you have changed my luck."

"Karibu, I hope your day improves."

English raised his eyes hopefully, nodded, and returned to the cruiser. He handed one of the phones to Sammy, and they both climbed into the vehicle.

"The man called your phone from mine, so the numbers are in the call directory. At least we can contact one another if we get separated. Unfortunately, I do not know any numbers besides Kelly and Alex, whom I asked to go into hiding until I figure this out. For now, let us see if we think L'osteria is worthy of Ginu's high praise."

Sammy excitedly nodded as he turned the key, and the cruiser's modified engine roared to life. He navigated back to the restaurant and deftly maneuvered the big vehicle into the only spot remaining in front of the eatery. The young man's broad smile returned to his face.

"I love obtaining a good parking spot."

English nodded. "Indeed." He laughed as Sammy's stomach growled in anticipation. "Come, Sammy. We will see if we can take care of that." The driver smiled as he placed a hand over his complaining abdomen.

CHAPTER 12

Upon entering the grand doors, English thought the L'osteria di Malindi certainly gave the impression it would live up to its vaunted reputation. The lime plaster coating the walls was strategically removed in the perfect locations to expose the gorgeous stone lying beneath it. Rich, dark wood was used throughout the interior and for the thick beams supporting the ceiling. The dim lighting cast by the heavy wrought-iron chandeliers was caught and reflected from hundreds of highly polished surfaces. All thoughts of the décor were quickly washed away, and mouths set to watering as smoke from the wood-burning ovens mingled tantalizingly with the heavenly scents of tomatoes, herbs, breads, and meats roasting to perfection.

The well-appointed maître d's initially enthusiastic smile quickly dissolved into a grimace as he looked the pair up and down. He raced from behind his station to ensure they were unable to gain further entry into the famous eatery.

"Perdonami," the man's thick Italian accent was noticeable even though he spoke only one word. "I'm afraid the L'osteria di Malindi has a strict policy on acceptable attire. I'm sure you understand." The maître d' held his hands wide as if he feared these vagabonds might attempt to race past him.

English and Sammy looked themselves over and had to admit they appeared particularly down at heel, especially next to the tuxedo-wearing man confronting them. Sammy's ever-present smile mutated into something snarl-like, and his stomach growled in protest. English had to admit between the dirt and tears in their clothing and the blood-soaked rag wrapped about his hand, they were quite a sight. His parents had ingrained in him the importance of appearances and first impressions, so he rarely went out looking less than presentable. It had not occurred to him that he might look bad enough to be kicked out of a business. He shook his head. *Mother would be most displeased*, he chuckled to himself. English regretted not buying them a snack at the petrol station, but he knew he barely had enough money to eat here as it was.

"Of course, sir," Safari said, acknowledging the man's justified concerns. "Come, Sammy; we will find another place to eat." Disappointed, the driver turned to go. As English followed, an idea struck him, and he spoke to the smaller man in an overly loud voice. "Perhaps Ginu could make a different recommendation. He surely knows some other restaurants."

The maître d's ears perked up at the mention of Ginu's name, and he raced to stop the departing men.

"Ginu? He sent you? Scusi, are you Deputy Commissioner Safari?"

"Hmm? Oh, yes, I am Deputy Commissioner Safari."

"Perdonami, Deputy Commissioner. Ginu alerted us that you might be coming to our establishment, but he gave no warning about your…situation." The maître d's nose wrinkled slightly in disgust or discomfort; English could not be sure. "Please, signori, allow me to find you a table. Perhaps a private room in the back?"

English was about to agree gladly, but Sammy spoke up before he had the chance. "Would a front window table be possible? I want to keep an eye on my vehicle." He wisely did not mention that since the window was shot out, it was an easy target for theft.

The maître d' let out his breath in a huff but managed to keep his tone amiable. "Of course, signore, I have just the table." The man led the disheveled pair to a table with a view of Sammy's cruiser. "Will this do?"

Sammy leaned over the table and verified he had a clear sightline before answering. "Yes, this will do nicely, asante."

"Perfetto," the maître d' said as he placed their menus on the table. "Sebastianu will be your waiter. May I take your drink order while you decide?"

Safari only now realized how parched he was and knew what would best quench his thirst. "Cold Tangawizi if you have it. Water if you do not."

"Very good, signore. E tu, signore?" the man directed towards Sammy.

"The same, asante."

"Eccellente, Sebastianu, will be right out with your Tangawizis." The sharp-dressed man quickly departed. English humorously thought the man's rapid egression was fueled by a worry his clothing would be infected by theirs.

English decided he desperately needed to wash up, but his manners dictated he offer Sammy the chance to go first. "Sammy, would you like to use the facilities while I watch your cruiser?"

"No, sir. I can wait. That hand of yours needs to be washed."

Safari looked down at his hand and nodded appreciatively. He painfully returned to his feet and stretched his back before making his way towards the washrooms. He noted on the way that boisterous laughter was emanating from one of the closed-door private rooms. English idly thought if he and Sammy had taken the maître d' up on his suggestion of sitting in one of these rooms, they could close the door and pretend none of this was happening. He grimaced as his father's admonition about *'wasting time wishing'* whispered through his memories.

"If you want better times, make them come about, English," Safari muttered to himself as he pushed the door open with his good hand. He went immediately to the sink. The mirror's biting criticism warned him to be more careful in the future. English slightly winced as he removed the bandage from his hand and tossed it in the receptacle. Dirt was caked into the wound, and he washed it out as best as he was able without risking a new round of bleeding. Next, he set his glasses down and washed his face. When he looked back in the mirror, he felt almost human again. He quickly used the facilities, rewashed his hands, and wiped the sink down to ensure no blood remained. The waiter was speaking with Sammy as English reached their table.

"Here he is now," Sammy indicated English with a tilt of his chin, and the waiter turned around to greet him.

"Buon pomeriggio, signore," the waiter said exuberantly. English nodded and slid into his chair. Immediately upon taking his seat, Safari was surprised by a loud cry of "quattro stagioni" in an exaggerated Italian accent. It came from the same private room he had heard on his trip to the restroom. Sebastianu hung his head slightly with a whisper of a sigh before perking back up.

"Perdonateci, signori, a *spirited* group of Americans has been here since opening and enjoying our extensive collection of … adult beverages. They are having quite a good time and laugh hysterically each time one yells, 'quattro stagioni.' We don't understand why the four seasons pizza is so funny, but it's good to see them enjoying themselves at our fine ristorante."

English dismissed the waiter's concerns. "Hakuna matata, Sebastianu. We are just grateful to be seated, and the heavenly aroma surely portends a wonderful meal." Sebastianu gave a slight bow of appreciation as Sammy smiled and rubbed his hands together in anticipation. Safari looked down quickly at the menu and decided on his choice. "I intended to have something else, but now that I have heard such a thunderous recommendation, I will have the quattro stagioni. A good pizza sounds deeply comforting at this point."

"Eccellente, e tu signore," the waiter said, addressing Sammy.

The driver pursed his lips, and his head moved back and forth as he weighed the options. "I was thinking about the saltimbocca, but I must admit, the quattro looks good. I will have that as well."

Sebastianu chuckled. "Molto bene signore. I will have those orders out immediately." The waiter nodded at someone, and they brought a basket of fresh-baked bread and poured some olive oil for dipping on a plate.

The diners could barely wait until Sebastianu departed to tear into the bread. Sammy excused himself and headed to the restroom even as he was still chewing. English moved closer to the window to keep an eye on the cruiser. Between the delicious bread and the Tangawizi, English began to relax, almost forgetting that he had spent the past day narrowly avoiding death. He idly chewed as he watched life in Malindi casually stroll by outside. English smiled up at Sammy as the small man returned to the table.

The driver immediately tore off another hunk of bread and took a bite. He held up the remaining piece and voiced his pleasure. "I never thought bread could taste so good," he said with a smile before popping it into his mouth.

"Absence makes the heart grow fonder," English rebutted jokingly. "I am sorry to have put you through these tribulations. I am certain this is not what you thought you signed up for when you took this job."

Sammy waved his hand in dismissal. "It is *definitely* not what I expected, but it has been exciting, to say the least."

"Exciting is one way to put it. Dangerous, deadly, any number of other adjectives might be more appropriate."

The driver chuckled. "No more so than my previous job, but I was usually more prepared in that one. I always had food tucked away for when the tourists wanted to stay longer than the agreed-upon contract. I wish I could say that being shot at was a new experience, but on several occasions, I came upon poachers in the parks and had to flee as well. The animal encounters were also more frequent. So, all-in-all, I would say this has been on par with my work experience, just without a packed lunch." Sammy's smile elicited a laugh from his boss.

"You have most definitely lived an adventurous life. I must admit I am not quite used to this much excitement packed into such a small span of time."

"To be fair, sir, I was not with you for your adventures on the port. It sounds like that was an even closer call than we had last night. You are lucky the port security director showed up when he did, not to mention the police commissioner. I might be investigating *your* disappearance if they hadn't been there."

"True, Sammy. Poor Tsumbe. I had wondered what side of the law he was on since I met him. He proved to be true in the end. His cavalier mannerisms were a clever tool for disarming people. I hope to bring him some justice also before this is over. As for Commissioner Chongoi, when last I saw him, he was diving into the harbor. I know not if he survived the experience. I plan to call him from the payphone near the front door once we finish. If our pursuers are aware of his identity, they may have his line tapped. I would rather be on our way before anyone could be sent to look for us here."

"Wise decision, sir. Even if I am accustomed to significant excitement, I would prefer to steer clear of another shootout if it can be avoided." Sammy smiled in such a way that English wondered if it would bother the happy-go-lucky man either way. He secretly wished, not for the first time, that some of the young driver's unflappability would rub off on him.

The two shared stories and laughs while they waited for their food. Sammy told a story about a group of Dutch tourists who were loud, harsh, and abusive the entire time he drove them around. That all changed when a pack of lions noticed the loutish group standing in the van with the roof raised. Sammy sheepishly admitted he took a little longer than usual before lowering the vehicle's roof back down. "They were much better mannered for the rest of their visit." Both men laughed again.

English shared an animal story of his own. "It was nowhere near as dangerous as lions, but Elijah and I were forced to hide in a trailer hauling goats to a farm outside of Nairobi. We would have been in grave danger had we been discovered." English paused as he chuckled at the memory. "Unfortunately for Elijah, one of the goats took a particular liking to him, and it made for, shall we say, a rather uncomfortable situation for my friend." Safari laughed so hard he was unable to continue, and Sammy joined in as he imagined the scenario. English caught his breath and felt so much better. He had not enjoyed a good laugh in such a long while that he could not remember the last time he did. Their stories were interrupted by Sebastianu arriving with their pizzas. English had to suppress the urge to yell out "quattro stagioni."

"Two quattro stagioni pizzas. Is there anything else i signori need at this time?"

English looked at the pizzas and deeply sniffed the enticing aroma. "No, Sebastianu, these look and smell fantastic, grazie."

The waiter bowed slightly. "Prego, eccellente. I will check on you soon. Do not hesitate to call out if you need anything else."

The two men barely waited until Sebastianu left before each tore off a slice and took a bite. Both of them immediately reached for their Tangawizis to quench the damage caused by the oven-hot pizza. The incredible flavor and their hunger had them blowing on their slices to get the next bite in as quickly as possible. The men were all smiles as they wolfed down their meals in silence. They momentarily stopped eating when Sebastianu brought out a second Tangawizi for each of them. They both muttered a "grazie" before digging back into the next season of their meals. Only when they finished the fourth season did English sit back. With his young man's appetite, Sammy grabbed another piece of bread and munched it slightly less urgently than before. Once finished, the driver leaned back with a satisfied sigh before looking around the restaurant.

"That was fantastic, sir. The way that artichoke was seared…"

"Delizioso?" English bantered.

"I can think of no better description, sir." The driver's enormous smile seemed to fill his entire face.

"Agreed. I am glad you enjoyed it. Unfortunately, I fear it is time to get back to the business at hand." The driver's smile faded slightly as his eyes roamed back to the last piece of bread in the basket.

English chuckled. "Help yourself, Sammy. I am quite full." The driver's hand darted out and snatched the bread before his "thank you" was all the way out of his mouth. English chuckled again as he looked over his shoulder at the pay booth near the restrooms. "I am going to see if that pay booth is functional." Sammy nodded an acknowledgement as he finished off the bread. "Well, wish me luck, Sammy. I will first see if Commissioner Chongoi survived our last encounter."

"Good luck, sir. I hope he did survive now that we know he is a good man." English nodded before slowly heading to the maître d' to ask for some change to use the nearly obsolete technology.

Just before reaching the maître d' stand, the door to the private room opened, and English looked over to catch a glimpse of the party, which so enjoyed themselves while he was here. Shock registered on his face as he met eyes with none other than John Collette. He looked at the others in the room and saw it was John's team. His brief hope that John would not recognize him was dashed as the American shouted in a volume enhanced by drink. "English!" Eric and Phil turned as one and added their greetings. "Jambo!"

English panicked. If John's team was part of this criminal conspiracy, they might know English was investigating them. They did, however, seem genuinely happy to see him. He had known John for years. It was hard to believe he was involved, but his man Spencer was at Tsavo. It was irrelevant right now. Either John was involved and did not know English was on to them, or he was innocent. The only choice was to go over there and talk to the Americans. He looked back at Sammy, who was watching the entire exchange. The two shared a slight nod. English knew Sammy would have his back if things turned ugly.

By the time English reached the Americans' room, he had plastered a smile firmly on his face. "John," he said with fake enthusiasm, "Eric, Phil," he nodded towards each man as he said their name. "What on earth are you doing up here in Malindi?"

"Enjoying what is probably our last trip to Kenya, my friend." John's words slurred slightly, but he seemed more annoyed than inebriated. "Look at this," he said as he held his iPad towards English. "Some idiot did this and probably got to keep his job." Safari took the iPad and looked at the image. It was a collapsed stack of containers on a ship with a big void where containers usually sit.

"What am I looking at here?"

Eric spoke up. "That's a container ship out of Altamira in Mexico. I was down there doing security work, and some idiot thought he could open one of the containers to steal something, and the whole shebang collapsed." The men shook their heads in unison as they chuckled. "I grabbed a couple of pictures, but these are from the news down there. They tried to claim container integrity was the cause. Most people don't realize the container's doors are part of the structure, and they can't support the same amount of weight if they're open."

English nodded his head as he pursed his lips in thought. "It has been a while since I studied the stacking regulations, but I know the weight limits are affected by container integrity." He looked at the table, saw only three settings were placed, and decided he should venture a question about their missing comrade to gauge their response. "Where is your new friend? The big man with the weak stomach?"

John nearly leapt out of his seat in anger. "Friend? Friend? That jackass is the reason I'm losing my job."

Safari felt hopeful that this meant John was not involved and tried to elicit more information. "What do you mean? Losing your job? I know I am not fully versed in American culture. Still, I *do* know it is virtually impossible to lose a government position, especially one as important as yours, my friend."

John calmed down a bit and took a sip of his beer. "Well, true; technically, I'm not losing my job. I'm being moved to a position where I will never see the light of day again and can do no further *harm*," he added air quotes around harm for emphasis.

"No. Are you telling me you will no longer be visiting Mombasa? Who will sing 'Jambo Bwana' to me?"

John chuckled. "At least you appreciate my talents. This really sucks, but that's why we're up here. I always wanted to eat at L'osteria di Malindi, and it's literally now or never. You should join us."

English balked at the suggestion. "I am afraid that we cannot. We just finished eating and must be heading back to work soon. We only stopped here because we ran into some trouble on the road and needed a place to collect ourselves before heading back into the breach, as it were."

Eric nodded towards Safari's injured hand. "That does look like quite a nasty cut there."

English looked down at his hand as he answered. "Yes, I sliced it trying to open a stuck gate. I would say it looks worse than it feels, but that would be a lie. It hurts quite a bit." All the men shared a laugh. "So, tell me why you are *losing* your job, my friend."

John's head shook slightly in agitation, and he let out a puff of air before answering. "That fucker, Spencer. Excuse my French." English shook his head to indicate he was not offended. "Remember how I told you some muckety-muck of a relative of his got him onto my team?"

"Yes."

"Well, it turns out there was a reason he was so desperate to be on this trip."

"What was that?" English was hopeful he was finally about to get some answers.

John tsked. "He was being investigated back home for suspicious behavior. They pulled his security clearance after intercepting some communications, and I understand he also emptied his bank accounts. The reason he was so keen to stick close to me on the way over here is customs had word to stop him, but they don't check as closely when you're travelling with someone who has a diplomatic passport. Which, I'm told, I won't have anymore once I get back. Now he's disappeared. That mother f..." John's words were muffled by a growl-like noise he made as he ground his teeth.

"That is awful. I am so sorry, John. Is there anything I can do to help?" English decided to hold back his awareness of Spencer's location. It was an extreme coincidence John and his team came up here, and English did not like coincidences.

John perked up a little. "No, English, thank you. Are you sure you won't join us? This is the last time I will be here and be able to use my entertainment expense account."

Safari smiled slightly. "No, I am sorry, John. I must be leaving soon. If I had known it was you in here having such a good time, I would have joined."

"Well, I'll have your meal added to our bill anyway. Might as well get as much out of me while you can." John motioned for their waiter and explained that he wanted Sammy and English's bill added to their own.

"Asante, friend. I will be sorry to see you go." A thought suddenly struck English, and he looked back at the image on the iPad still in his hand. "You say someone who opened the door on this container should have known it would collapse?"

Eric answered him, "Yes. If they work on a port or a container ship, they should know enough not to take that chance. I imagine a layperson wouldn't know, but the individual was on the ship when it happened. Either they are ignorant of that information, or it was sabotage."

English whispered, "Indeed," as he looked at the photo again. "Would you be able to look up the images of the ship that was hit by pirates in the Indian Ocean a few months back?"

Eric nodded and reached to take the iPad back before typing in a search. After a few clicks and scrolls, he looked at the screen and added a "hmm" before handing it back to Safari.

English looked at the images in the feed, and his hunch was correct. The containers visible in the pictures that had been opened were either high in the stack or had no containers stacked above them. "Now that is unusual."

Even though English was speaking to himself, Eric answered him. "Yep, you don't see container ships very often that aren't loaded to the brim. I'm guessing your pirates were either former port workers or were coordinating with the workers who loaded the ship. Like I said, not many laypeople would know to avoid opening the bottom container of a full stack."

English muttered an acknowledgement, but his focus was fixated on the images. Was this how Elijah had stumbled upon this case initially? He would need to find the report to see if the container numbers were listed and compare those numbers to the scanner images Elijah had collected. Safari zoomed in on the photo, but the numbers were either obscured or too blurry to make out. He was pulled out of his concentration by the annoying sound of something rolling around on the table beneath him. He looked over the iPad to see what it was. Fury ignited in English as he saw John idly rolling a small glass jar with some yellow powder back and forth in front of him. He knew he should hide his reaction, but such a betrayal by one he considered a friend was too much. He lurched forward, grabbed John by the collar, and hoisted him from his seat.

John was utterly discombobulated as he flailed helplessly against Safari's iron grip. "English, what the hell?" he yelled out. Eric and Phil had jumped up, ready to save their boss from this unexpected attack. English sensed Sammy come up behind him as he shouted back at his one-time friend.

"What the hell, indeed! You dare to call me friend and then taunt me to my face with the reason Elijah was murdered?" English saw the confused look on John's face, but his anger would not allow him to let go of the man's shirt.

"Murdered? English, you've gone insane. What makes you think I had anything to do with Elijah's murder? He was my friend, for Christ's sake." English saw that John was waving Eric and Phil back with one hand as he tried to free himself with the other.

English tilted his head down at the table to the small jar John had been playing with a moment ago. "You have the evidence right there." John looked down in a very confused hurry before he laid eyes on the jar.

"The jar?"

"Of course, the jar."

"English, that is just a training aid I forgot to take out of my pocket before we came up here. You would know that if you attended the training session you were supposed to attend yesterday."

Safari loosened his grip slightly as he looked more closely at the jar. It had a sticker on it that said: "For training only." He completely let go of John's shirt when he fully absorbed what the man had said. "Training?"

John's voice showed his irritation, "Yes, training. The entire KRA leadership was supposed to attend our training session yesterday. Your colleagues made an excuse for you that you were out on KRA business. What the hell has gotten into you? As if I'm not already having a bad enough day, someone attacks me over a training aid. Jesus H. Christ, English. You better have a damn good excuse for that." John smoothed out his shirt as he sat back down.

"So you are really not involved?"

"Involved in what, English? Murdering people? No, I'm not a murderer. What the hell?"

"Sorry, my friend. This case has me doubting everyone and everything. When I saw that jar, I assumed you must be involved. It looks just like the ones I saw last night."

"You saw something like this?" John held up the training aid.

"Yes, exactly like that," Safari confirmed. John exchanged a worried look with Eric and Phil. "Why, what is it?"

"English, this is uranium. What is known as yellowcake, to be exact. For some reason, smugglers almost always have it in small glass jars like this. It's not necessary to transport it like this, but it's probably on some website or something. You say you saw this last night?"

"Yes, Sammy and I saw cases and cases of those jars." The Americans exchanged more worried looks as English paused while he decided if he should share who was inspecting the yellowcake. "John, there is something else you should know." John's eyes grew wide in anticipation at Safari's tone. *What could be worse than what he had just heard?* "Your man, Spencer…"

"What about him?" The mention of Spencer's name changed John's tone from worry to anger.

Safari cleared his throat before continuing. "He was handling the yellowcake."

Full-blown panic was now rampant among the Americans.

"I knew I hated that guy," Phil's voice was full of vitriol.

Eric shook his head in agreement. "That son of a bitch. You know his grandfather was on the Manhattan Project? That's why everyone always treated him with kid gloves. I should have decked him the other night when he was going on about how he could kick everyone's ass because he played rugby in college. That piece of shit."

John was much calmer than his colleagues when he spoke. "Are you sure it was Spencer you saw?" English nodded. "We need to get headquarters involved. There is a recovery team that can be mobilized. It's their job to retrieve dangerous materials from unsavory individuals. What else can you tell me about this?"

"Spencer was at Tsavo Park. They have huge tent

structures with lots of lighting and machinery. We could not see inside before we were chased off, but they had many industrial generators and personnel. They were very well-armed. We barely made it out alive." English looked over at Sammy, who confirmed his story. "Another strange thing, we saw Lord Anson there with Spencer."

"Why is that strange?"

"Lord Anson's death was announced a short time ago. The Vice President closed Tsavo Park as a precaution until his murderers could be brought to justice, or so we have been told. I think they are shipping the yellowcake out of the Port of Mombasa and having it picked up by pirates. That is why only certain containers are being opened. It is also why they murdered Elijah. He must have become aware of this smuggling. During his investigation, Elijah had pulled the scanner images of specific containers. They each had curious blank spots, which I now suspect were shielded yellowcake vials."

John agreed, "Right, that seems likely. If these men are working with someone like Spencer, it makes sense that they know what they are doing. I've got to contact HQ immediately."

Safari held up a hand. "Make certain they are not able to trace you. I do not know if your phones are being monitored or not, but I suggest acting as if they are until you learn otherwise. These men are vicious and have no qualms about killing. They killed Elijah when he learned the truth. They attempted to kill Sammy and me last night, and they killed the Director of Port Security, Michael Tsumbe, in front of me when I was investigating the port the other night."

"Michael's dead?" English nodded. "We met with

him just the other day. He was a funny guy…OK, we need to be careful when contacting HQ. Any ideas?"

Eric and Phil seemed to bounce ideas off each other with a look. Eric finally spoke up, "I can send an encrypted email from my laptop. We have that emergency satphone, which is secure, but it's back at the hotel. I haven't lugged it around since our first trip here, and we determined it wasn't as dangerous as the Embassy's security officer made it out to be."

"Yeah, OK, I think I have the rapid response email somewhere on my phone," John said as he looked through his phone's contacts. "We can send the email, hurry back to the hotel, and grab the sat phone. By the time we get there, everyone will be alerted. That is if we're lucky enough that someone checks the email."

English pulled out his burner phone and looked up his number. "Unfortunately, this is incapable of international calling, or I would let you use this. I am trying to stay below their radar, but once you get hold of your people, call me on this number." Safari grabbed a pen and wrote his and Sammy's temporary numbers on a napkin.

Eric had his laptop open and powered it on. "Boss, it's ready." John found the recovery team's emergency contact information.

"All right, pass it over." Eric pushed his laptop over to John, and the man began typing a message. He looked up at English gravely, all vestiges of inebriation wholly shed. "You're sure about this?"

"Very sure. Sammy and I saw the vials with our own eyes and were nearly killed for it."

"All right." John took a deep breath and held it as he pressed the send button. "Part of me hopes you're right, and part of me prays you're wrong, English."

"I wish I were wrong, but I think this is the last piece of the puzzle." English held up the jar of yellowcake and looked at it intently.

John held out his hand, and English passed the jar back to him. "It's funny about this. You know how much this is worth?"

English shook his head that he did not.

"Obtaining this legally? Not much. Somewhere around fifty bucks a pound. Illegally? Priceless if you find the right buyer. Wait. This is being transported through the Port of Mombasa?"

"I believe so, yes," English responded.

"Son of a bitch. That's why someone keeps damaging our equipment. If our radiation portals were set up, they would detect this no problem. Our system was designed so multiple agencies can verify the readings anytime. Port security, KRA, and the radiation protection safety board will all have terminals they can monitor. It would be too broad to control once it gets up and running. That's why we were setting it up this way, to combat corruption."

"Alex was right," English blurted out. "Alex Stoney, the head of Constructicon. Remember when I said he was complaining about someone sabotaging the project?"

John concurred, "Yes, it's all making sense now. Even if it's unbelievable, we set this equipment up all over the world to safeguard against rad material smuggling. In reality, you never expect something of this magnitude to cross its threshold. I *really* need to talk to my bosses."

"Of course," English replied, relieved to have an ally in this fight. "I need to call the Mombasa Police. Their commissioner rescued me when I was almost killed at the port, but I am unsure if he made it out. May I use your laptop to look up their number? I am going to attempt to use the payphone over there to contact him."

"Go for it." John pushed the laptop over, and Safari searched for the phone number of the Mombasa Police Headquarters. Once he found it, he programmed the number into his burner phone, thanked the Americans, and headed towards the phone booth.

"Excuse me, sir," English said to the maître d' as he held up a bill. "Would you be able to give me some change so I may use the payphone?"

"No, signore." Safari lowered the bill as his hope of a functioning pay booth was dashed. "Our phone requires no money. Feel free to use it." Relief flooded back to English.

"Grazie." Safari rushed to the booth and closed the antique doors to give himself some privacy. The sound outside was utterly cut off. *They took their discretion seriously in Malindi*, English thought, impressed. The phone was an old rotary, and English ruminated for a moment to remember how to dial using the obsolete technology. After a couple of rings, someone picked up.

A pleasant-sounding woman's voice recited a standard greeting. "Mombasa Police Headquarters, how may I direct your call."

"Yes, I need to speak with Police Commissioner Chongoi, tafadhali."

"May I ask who is calling?"

English did not wish to say his name in case someone working for Chongoi was involved. "Tell him it is his friend from the port. He asked me to call him when I had a chance."

The voice on the other end paused for a moment. "Of course, sir. I will see if he is available to take your call. Please hold."

The phone went dead as Safari was placed on hold. After a moment, Chongoi's voice came on the line in a frantic whisper. "English, is that you?"

"Yes. I am glad to hear you survived our last meeting."

The police commissioner harumphed. "Barely. One of their bullets grazed my shoulder, but the damage was not too serious. I am glad to hear you made it as well. What happened to you after we separated?"

"A lot, to be quite honest. We discovered the cause of all of these troubles."

"Do tell. I have been racking my brain to figure out what could be valuable enough to justify killing so many high-value targets. What have you learned?"

"It all ties to Tsavo Park. They have set up a uranium enrichment facility…" English paused as he noticed the line had gone dead. "Abasi, are you there?" Safari waited a moment to verify he had lost the connection. Just before he hung up, a man with a posh British accent spoke on the other end of the line.

"English Safari, what a most interesting name. So pleasing to the ears of one of His Majesty's subjects. Your name conjures up images of adventures on the great plains of Africa, blissfully kept safe by an army of locals, all while sipping on a gin and tonic. If only you could have been as accommodating as your name." The man sighed as if he genuinely wished English had just turned a blind eye to this investigation. "Alas, you seem incapable of minding your p's and q's. Mr. Safari, you have caused us no end of grief these past few days. Fortunately for Mr. Chongoi, we were able to cut off your call before he learned anything of significance that would force us to take action against him. You, however, are not so lucky. Where are you, Mr. Safari? It is a fascinating trick you have managed to pull off. We have the best technology available, yet the number you are calling from does not seem to exist. In fact, the phone you are calling from appears to have no number at all. I have never encountered such a thing in all my years of doing this sort of work. Bravo, it is not often that I am surprised."

English silently thanked the proprietors of L'osteria di Malindi for their dedication to secrecy. "I am glad I was able to give you a new experience. You seem to have me at a disadvantage, though. You know my name, but I do not know yours."

"Were it only that simple, Deputy Commissioner. For now, you may call me Harry. Now that we have gotten to know each other, I am saddened to inform you that you can no longer be allowed to traverse the path you have set yourself on. Have you mentioned our little operation you discovered to anyone?"

English thought it best to keep the Americans out of this. He knew, at the very least, they would put an end to the smuggling operation if John's superiors received the message. "Not yet. You managed to cut me off right as I was getting to the good bit, Harry."

"That is excellent news, English. If you speak the truth, we will not be forced to kill anyone else once you turn yourself over to us."

Safari guffawed. "Why on earth would you think I would turn myself over to you? I am going to bring you all to justice for killing my friend, Elijah."

"Ahh, Mr. Safari, there *really* is no justice in this world. You should know that by now. It was a shame your man, Elijah, had to die. He showed genuine intuition. We thought he had eluded us when his body was not found. Ironically, you have to die now because he had managed to hide himself from us that night. Had we found him when he was shot, you would have never known his fate, and this little investigation of yours would have never been undertaken. C'est la vie, n'est pas?"

English's blood boiled at the casual manner in which *Harry* spoke about Elijah's murder. "You bastard," English seethed. "I will come for all of you. I will put an end to your operation and make certain you all spend the rest of your days in prison."

"No, Mr. Safari. As I said, you will turn yourself over to us, and that will be the end of this unseemliness."

"And why would I do that?" English couldn't hide his disbelief if he tried.

"Because Mr. Safari, I have studied you very carefully, and I am an excellent judge of character. You would not want an innocent life to be taken in exchange for your own. Especially when it is a life as lovely as that pretty little woman of yours."

"I think you have not studied me carefully at all, *Harry*. I do not have a woman. Now, if this farce is over, I will be saying goodbye."

"Please, Mr. Safari, do not try to deceive me. Our men tracked down your woman…," English heard the man speak to someone offline, "her name?" Safari could not hear the response, but *Harry* spoke again, "Kelly, at her grandmother's house. If you do not turn yourself over there by midnight tonight, we will kill her.

Or you can deny she is your woman again, and I will call my men and have them kill her immediately. I think we will find you soon enough either way. This just makes it a little less messy for those around you."

English panicked fully now. They found where Kelly had hidden herself. He was unsure where she had gone, but it made sense she would stay with her grandmother. Kelly's grandmother lived in the slums outside of Nairobi, the last place anyone would look for her. At least, that is what Kelly must have assumed. English would not let them kill Kelly to save himself, and they knew it. Maybe they would let her live if he turned himself over, along with any evidence. They had no reason to kill Kelly once he was gone. She was not in a position where she could threaten them. Safari resigned himself to his fate.

"Promise not to hurt her, and I will exchange myself for her," English said dejectedly.

"I am a reasonable man, Mr. Safari. I see no reason to harm her if you comply."

"I am on my way," English said before hanging up. *At least the Americans will be able to disrupt this operation*, he thought as he exited the booth. He walked over to the maître d' station and addressed the man. "Is your phone capable of international calling?"

"Ma certo, signore. Our clientele frequently call back to madre Italia."

"Eccellente," English replied as he tapped the podium, walked over to where he had a clear view of the private room, and called out loudly. "John!" The man's face poked out from the chamber, looking much more solemn and haggard than English had ever seen him.

"English?"

"John, the L'osteria's phone is secure *and* capable of international calling." Safari looked over at the maître d', and the man bowed slightly.

John hurriedly grabbed his phone to find the emergency recovery team's number and raced to English. "Thanks, English. I'll get the team on it right away. You may have stopped an international threat."

English smiled. "I hope you can stop them. I fear it may be the end of the road for me," he whispered. When John's puzzled look met Safari's eyes, he continued. "They have Kelly. They agreed not to hurt her if I turn myself over to them. I cannot allow another of my friends to die when I can stop it. If there was more time, I might be able to arrange a rescue, but they said they would kill her by midnight. Just promise me you will stop them, John. You are my last hope. They, whoever they are, appear to be ignorant of you and your team. As soon as you alert the recovery group, I suggest you leave Kenya for safer waters."

"English, I'm so sorry. I could try to get you some assistance from the Embassy, but the probability that they would get involved seems pretty low to me. If Kelly was a US citizen, maybe, but otherwise…" John let his thought trail off rather than describe the likely outcome. "Well, English, I hope this is not our last meeting. You've been a good friend, and I admit you're a much braver man than I am. I hope Kelly's all right. Until next time, my friend." English gripped John's outstretched hand in a firm shake and signalled for Sammy. The driver jogged over, and the pair left with John looking after them with genuine sadness in his eyes.

Safari clasped Sammy on the shoulder as they neared the cruiser and quickly explained the situation.

"Tell me, Sammy. How fast can you get to Nairobi?" The driver smiled suggestively, and English felt reassured. "I was hoping you had another trick up your sleeve." Both men chuckled as they hopped into the cruiser. Sammy whipped out of his parking spot, and the pair were rocketing towards Nairobi before English finished buckling in.

CHAPTER 13

As Sammy deftly maneuvered the cruiser through the moderate traffic of Malindi, English tried in vain to remember where Kelly's Grandmother's house was. He knew she lived in the Kibera slum outside of Nairobi, but it had been several years since Kelly had asked him to have dinner at her Bibi's house. Kelly had unsuccessfully tried to get her Bibi to move after her husband died, but the woman was strong and stubborn. Her husband had been a mighty warrior in his youth. For some reason unknown to English, they decided to give up their nomadic ways and moved to Kibera. The man's reputation as a warrior had ensured a certain level of respect that lent itself to his wife long after he had passed away. As a result, Kelly's Bibi was as safe in Kibera as a prince in his palace, or so they thought. This is why Kelly felt she would be safe staying with her, but the amount of money these villains were willing to throw around could overcome any loyalty in the slums. Everyone has a price, it seemed. Well, thanks to John paying for their lunch,

English had a few shillings to throw around to pinpoint Kelly's location.

"Sammy, Kelly's Bibi lives in the Southwest section of the Kibera slums. Do you know the area?"

"Of course, sir. Sammy has been to Kibera many times."

"How long will it take us to get there?"

Sammy furrowed his brow in thought for a moment before answering. "It depends, sir. If we were to drive the speed limit from Malindi, it would normally take eight and a half hours, taking the one-o-three to the one-o-nine. We could do it in just under seven if we push it, and the truck traffic on the one-o-nine is not too backed up. I know a shortcut across the southern portion of Tsavo East that would shave another forty minutes off our journey if we risk returning to Tsavo."

"It would be best to arrive as quickly as possible. I am willing to risk it, but I would not ask you to risk yourself if you are not comfortable. We would still make their midnight deadline by sticking to the highways."

"Tsavo, it is then, sir. Sammy is not afraid. Besides, Kelly needs us."

English knew Sammy would say as much, but it still amazed him. He felt the need to thank him once more. "No matter how this turns out, I want to express again how much I appreciate all you have done."

Sammy smiled. "Of course, sir. This has been a most fulfilling position. It feels much more important to be doing this work rather than hauling tourists around to see animals for the thousandth time."

Before long, their cruiser was blowing past Ginu and the makeshift checkpoint. The pair waved acknowledgement as the beefy guard leapt from his chair. If they survived the day and needed to return to Malindi, it would be best to have Ginu on their side. Once Ginu realized who it was, he returned to his seat, a bit disgruntled about being disturbed but not overly angry. Once Sammy had cleared the edge of town, he pushed the beast to its limit, and English felt as if he was being pressed into his seat as they accelerated. Twenty minutes at this frenetic pace saw the cruiser arriving in Kakoneni. Sammy only moderately slowed as he peeled off the one-o-three onto a dirt road. English worried this would be like last night's deeply potholed dirt road, but it was well-packed and smooth.

Sammy spoke up as he kept his eyes peeled on the terrain for surprises. "This road cuts through Tsavo East and leads out into Kibwezi. From there, we can get back onto the one-o-nine. It is smooth like this for most of the drive."

English was relieved. His body still remembered the jostling from the roads near Marekani and feared these roads would be worse. Sammy sat up, and every muscle in his body tightened.

"Hold on, sir. This is one of the rough spots coming up."

Safari looked ahead and saw what looked like a riverbed fast approaching. His eyes grew wide as Sammy showed no signs of slowing. "That is the Galana River, sir. It is almost never full this time of year, and this is a naturally shallow area even during the rainy season."

"Almost never?" English's voice held a hint of concern.

"It will be fine, sir, as long as I do not slow. Watch for animals with me. A big hippo taking a mud bath in the wrong place will end our journey rather quickly."

Even as he focused his eyes on the river ahead, Sammy flashed his big smile again. English whipped his head forward and began scanning the horizon for any animals in their path. Before long, the cruiser was plowing its way through the quaggy ground as the beast's tires flung mud in every direction. The cruiser slipped sideways several times, but Sammy's expert hands promptly corrected their path. Halfway across the river, English did indeed spy a hippo raising itself out of the mud enough to see what was disturbing its sleep. He said nothing for fear of distracting Sammy with irrelevant information, as it was not close enough to cause them trouble.

Once they cleared the far riverbank, Sammy relaxed; moments later, English followed suit. He wiggled his jaw back and forth to release the tension that still lingered from clenching his teeth. "See, sir. Nothing to worry about," teased Sammy.

English nodded along as he widened his eyes, eliciting a small chuckle from the driver before he added, "You should see the crossing during the rainy season."

"I can only imagine. Will this road be smooth from here out?"

"Yes, sir. This dirt road is better than many of our paved ones from here until we cross the Galana again."

"Then I think I will make a call. If we are to have any chance of rescuing Kelly and me surviving, we will need more guns than just your rifle. I will try to contact Alex. I know he will come to our aid. Now, I need to figure out how to message him without alerting anyone who might be listening to his phone."

English dialed Alex's number, one of the few he had memorized, and when the voicemail answered, he spoke in his poshest British accent. "Yes, good day, sir. This is Reginald calling on behalf of the Oxford University Boat Club to thank you for your previous support of the rowing crew. We are hoping you are able to continue your generous benefaction of the sport you so revered when you attended our beloved University. Please contact me at your earliest convenience to work out the details of how you may best support us at this time. I look forward to hearing from you. Ta-ta for now."

Sammy looked questioningly at English but said nothing. Safari explained, "Alex hated the rowing team and all of the "*wankers*" who were obsessed with the sport. I believe he will realize it was me calling and use one of his burner phones to call me back. My only concern is that he will not check his messages in time since I warned him of the danger." Safari hunted around and found a scrap of paper. He began writing on it as he spoke, "This is Commissioner Sambu's address in Nairobi. If something goes awry in Kibera, I want you to get to her home and relay what we have uncovered." Sammy began to protest, but English stopped him. "Listen, Sammy, there is a genuine chance this will go poorly for me, but if I can save Kelly, I will risk it. I need to know that Commissioner Sambu will at least know what is happening. If she determines nothing can be done, or it is too great a risk, then so be it. I would hope she would see justice done, but the world of politics is one in which people continuously weigh the odds. If our own government fails us in this, at least we alerted the Americans, and they can intercept the shipments once they reach open waters."

"If you wish me to inform the commissioner,

consider it done. I do, however, believe you will make it through to see tomorrow, sir, especially with Sammy watching your back."

"I am very fortunate to have such loyal friends, and I could think of no one better to have on my side." Safari clapped Sammy on the shoulder before looking around in the back. "You do not happen to have another firearm back there, do you?"

"No, sir. I have never had need before this week. I only armed myself to protect my passengers in the event of an animal attack. We might be able to purchase one in Kibera."

"I was thinking the same, though the weapon's pedigree and functionality might be questionable. It will not matter if we only need it for brandishing purposes, but if we have to use it…" English sucked air between his teeth while making an apprehensive face to show how he felt that situation would turn out.

"At least it is a possibility, sir. We have a few hours to think of other options if Mister Alex does not respond."

"True. I suppose I could arm myself with your machete and hammer, but going up against thugs equipped like those we faced last night with such armaments is a fool's errand. The problem with Kelly's Bibi's house is it is essentially a one-room shack. We have no options other than breaching the front door and hoping to catch them off-guard. There are no windows, and any attempt to cut or break our way into another wall would alert Kelly's captors immediately. We do not even know how many are guarding Kelly or if any are lying in wait outside in the streets. This might very well be more of a hostage exchange than a rescue operation unless our luck really did change back in

Malindi."

Both men fell quiet and began to scan the road ahead, looking for any issues that might impede their progress. English spotted something large in the distance and pointed it out to Sammy.

"What is that up ahead?"

"Hmm, it looks like it might be an elephant. Hopefully, it is far enough from the road to not cause us problems." Even as he said this, Sammy slowed the cruiser ever so slightly. Both men watched as the behemoth grew ever closer. Sammy swore lightly under his breath as it became evident that the elephant was in the roadway, and a glance to either side showed no obvious alternate pathway.

Sammy coasted the cruiser to a stop and stood on his seat as he hung out of the car door, looking for a way around the massive bull elephant standing approximately thirty meters directly ahead. The animal began throwing dirt around with its trunk, and English felt as much as heard a deep rumbling sound emanating from it. Sammy lowered himself back into the vehicle.

"He is a bit perturbed by our presence and is letting us know," explained Sammy. The driver looked behind the vehicle and found a nice flat area a short distance away. "I may be able to antagonize him to the point he chases us. We can pass here if we reach a place with enough width to dodge around him."

"*If?* What happens if you manage to antagonize him and we cannot reach that wide spot?" English asked as he looked at the location Sammy had indicated.

"That would be bad, sir. I have seen one of these large bulls completely crush a safari vehicle much bigger than my baby here." Sammy patted the steering wheel as if trying to reassure the cruiser he would not let anything so horrid happen to her.

"Other options?" English asked as he eyed the enormous creature before them.

"We can try off-roading here, but I am unfamiliar with the landscape beyond the road. I have only travelled on this path a few times before and never explored further. There may be another way, but it would take us some time to find it."

English weighed the options and decided since he would likely be dead by midnight tonight, they might as well go for it. "All right, Sammy, let us see if we can make an elephant angry with us."

Sammy smiled and added, "No problem, sir," as he crept their vehicle forward. The driver stopped progressing once the elephant began pawing at the ground with one of its front feet. He looked over at Safari, "Are you ready, sir?" English nodded, and Sammy revved the engine loudly as he laid on the horn. Almost immediately, the elephant charged, and Sammy slammed into reverse, and the cruiser hurtled backwards. English felt like they were flying, but the elephant was gaining on them, trumpeting its challenge as it raced forward. Their vehicle reached the broader part of the path just as the great beast closed in, and Sammy spun them out of its way. A glancing blow from the elephant on the cruiser's rear nearly tipped them, but Sammy managed to get all four wheels back on the ground as he tore down the path.

"Phew," the driver said as he wiped the back of his hand across his brow.

"Indeed," English said as he smiled back. He had never been so close to a fully grown elephant before and never wanted to be again. "Seeing one of those animals this close…their power is indescribable."

"Yes, sir. That was definitely one of the largest I have ever seen. Hopefully, I can appreciate them from further away in the future."

English smiled again. "Yes, if I survive this, I think I am going to take a vacation where the only large things I encounter are the drinks."

"Cheers to that, sir. I could use a drink myself."

After an hour on the road, English's phone began ringing. The pair looked at the phone in apprehension as Safari slowly raised it to his ear and answered it in his fake posh accent. "Oxford Boat Crew Alumni, Reginald speaking."

Laughter greeted him on the other end of the line. "English, that is the worst accent I believe I have ever heard. You never could get that one down."

English felt relief pour into him. "Oh, Alex, it is excellent to hear your voice," he declared as he gave Sammy a thumbs up.

"Yeah, mate, I've been worried sick about you. I had for a moment hoped it was Reginald from the boat club calling so I could take my frustration out on that bloody wanker."

Safari smirked. "Yes, I thought you would like Reginald. That is one of the advantages of knowing someone as well as I know you, old friend."

"What's with all the cloak and dagger? Is your phone being monitored?"

"Not this one. I picked up a pay-as-you-go from a petrol station in Malindi. Mine was destroyed at the port. Someone was monitoring calls. They broke into a call I made from a Malindi payphone to the Mombasa Police Commissioner." As English paused to try and prioritize all the info, Alex jumped back in with more questions.

"Malindi? What are you doing over there? Is that where Elijah was killed?"

"No, no. Sammy and I just needed a place where we could safely collect ourselves and plan our next move."

"Malindi, safe? I would never think of Malindi as safe unless…"

"Exactly, the government appears to be behind all of this. Oh, and you will love this tidbit. Lord Anson is alive and well and intricately involved in this conspiracy."

Alex pshawed, "Oh, that dirty mzungu. Making me feel sorry for him."

English chuckled before adding a little more fuel to his friend's fire. "Then this will make you like him even less." He paused a moment to give time for Alex's imagination to conjure up various horrific scenarios in which the newly risen Lord Anson could be involved. "They are the ones who are sabotaging your project on the port."

Sammy and English laughed as Alex's rage exploded over the phone. "What?! Why on bloody earth are those bastards screwing with my project and my company's reputation?! Wait…" Alex stopped shouting as the significance of this revelation entered his cognizance. "This has something to do with radiation?"

"It does." Safari proceeded to break down the events of the past few days. "Elijah was killed because he had uncovered a massive smuggling operation. From what I have gathered, they also killed the Waliangulu tribe to justify closing Tsavo after discovering the mines had uranium, not just tsavorite. That is why Elijah had the tsavorite ring on him when he died. He had found some of the tribe's bodies and took evidence."

"Poor Elijah and the Waliangulu. Uranium? I don't like where this is going."

"You are not wrong, Alex. Lord Anson and an American, Spencer, who came in under John's diplomatic umbrella, were at Tsavo. They have set up huge facilities and are processing the natural uranium into yellowcake. They are shipping it out through the Port of Mombasa, and pirates are transferring it off the ships in the Indian Ocean. I think that is how Elijah originally figured out something was wrong. The pirates were only opening specific containers. All of the containers were either low-stacked or at the top of the stacks. This meant someone at the port was collaborating to ensure these could be safely opened. The X-ray images of the containers that Elijah directed the team to take not only showed some of the Waliangulu but also shielded boxes holding the uranium."

"Ahh," Alex added as he recalled the scans English had shown him.

"I went to the port to investigate and found blood in the container we thought was used for human smuggling. Now, I am certain that is how some of the Waliangulu were disposed of after they were killed."

"That's bloody awful."

"It is. The container was over near Shed 13."

Alex nodded as he envisioned the area. "Makes sense. If I wanted to do something illegal on the port, that'd be where I'd do it."

"It most definitely is the place for illicit activity. Unfortunately, I was discovered and only survived through the intervention of Michael Tsumbe. He was killed saving my life."

Genuine remorse filled Alex's voice, "Oh no, not Michael. I really liked him. He was a funny guy."

"Regrettably, I never got to know him that well. Police Commissioner Chongoi also showed up in time to rescue me after I got locked in a container."

"Inside? Oh, mate, that must have been a nightmare for you." Alex, of course, knew of English's extreme dislike of confined spaces.

"Had Chongoi not shown, I would not have had much longer to worry about claustrophobia. Long story short, this led me to Tsavo. Sammy took me to the tsavorite mines, where we discovered the uranium enrichment operation, Lord Anson, and the American Spencer. They were heavily guarded by military special forces, leading me to believe Lord Anson's good friend, the Vice President, is deeply involved. We barely escaped, thanks to Sammy's driving and his badly shot-up cruiser. That is why we fled to Malindi."

"Understandable. Where are you now? It sounds like you're in a car."

"That is the reason for the call, my friend. I told you how they broke into my call to Chongoi."

"Yes?" Alex added with some uncertainty as to where this was heading.

"A very posh Brit came on the line and told me they had Kelly, and if I did not turn myself over to the men holding her at her Bibi's house in the Kibera slum by midnight, they were going to kill her or do worse."

"These guys are right bastards. Midnight, eh?" Alex paused as he looked at his watch. "I'm out at the ranch. I figured it was safer than my house in town after I got your call. I can get to Kibera before midnight. What do you need?"

English grinned. He knew he could always count on Alex, no matter the odds against him. "Have I told you recently what a good friend you are?"

Alex laughed, "Not recently enough, but there'll be time for that later. If we make it through this, I will graciously allow you to lavish praise upon me. For now, let's make sure Kelly is safe. Then we'll take care of the rest."

"The praise will be generous and public; have no fear, my friend. I may even buy you a Tusker or two. Sammy and I were speaking, and the first thing we need is more guns. We only have Sammy's rifle right now, but, as I learned last night, he is a very good shot. I assume whoever is holding Kelly will be armed, and from what we saw last night, they will have the latest military-style armaments."

"I can bring a few pistols and rifles, English, but I don't have anything fancy. I've only ever needed those. I might be able to make some calls if you think we need more firepower, but in the timeframe we're looking at, I doubt I would have much success."

Safari was shaking his head before Alex finished speaking. "I think we will be fine with what you have. I am mostly counting on the element of surprise. I have no intention of getting into a full-fledged gun battle with Kelly caught in the middle. We had an idea to even the odds. If you could bring a few shillings, we might be able to hire some backup or possibly bribe the guards." English hated asking Alex for money. Most people who interacted with his friend wanted to get their hands on his fortune, and English had always made a point to let him know he was not interested in it. These were extraordinary circumstances, though, and he would pay him back if he were able.

"That makes good sense. I'm sure Kibera has more than a few armed fellows willing to earn a shilling to look menacing. All right, I can scratch up a bob or two. Anything else?"

"I think that will do unless you have any other ideas. As a last resort, I can trade myself for Kelly, but I am hoping it does not come to that."

"None of that talk, English. We'll get her back without sacrificing my best friend. Who else will listen to me complain about the struggles of being a Mzungu in this day and age."

Safari laughed again, "Not many would be able to bear such a burden."

Alex joined him in a laugh. "True, you are made of strong stuff, English Safari. Right, let me gather my resources and head to Kibera. I'll call when I'm getting close."

"Asante sana, Alex. I will also text Sammy's number in case you cannot reach this phone. See you in Kibera."

"See you there." Alex hung up and went to his safe to collect his guns and the cash he had stored there. English texted Sammy's disposable number to his friend and returned the phone to his pocket.

"Well, Sammy, it looks like we have a plan."

"Yes, sir. I think we will recover Miss Kelly. They are most likely not expecting us to attempt a rescue, and unless they thought to bribe some of the locals, we will greatly outnumber them. Do not worry. It is a good plan."

English wished he could be as confident, but these men had killed many who might have impeded their plans. They did not hesitate to kill Elijah or Tsumbe, not to mention the countless dead from the Waliangulu tribe. Kelly might not even be alive at this point. Safari mentally chided himself. *Do not go down that road, English. She has to be alive.* He shook his head to clear his thoughts before speaking aloud. "Yes, we will get her back, Sammy. Thank you."

The driver nodded before focusing back on the road and the rapidly-approaching river crossing. "Do you see any animals in our path, sir?"

Safari scanned the river ahead of them and did not. "The way looks clear, but crocs are not easily spotted in the water."

"Crocs are not big enough to impede our way. As long as no hippos are near, I am going for it." Sammy gunned the cruiser's engine, and they launched into the water, powering through the door-high water and mud with only minor slippage before tearing up the far side of the riverbank. A hundred meters saw them back on the flat, dirt road, and Sammy smiled as the cruiser began picking up speed. "Now we should be able to make some good time, sir. We will be on the one-o-nine before long. Then our only concern will be the truck traffic."

English nodded. He knew the traffic between Mombasa and Nairobi well. It was why he almost always flew when he needed to go up to headquarters for face-to-face meetings. He was looking forward to the day when the internet in Mombasa was improved enough that he could reliably hold virtual meetings. It might take some time for the powers-that-be to accept virtual meetings as regular order, but the option would be welcome from Safari's end. Some things must be done in person, but there are other times when a meeting is only required because someone higher on the food chain insists on one. English refocused on the road ahead. He would worry about meetings when or *if* he ever got back into the office.

Sammy was not wrong. In just a few minutes, they were practically launching onto the paved surface of the one-o-nine. Dread filled English. He hated dodging between the trucks on the only highway between the port city of Mombasa and Kenya's largest consuming city, Nairobi. It would be tortuous at this hour since most trucks tried to time the journey to ensure they arrived in Nairobi in the late evening. That way, they would have minimal traffic in the capital city. Unfortunately, anyone needing to drive between the two cities during this time must dodge between the slow-moving trucks heading uphill towards Nairobi and those barreling downhill back to the port.

They were travelling at break-neck speed for only a short while before they had to slow as they caught up to the convoy of trucks making their nightly procession. Sammy edged towards the centerline of the road until he could see around the first truck. Once he was assured there were no oncoming vehicles, he crushed the accelerator and passed as many trucks as possible before an oncoming truck forced him back into the northbound lane. The pattern continued where they slowly crawled ahead amidst the lorries and then tore around them each time there was an opening in the oncoming lane. *A person with a weaker stomach would find the lurching nauseating,* English thought as he tried to take his mind off it.

The space between trucks lessened with each mile closer to Nairobi. They experienced long bouts where insufficient gaps in the oncoming traffic kept them trapped in the slow-moving truck convoy, but once an opening appeared, Sammy had them moving again at a decent pace. The young driver was taking chances that English would not have dared had he been behind the wheel, but Sammy knew his baby well and its acceleration capabilities. If Kelly's life were not in danger, Safari would have insisted they use greater care. They were likely racing to their deaths anyway, so he figured they might as well throw caution to the wind.

No sooner had English had that thought than a particularly close call had him catching his breath as he locked his arms and legs, thinking a collision was imminent. Sammy laughed when he saw his boss's reaction. "No need to worry, sir. Plenty of room on that one." The driver smiled again as English chuckled nervously at the young man's assurance.

After a few more rounds of passing, English felt his heart rate slow a bit. Unfortunately, the calm did not last long. While overtaking another lorry, the rig in front of it slammed on its brakes, rapidly swallowing the space Sammy was aiming to occupy. He had to accelerate again to attempt to reach the opening in front of that truck. The driver of the truck coming towards them began laying on his horn as he realized a cruiser was directly in front of him. Safari closed one eye and involuntarily leaned towards Sammy, who was crushing the gas pedal against the floor. The cruiser whipped back into their lane just as English said goodbye to this life. The semi sideswiped the cruiser, taking the side mirror with it and forcing them to overshoot the road.

Once Sammy got the cruiser back under control, he was smiling again. "Okay, sir, now you can worry." English laughed as relief of being alive flooded his body, and he pried his fingers from the dash.

"Phew," was all he managed as he copied Sammy's

habit of pretending to wipe sweat from his brow. Although Sammy feigned nonchalance, English noted his young driver was now only passing when there were sizable gaps in the oncoming traffic. It was fine with Safari. He was not sure he could take another close call like the one they had just survived. He looked at his watch. The pace they had been on practically ensured they would arrive several hours before their deadline. Now, he could shift his worry to what would happen when they arrived. English looked over his shoulder at the rifle sitting on the back seat and wondered whether or not he was ready for what was to come. Safari took a deep breath and centered himself. Kelly was counting on him. He was not about to lose another friend to these bastards. Anger welled up in him. Whether or not he survived, English would damn sure see her walk out of there.

Several hours passed as they continued at this more relaxed pace, and English spotted the highway sign. Only one hundred kilometers remained until reaching Nairobi. He checked both his and Sammy's disposable phones, but neither had received a call from Alex. Safari hoped his friend had a less exciting drive from his ranch than they had, but Alex had to catch the one-o-nine at some point, even though his starting location was much further north than theirs. The last hundred kilometers passed without issue, and Sammy turned off the highway towards the Kibera slum. They made their way to the Southwest entrance, and Sammy drove around until he found a place to park.

English rechecked his watch. "I will call Alex and see where he is and if he thinks he will make it in time." Safari pulled out his wallet and checked how much cash he still had on him. "If not, we will see how much backup we can get for the price of a couple of chicken masalas." He looked doubtful about those prospects as he hit the redial button. Several rings and worry began to set in, but soon, Alex's voice answered.

"English?"

"Yes, Alex, it is me."

"Thank God, this bloody phone isn't hooked up to my blue tooth, and I can't see the bloody buttons."

English smiled. "Heh, getting old is not fun, is it, my friend?"

"Old? Old has nothing to do with it. This phone is a cheap piece of garbage, and the keys don't light up. Where are you?"

"We have arrived and parked near the Southwest entrance to Kibera."

"Woah, you boys made excellent time. That Sammy's one hell of a driver."

"Yes, he is. Our journey was not without some close calls, however. The important thing is we made it here in one piece. I fear my paychecks for the next year will be spent repairing Sammy's cruiser."

"Ooh, that close, eh? Well, I can believe it with this traffic. I'm another forty-five minutes or so out, but I'll be there in plenty of time. I got a couple of pistols for each of us and a bag full of cash. Hopefully, it's enough to get us plenty of help."

"You are a lifesaver, Alex. Call me when you get close, and I can guide you to our location. Kwa heri."

"See you soon, mate." Both men hung up, and English exited the cruiser to stretch his legs.

"Sammy, I have no idea how you were able to sit in a vehicle all day, taking the tourists around. I am stiff as a board."

"You get used to it, sir. I admit I am a little out of

practice since I started working for KRA." The young man smiled as he joined English in a bit of stretching. After a few toe-touches, Sammy grabbed the rifle from the backseat and headed to the cargo bay to add more bullets. Once finished, he returned to the front of the cruiser, placed the gun on the hood, and jumped up beside it. An awkward silence filled the air, but neither man felt like talking. Sammy kept an eye out for strangers from the front, slowly kicking his legs as they dangled. English guarded their rear as he paced back and forth with nervous energy. Both men jumped when Safari's phone rang out.

English checked the number. It was Alex. "Habari, friend. Have you arrived?"

"Yeah, mate. Where are you guys at?"

"Hold on. I will let Sammy direct you." English put his driver on the phone, and the young man guided Alex to their location. He parked his exquisite vehicle next to Sammy's practically destroyed cruiser, and the comparison made it look all the worst for it. Alex jumped out once he stopped and looked over their car before letting out a whistle.

"Wow, you boys have had quite an adventure. I guess you weren't kidding when you said these men were dangerous. It's one thing to imagine what happened and another thing altogether seeing the evidence first-hand." Alex circled the entire cruiser, taking in all the damage before shaking his head in disbelief again.

"Yes, it has been nonstop. Sammy has saved my life multiple times in the past day. You can see the bullet holes and the damage from the truck, and he even had to shoot a leopard that was preparing to pounce on me. Adventure is putting it mildly, I would say." Sammy nodded along as he wore a pleased smile on his face.

"Nice work, Sammy. I don't know what I'd do if my best friend were to kick the bucket suddenly. Thanks." Alex gave the driver a slap on the shoulder.

"My pleasure, sir. It has been a fairly exciting week at work."

Alex shot a bemused look back at the smaller man.

English laughed. "I have learned that our Sammy, here, is quite unflappable. I look as if I have survived a zombie apocalypse, and he acts like it has been just another day at work."

All three men shared a laugh before the situation brought them around to being serious again. Alex looked around cautiously, then went to the back of his vehicle and opened the hatch. He popped open several cases to display a selection of guns. He strapped on one in a holster and picked up a second to keep in his hand. English followed suit, and both men checked their weapons were loaded. Safari cocked his head at his friend to ask if he was sure he wanted to be involved. Alex gave a quick nod of confirmation and handed another pistol to Sammy. Sammy tucked it into his waistband and retrieved his rifle. Alex pulled out a sling bag and donned it diagonally across his chest. He patted the bag and whispered, "Money." The trio headed off in a cautious jog towards the slum's entrance.

CHAPTER 14

English, Alex, and Sammy slowed to a walk as they neared the commonly accepted southwestern entrance to the Kibera slum. They could have attempted to enter through a less formal entryway, but that would invite more problems. The only other way would be to cross through the outer shacks' waste dumps and risk invading one or more squatter's personal areas. This would be provocative in the extreme as the hard-fought ownership of each space, especially choice outer ones, would be violently defended—no need to risk such a confrontation when they were seeking help from the locals. The best path here would be the open and direct one. Although English and Sammy presently looked rough enough to pass as residents, Alex stood out like a sore thumb. Mzungus were rare in the slums, but even the brave tourists and missionaries who visited would never do so this late at night.

Arriving at the opening between shacks that served as the official ingress, the threesome was fully immersed in the sounds and smells that accompanied hundreds of thousands living in close proximity without essential services. Smoke from charcoal fires did little to mask the need for improved sanitation. They did their best to keep that fact from their faces as they looked around for someone who might be able to help them.

English scanned the people loitering near the entrance and spotted one who stood out. He was lying near a wall on the far side of the entryway, and Safari knew almost immediately he was not the homeless man he was pretending to be. He drew Alex and Sammy in close and whispered to them. "You see the man lying against the wall directly behind me?" Both men looked in the direction English indicated and nodded. "He is too well-dressed to be homeless in Kibera and watches everyone who enters intently. I believe he is the lookout for the gang that controls this region of the slum and our best bet at finding Kelly and getting some hired hands. I am going to approach him but be ready. One never knows how volatile the situation in Kibera is at any given moment." Both men nodded again and readied themselves for the possibility that this introduction would go poorly. Sammy lowered his rifle from his shoulder, and Alex added his left hand to the pistol he already carried in his right. Safari looked up at the night sky and took a deep breath to center himself before moving out.

English approached the man he had identified with his hands raised to indicate he meant no harm. The gate guard sat up and readied his pistol when he realized Safari was heading towards him. English tried to remain calm as that pistol was pointed in his direction. "Habari," English said in a friendly tone.

The guard's eyes squinted with suspicion. "We mean you no harm," Safari said as he indicated his friends with a nod of his head. The man lowered his gun slightly when he saw Sammy and Alex were ready for a fight. They had not attacked, and Alex was obviously not from a rival Kibera gang.

"What do you want?" the guard asked gruffly.

"We need some help," English started. The man pshawed. Safari used his hands to quell the negative reaction and ask for a moment before being dismissed. "Actually, our friend needs some help. Some men have taken her and her Bibi captive right here in Kibera." The guard started to dismiss English, but he pressed on in the hopes his story or the promise of a payday would win him over. "Would you know Nalutuesha Sironka or know someone who might be able to guide us to her home?" The guards sat up at the mention of Kelly's Bibi's name. Safari took that as a good sign. "I remember it being around forty homes in on the southern perimeter. We can pay for directions if need be."

"Are you saying someone is holding Nalutuesha Sironka captive in her home?" The guard's voice dripped with skepticism.

"Yes. We were told she and her granddaughter, Kelly, were being held there, and the men responsible would kill them both at midnight.

The guard made an incredulous snort. "I cannot believe anyone could take Nalutuesha. In her own home, no less. They would need a small army. She is one tough old mbuzi."

English laughed. Kelly's Bibi was indeed tough and a bit frightening, but their captors were armed men and had the element of surprise. "Yes, she is. That is the reason we believe we need help beyond just directions." The guard raised an eyebrow in curiosity. "We do not know how many men have taken these women and need to hire some, shall we say, muscle. I thought it best to ask those who control this area for assistance as it behooves you to ensure no outsiders can threaten anyone under your governance."

The guard looked English up and down, then looked over at his two companions, suspicious eyes pausing on Alex before turning back to the man standing in front of him. English decided he best sweeten the pot before a decision was made.

"I forgot to mention. We can also pay a small stipend to anyone who shows up on Nalutuesha's behalf. Of course, your boss and yourself can also expect compensation for the inconvenience." The guard smiled and signalled to two men standing in the shadows who sauntered over to get their instructions.

The guard pointed to one of the men. "Take these men to Nalutuesha Sironka's house. They think she and her granddaughter are being held captive." The guide made to protest, but the guard cut him off. "No arguments," the guide nodded sullenly but perked up as the guard continued, "besides, they have promised a tip to whoever shows them to her home." The gatekeeper pointed at the other man, "You, go to the boss, tell him the situation, and ask him to send backup for our friends here." He indicated English with the back of his hand. "Tell the boss they also promised a fee for him and anyone who aids them." When the man stood motionless, the gatekeeper jumped to his feet and shooed the man on his way. "Go! Now, and hurry!" The guard's tone and wild gesticulation spurred the man into motion, and he ran down the northern row of shacks.

English thanked the guard and turned to go but was stopped by an outstretched hand. "Bup bup bup bup," Safari looked down at the man's hand, which was indicating he should be paid now.

"Ah, of course, sorry," English grabbed all the cash he had in his wallet and placed it in the man's hand. He thought it wise not to let them know how much money Alex had on him until the job was done. The man saluted Safari with the bills before stuffing them inside his pocket.

"Pleasure doing business with you. Hope it works out. I kinda like the old mbuzi."

"Thank you, so do I." English turned to follow their new guide and nodded for Alex and Sammy to join them. The three men trailed a few steps behind their escort. Alex asked the question he and Sammy had been wondering about throughout the entire transaction at the slum entrance.

"Backup?"

Safari nodded. "He sent a runner to get men from their boss. Hopefully, they will meet us where they are holding Kelly."

"A lot riding on *hopefully*, mate."

"I agree, Alex, but there is not much else I can do. If no one shows up, we will have to devise a 'plan B' and deal with these kidnappers on our own."

"All right, but I do like the idea of having some backup."

English grunted his agreement. "Keep an eye out. I imagine their captors have a watch." Sammy and Alex both began scanning the path ahead. Looking for a person would be difficult enough in the dark in any setting. Regrettably, Kibera's structures were so inconsistent in size and placement that it would be nearly impossible to discern a person hiding amongst the chaos. Their guide seemed unfazed by any worry of gunmen lying in wait and kept marching forward at a consistent pace. He passed a small intersection with another path leading north and stopped short beside a large, ramshackle wooden structure. The guide signalled for them to join him.

"Nalutuesha's home is the third one on the right," he said, pointing in the direction of one of the sturdier-looking buildings they had seen since entering Kibera. "This is as far as I go," he added, holding out his hand in anticipation of his tip.

Alex took a thousand shillings from his bag and handed it to their former guide. "Do you know if anyone will be coming to back us up?"

The escort shrugged his shoulders as he took the money. "If the man at the gate said some would show, they will show. If not…" the man finished his thought with another shrug before fading quietly into the shadows.

Alex was not too happy with the cavalier answer. "Thanks for clearing that up," he whispered into the darkness.

English looked after the guide for only a moment, then returned to the task at hand, rescuing Kelly. English scoured the area but could see no guards. He was unsure if they did not exist or if they were well hidden. Perhaps they felt he was so isolated he was not a threat worth too many of their men. He forced the thought from his mind that there were many men, but they were inside doing unspeakable things to Kelly. Men who might be involved in something like this would not be of the gentlemanly sort. English shook his head to snap himself out of the dark hole he was falling into, then began sneaking down the lane opposite Nalutuesha's home. He stuck to the shadows as much as possible, carefully avoiding stepping on or kicking anything that might alert an otherwise inattentive guard. Sammy and Alex followed his lead, and all three crouched behind some rusty barrels directly across from their target. Alex and English studied the area from either side of what appeared to be makeshift firepits while Sammy snuck a look over the top.

"I see no guards anywhere or even indication that anyone is inside. There is no movement. Surely, if they were inside, we would see something," English whispered concernedly.

Alex agreed. "Yeah, something's not right, mate. I wish we could get eyes in there. I mean, if I were set on holding someone in that house," he nodded his head towards the house opposite them, "I'd have a man right here watching for, well, for us, frankly." Sammy was nodding his agreement vigorously.

English thought a moment. "All right, wait here. I will try to get a peek inside. If anyone comes up to me or gets the drop on me, please shoot them." Safari smiled at them both, slid further onto the ground, and began crawling towards the house when they heard a large group of men chattering from around the corner they had just passed. English pushed himself back behind the barrels, and all three men turned to face the new, potential threat. The din was getting louder as a troop of armed men came into sight. The ragtag men carried a hodgepodge of weaponry, some modern, some looking to be World War I relics. They certainly were not as well-armed as those guarding Tsavo, but no less deadly if they caught the three of them. English held a finger up to his lips, then indicated they should stay down. If they were lucky, this group would just pass them by. Safari silently cursed his luck when a pair of the men advanced in front of their hiding place and stopped to light cigarettes.

The smell of cigarette smoke filled the air as the men began arguing. "Where are they, Ochieng? You said they would be here." A menacing tone permeated the speaker's voice.

An apology quickly escaped the second man's lips. "Sorry, bosi, they should be here. Let me check if they were delivered to the correct house. Natori!" the man shouted. The three hiding men could hear a man run up to the others.

"Yes, sir?"

"Natori, where are the men I told you to deliver to Nalutuesha's house?"

"I brought them as you asked and left them right here."

English slowly stood up to avoid startling anyone into shooting him. "We are here," he said calmly. The men who had been trying to explain the situation to their bosi jumped at Safari's sudden appearance, but their leader hardly reacted. He was a hard-looking man with a deep scar running down the left side of his face. English immediately knew he did not want to be on this man's bad side. "Sorry, we were not certain who was approaching and thought it best to hide until we figured it out." Sammy and Alex stood up to join their friend. The gang leader looked over each of them before feigning a smile.

"Hakuna matata, it was probably wise though I thought there was a woman in need of your rescue."

The man's words said no trouble, but his tone exuded anger at whatever slight he felt at having to wait for English and his friends to appear. Safari knew he would have to tiptoe around this one. "Yes, sorry again. We were expecting guards when we arrived and, finding none, became suspicious. I was just about to go take a look in the house when we heard your party arriving."

"Okay, now you know it is us. Go take a look so we can get paid and get back to enjoying our evening."

"Right, I will do that now." English's eyes followed the butt down as the man threw the remains of his cigarette onto the ground to crush it out with his boot. "Wait, what is that?" he said, pointing to the ground beneath the gang leader's foot.

"What is what?" The man's tone was becoming even more flush with anger.

Safari stepped closer to the man and turned back to his companions. "Alex, let me borrow your phone. I need a torch."

"All right, mate," Alex said as he turned on his phone's flashlight and handed it to English. Safari stooped to the ground and shined the light all around the area before dipping his fingers into the muddy earth. He examined them closely under the phone's light.

"Blood, and a lot of it. Someone died here in the past few hours." English stood up and looked about. "Maybe that is why we found no guards. Someone has already taken care of them." Safari looked at the callous man before him to ask if it was his men.

The man turned down his lip as he shook his head. "It wasn't us, but we expect to be paid as if it was." English nodded his understanding. "We will wait here as your backup. You go into the house and get your women. If anyone but you comes out, we'll kill them. Deal?"

Safari realized he did not have a choice in his answer. "Yes, sounds like a plan." He signalled Alex and Sammy to follow him and crept to Nalutuesha's home. English briefly listened at the weather-beaten wood that served as a door to the small building. Hearing nothing, he turned and gave his companions a thumbs-up. He mouthed on three as he held up three fingers. Both men nodded their understanding. English held up one finger, then a second, and when he got to three, he kicked the door in, and all three men rushed into the room. A confusing scene met them. A wooden chair was in the middle of the room; rope and blood were strewn around the chair. English's mind feared the worst. They were too late. Kelly had already been killed. He scanned the room for clues as to what had happened but was immediately distracted by Alex calling out.

"English!" Safari turned to see Alex, hands in the air, with a spear at his back.

"English?" a woman's voice called out from the other side of the room. "Bibi, no!" The old woman holding the spear paused momentarily, then let the weapon relax away from Alex's back.

Alex, eyes wide, let out an audible sigh of relief.

The woman who had called out stepped into the light. It was Kelly. English had to choke back tears as he rushed forward to hug the woman he thought dead just moments ago.

"Oh, English, you came for me. You brave or stupid, man." They both laughed.

"I think I will choose to remember only the brave

part of that when I retell the harrowing tale." English smiled at his assistant. "What happened here?"

Kelly nodded towards her grandmother. "Bibi happened." Kelly smiled at her Bibi. "Several men came and grabbed me. They tied me up and told me if you did not turn yourself over to them by midnight, they would kill me. They either did not see Bibi or decided she was harmless. As soon as they turned their backs on her, she grabbed her spear and killed them before they could call out. She snuck out through an opening in the back wall and, when she came back, told me she had taken care of the guards outside also. She is amazing." English looked over at Kelly's Bibi. Though the woman was showing age on her face, he could see her one exposed arm was still taut with muscle. He nodded at the older woman.

"Indeed she is. I guess we were not needed at all." Safari smiled at Kelly. "I am so relieved you are well. I am also so sorry you were placed in harm's way."

"It is fine, English. I am all right."

Alex jumped in, "I'm not. Why did your Bibi pick me to play pincushion with? Bloody hell!" He felt around his back to ensure the spear had not punctured any skin.

Everyone had a quick chuckle at Alex's expense as Kelly translated for her Bibi. The older woman let out a huff of air through her nose before explaining. Kelly translated for the group. "She says it is always the mzungu who is in charge. Bibi figured if she held you at speartip, the others would have to drop their weapons."

"The curse of the mzungu strikes again," Alex laughed as he kept prodding his back to ensure blood was not pouring through a giant wound. They all stopped as a voice from outside shouted a question.

"Everything all right in there?" English recognized the gate guard's voice. He had almost forgotten a gang of heavily armed men was waiting outside to kill anyone who was not them as they left the building.

Fear came across Kelly's face, and her Bibi again took up her spear. Safari waved her off. "It is the men we hired as backup in case those inside were too much for the three of us. I should have known Nalutuesha would not tolerate someone disrespecting her granddaughter in her home." English smiled at the older woman when she looked at him. "She is one tough woman."

Kelly laughed. "You have no idea," she said as she hugged her Bibi.

English turned to Alex and Sammy. "Do you think the two of you can negotiate the fee with our friends outside?"

"Uhh, sure, mate," Alex said as he recognized his friend wanted to speak to Kelly privately. "Come on, Sammy, let's see if we can save me a few shillings." The driver flashed a big smile as the always boisterous Alex ushered the young man out of Nalutuesha's home.

English hugged Kelly again as her Bibi smiled on. "How are you, really?" he said.

"I am *fine*, no, really," she added when Safari's eyes displayed his doubt. "It was disturbing, to say the least, but Bibi was so great. I had no idea she had such capacity for violence or that she could still move like that. She never talks about her or my Babu's past, but I think they lived through some difficult times." Kelly once again smiled at her grandmother before turning back to English. She seemed to notice for the first time how beat up he was. She took his face in her hand and turned it this way and that to inspect the damage before letting out a disapproving tsk. "Have you figured out who's behind all of this?"

English nodded, "I believe I have. It looks like Elijah uncovered a uranium smuggling operation, and they killed him for it."

"Uranium?" Kelly asked with a puzzled look on her face. "If I had one million guesses as to the cause of our troubles, I am not sure that would have made the list."

Safari chuckled in agreement. "I know for a fact it would not have made mine. I guessed everything but that. You knew Elijah and his hunches, though."

The young woman nodded. "He had always seemed to know when something was not quite right and dug around until he solved the mystery."

"Well, this must have been one doozy of a hunch. It looks like every corrupt politician in our country is in on this. Elijah had pictures of the Vice President and that English Lord who was supposedly killed." Kelly squinted her eyes to question his candor. "I am serious. They appear to have faked his death just to close Tsavo and kill some or possibly all of the Waliangulu tribe." Kelly gasped at this horrific revelation. "They have set up a processing plant near the tsavorite mines. I even saw that large American who was sick in our office. He fled some suspicious activity charges back home using John's diplomatic connections."

English thought about sharing how close to death he had come in the past few days but decided Kelly needed nothing else to worry about at the moment. He could fill in the rest of the details at a later time. "Needless to say, it has been an exciting few days since

I asked you to take time off from work."

Kelly looked him up and down again and knew there was more to the story explaining how English looked so maltreated but left it alone. "How did you know we were in trouble?"

"The ones behind all of this intercepted a call I made to the police commissioner. Turns out he is a good man. He got me out of a spot of bother at the port. I called to inform the commissioner of what I discovered, and a very posh Brit came on the line and said I had until midnight to turn myself over here or…" he left the threat unspoken.

Kelly nodded her understanding. "You came for me?"

"Of course, Kelly; you know I would never let anything happen to you if there was any way I could prevent it." The young woman smiled up at him just as the front door reopened.

Alex looked embarrassed when he saw how close English and Kelly were standing. "Oh, sorry, we can go back outside if you need a minute."

Kelly stepped back. "Not necessary, Alex. How did your negotiations fare?"

"Perfect. I mean, I am now poor, but at least Sammy and I were not shot, right Sammy?"

"That was my preferred outcome, and here we are. Since it was not my money…" The driver's face lit up with an impish grin, and his shoulders and face indicated a laissez-faire attitude about how much the operation cost Alex. The bigger man feigned outrage as he pretended to reach for Sammy.

"Why, you little traitor." Everyone in the house laughed as much from relief as the comic episode before them.

English turned back to Kelly. "I need to find you a safer place to hide out." He silenced Kelly's protest by waving his hand around the room. "They have already located your Bibi's home. Once the man who sent me here realizes I have not turned myself over to them, they will surely send more men here to find out why the ones Bibi dispatched are not responding."

Alex stepped forward. "They can be my guests out at the ranch." English began expressing his doubts, but Alex cut him off. "English, there is nowhere safer in Kenya. You know that. Besides, no one *really* knows about it. I bought it using an anonymous LLC. It would take some serious legal maneuvering to figure out who owned the property, and they would need to have an inkling about it to know to start looking. Trust me. Once we get to my ranch, the ladies will be safe as houses. If that isn't enough to convince you, Bibi there," Alex nodded in her direction, "and her spear will be present to dispense with anyone who pays us a visit."

English chuckled, then turned to face Kelly. "It does sound like the best option, but I will let you decide. I cannot be certain anywhere is safe. I never thought they would find you here in Kibera. Obviously, I have only just begun to realize how deep this conspiracy is rooted. At lunch today, we ran into the Americans, and had John not been playing with a training sample of uranium, I might not have known how dangerous this situation is."

Kelly looked back and forth between English, Alex, and her Bibi and nodded in agreement. "It does sound like the safest place if you do not mind having us."

Alex waved his hands to indicate how ridiculous that statement was. "Kelly, of course, you are welcome in my home. Any friend of English is always welcome, plus I imagine your Bibi has some incredible stories which will enthrall us all."

"That she does. Maybe she will tell you some of the ones she feels are too much for her granddaughter."

Safari looked over at his faithful driver. "How about you, Sammy? Would you like to stay out at Alex's ranch? You have done more than your fair share of this investigation, and we have seen the lengths these people will go to silence potential interlopers."

"No, sir. Sammy will see this through, besides those who have so badly damaged Sammy's baby must pay."

English nodded his understanding and thanks. "That settles it, then. Alex will take the ladies to safety while Sammy and I follow through on getting this shut down. Kelly, gather any things you or Bibi might need. I am unsure how long this will take or if we will succeed." Kelly began to protest, but English stopped her. "We must be realistic. This goes all the way to the Vice President if we are correct, so it is possible we might not be able to stop this cabal. If something happens to me, I suggest you leave Kenya. Alex can help you and get you set up somewhere else." English looked over at his friend, who nodded his head assuredly. "Oh, and no cell phones. They can easily be tracked."

Kelly was visibly upset by the thought of English not making it through this but said nothing. Instead, she packed bags for her and Bibi while explaining the situation to the older woman. To Nalutuesha's credit, she took the news in stride and, after looking Alex up and down, began helping Kelly pack.

Alex came close to English in order for his whisper to be heard. "So, what's your plan, mate?"

"Unfortunately, still working on it," he replied in hushed tones. "I am thinking our first step is to try and reach Commissioner Sambu. She lives in Nairobi, so we are close enough to meet her in person, and it is more than likely her phone has been tapped. We have to use stealth if they are watching her home, but she has powerful connections that may rival the Vice President. Beyond that, my only other options are my friends in the Navy. The military is independent enough from the Vice President's influence that they may be able to take down the operation. If not, Sammy and I might be leaving Kenya along with Kelly, at least until or rather *if* the Americans step in to stop the uranium smuggling. Since they could not remove the Vice President or the other major Kenyan players, we will only be safe if this is handled internally."

Alex scoffed at the likelihood. "Fat chance, English, but I know you will try until the bitter end, so I hope I'm wrong. Just be safe out there. If *even* you decide it is hopeless, come to the ranch, and we'll figure out our next move. That goes for you, too, Sammy. Maybe we'll all take a tour of Europe or get fake IDs and start a band or something." English clasped Alex's shoulder. He could tell his friend was worried and began joking around to avoid thinking about it.

Kelly and her Bibi appeared and announced they were packed and ready to go. The five of them departed the house, with Nalutuesha taking a moment to let her eyes sadly drink in every bit of the home she had built so many years ago with her husband. English tenderly put his arm around the older woman's shoulders and helped her through the door. Kelly relieved him, and the tough woman who had defended her granddaughter against three armed assailants melted into her embrace. They walked, senses on full alert, through the slums and managed to arrive unmolested back at their vehicles.

Kelly's face registered her horror as she looked upon the damage Sammy's cruiser had sustained since she had last seen it. She directed her worried eyes to English and hugged him fiercely. "You come back, English. You hear me?"

English hugged her back. "I will do my utmost to comply. If I am not able…"

Kelly would not let him finish. "That is not an option!" she said definitively.

English held up his hands in resignation, "Yes, ma'am," he capitulated to put her at ease.

"That is better. Sammy, I am trusting you to keep you both safe." She added a stern look to let the driver know she meant it."

"Of course, Kelly, the deputy commissioner could be in no safer hands."

Kelly looked over their vehicle again and added a dubious "mm-hmm" before getting into Alex's SUV. Alex looked at the badly damaged cruiser, shaking his head while curling his lip. "She's got a point, you know," he teased. Sammy's eyes narrowed in faux anger before smiling once again. "Stay safe, you two. Let us know when it's safe to come back or if it completely turns to shite." The man pointed at each of them, tapped the roof of his vehicle twice, then jumped in and drove off. English and Sammy watched them depart until the darkness swallowed the taillights, then returned to the business at hand.

Safari clasped the driver's shoulder firmly. "Shall we get on with it?"

Sammy nodded resolutely, "Yes, sir." English

returned the nod, and both men climbed into the cruiser. Sammy tore out of their parking space and began mapping out the best, most unexpected routes to the address Safari provided. Nairobi's silhouette was greeting them before either man had time to decide whether this was the best course of action or not. Once its congested streets had swallowed them, it seemed like there was no option to escape except to push on through. English looked up at the sky over the city and was even more determined to mete out justice. He vowed to reclaim the joy Mombasa's night sky had always given him.

CHAPTER 15

English looked over at Sammy as he confidently navigated the streets of Nairobi. Safari had been to the commissioner's house several times and would be hard-pressed to find it without GPS. Sammy did not seem to need directions to any location in Kenya, but English wanted to verify. "You know the way to Commissioner Sambu's house?"

"Yes, sir. Sammy has been to the area many times before. She lives in a very affluent neighborhood." English urged him to continue with a questioning look. "Most of the tours start in Nairobi. Wealthier clients tended to hire private vehicles, while those who were less well-off stuck to the group tours or buses. I started many tours from the commissioner's region. I think I know of an area near her home where we can easily park and walk. We must avoid those involved in this conspiracy and the private security patrols throughout the locale. I think poor baby, here," he patted the dashboard, "might draw unnecessary attention."

"Good point. I do remember being accosted by

some uniformed men the first time I visited the commissioner's home. It was for a party celebrating a large interdiction. Elijah and I were being given awards for our part, and two men checked our invitations. I assumed it was for the event, but they may have been the neighborhood watch."

Sammy turned down a small side street. All the trucks wending their way from Mombasa had finally reached Nairobi and were now blocking the main thoroughfares. There was no good time to drive in the big city as far as English was concerned. During the day, pedestrians and privately owned vehicles brought travel to a standstill, while at night, the trucks hauling their cargo took over. The plethoric traffic of Mombasa paled in comparison. He would have to remind himself of this the next time he complained about being stuck or late for a meeting due to the congestion. English chuckled to himself. He knew the instant he was back home, he would be grumbling about it again.

The outskirts of Nairobi, where they found themselves, was quite possibly the most disreputable area in Kenya. English felt that while the buildings in this region were more substantial than in Kibera, the souls of those who lived here had not fared as well. The rat's nest of power lines strung between the dilapidated buildings instantly conveyed a feeling of disorder. Street lamps with their bulbs stolen or burnt out made the roadways feel less safe than if no lighting had been installed. The people in the streets at this hour were involved in every manner of nefarious behavior imaginable. Those dark-hearted citizens of Nairobi with money came here when they wanted their various vices sated. English averted his gaze several times lest his hope for a better Kenya take another hit. Those dreams lay in near-tattered ruins as they were. Only his desire for justice for Elijah kept him from abandoning his mission as it was.

A few more blocks driven and English noticed a difference in the landscape. There was no demarcation on the road, but suddenly, they were in a better neighborhood. The change was palpable. No more illicit business dealings could be seen on the streets, which were wider and cleaner. Sidewalks, missing from the seedier areas, were now visible on either side of the road. Even the power lines took on a more organized look. The most noticeable distinction between the two areas was the conspicuous lack of people. It was not a rich enough area to allow its residents to shun work and not poor enough to resort to the activities taking place in the district they had just left. Safari guessed most people living in these houses kept bankers' hours. He felt a pang of envy.

Sammy slowed to read one of the few street signs they had seen, nodded, and sped up again. "Soon, we should be able to get back onto the main thoroughfares. The cargo trucks are only allowed on the primary streets up to a point. No one wants the workers or the wealthy to be forced to deal with truck traffic. Neither the noise nor the increased chance of blocking traffic during a breakdown would be good for business."

True to his word, in a few minutes, Sammy had them back off of the side streets. Quickly, English saw familiar landmarks. A hotel he had attended a conference in and several restaurants he had eaten in at various times, chief among them. He was now very familiar with this area of the city. KRA HQ was only a few blocks from their current location. Now, they just had to head towards the embassy district and Commissioner Sambu's estate.

"I was thinking about where we could park, Sammy." The driver gave a side-glance to English to let him know he was listening. "There is a hospital, a hotel, and a golf club near the Commissioner's home. All have twenty-four-hour parking and security. None of these places are on the lookout for us, meaning the security would be to our advantage. There is a casino further down, but it will be heavily laden with cameras. Besides, the men we are up against are more likely to be in a casino than a hospital. Since we are unsure who is involved in this conspiracy beyond the key figures, we should avoid locales of ill repute unless *absolutely* necessary."

"Great minds think alike, sir. I believe the hospital might serve us well. It would not be too great a leap for a vehicle as damaged as ours to be in the hospital parking lot." Sammy's heart dropped a little as that thought settled into his consciousness, and he sighed at all the repairs he would have to make to bring his baby back to her former self.

English noticed his driver entering the doldrums. "Do not fear, Sammy. If we live to see those responsible brought to justice, I will ensure this most trustworthy of chariots is restored to glory. For now, at least no one will try to rob us."

"Quite unlikely, sir. Might even get some donations if I hold out a cup." The driver's smile returned to his face.

Sammy turned onto the hospital's exit and rolled his window down to speak with the security guard. "My friend needs stitches," he said to the man pushing his face into their vehicle. English held up his bandaged hand as evidence. The guard looked around again, then raised the drop arm. "Asante," Sammy shouted and sped into the parking lot. The guard lowered the arm and returned to his shack to await the next customer.

Safari looked at his hand and the blood-soaked bandage. "You know, I probably do need stitches, but that will have to wait."

Sammy nodded, then parked the cruiser near the one operating light. Both men tucked the guns in their waistbands, English forgoing the holster this time to avoid drawing attention. "Ready?" Safari asked.

"Yes, sir," Sammy responded as he locked the vehicle. English raised an eyebrow at the futile gesture, but it was probably a hard habit to break.

The two men walked at a good clip across the parking lot and were back on the street in moments. They jogged across the boulevard and began cutting across town towards the Commissioner's neighborhood. As they passed behind a large warehouse, Safari pulled Sammy off to the side where a handful of wooden pallets were stacked. He took one off the top and threw it onto the ground before delivering a few kicks to break off some of the boards. English took one and handed another to the younger man. "The walls at the commissioner's house and those surrounding the district have broken glass glued to the top. Trust me. We do not wish to attempt to climb them barehanded." Sammy nodded as he took the proffered board.

They kept their distance from the few pedestrians and stray animals that eyed them suspiciously until they had moved past their respective threat perimeters. The one man who showed an overt interest in the pair suddenly felt the need to be elsewhere when English lifted his shirt to show the gun tucked into his belt. Thankfully, that was the only hint of danger in the entire walk, and they arrived in the estate district without incident.

English reached his board up to the top of the wall and used it to smash the broken glass at its crest, then lay the board flat over the shards. He tossed Sammy's board over the wall, then interlaced his fingers and offered his much shorter companion a boost. "Up you go, Sammy. Make sure your hands are only on the board. Your full weight driving a shard into your hand would not be pleasant."

"Yes, sir," Sammy responded as he stepped onto the proffered hands and easily pulled himself up and over the wall. English pulled himself up next, a little slower than it would have been in years past, but he got the job done.

Sammy approvingly nodded as he picked up the board English had sent over the wall. "I always assumed those walls were a more effective barrier. That was almost too easy to defeat."

English chuckled. "Yes, they look daunting but are not much more than that. Deterrence is usually more psychological than physical but often quite effective. This is just the outer barrier, though. We still have to evade any security forces and scale the wall surrounding the commissioner's estate without being seen. That will be the hard part. Keep an eye out for guards making rounds. I want to avoid them at all costs. If it proves impossible, we will tell them we are Commissioner Sambu's guests and are just out for a walk. Hopefully, they would just let us be, but if not, we will let them escort us to her home. I prefer to enter via the backdoor in case she is being watched, but there is only so much we can control. Ready?"

"Yes, sir. Sounds like a plan." The driver hefted the board onto his shoulder, and the pair moved out. English certainly felt like he was committing a crime as they crept through the upscale neighborhood. At one point, they hid behind a hedge as the private security force drove by in their patrol car. Safari could see no surveillance of the commissioner's home when they arrived, but he still felt it prudent to use the back entrance. He repeated his technique from the district wall, and both men were soon dropping into the commissioner's backyard.

"I wish I knew her phone number by memory," English lamented. Instead, he picked up some gravel from the landscaping and made his way to the area below the commissioner's bedroom. "Let us hope she is a light sleeper," he whispered as he tossed small rocks at her window. After four pebbles came back down, a light suddenly flooded from the window, and the commissioner's face could be seen scanning her yard. English backed away from the house, waving his arms to ensure she saw him. The difference in lighting conditions kept her from identifying him, but she opened the window to warn off the intruder.

"Get off of my property, or I will call security!" She waved her phone to indicate she was serious.

"Commissioner Sambu!" Safari replied in a voice that was some combination of a whisper and a shout. "It is English, English Safari."

"English?" the commissioner questioned. "What are you doing at my home in the middle of the night?"

"If you let us in, I will explain. Oh, and please keep

the lights off."

The commissioner gave him a puzzled look as she ducked back inside, but the light was extinguished seconds later. A few moments passed, and the commissioner, still fastening the belt on her robe, appeared to open the back door. She ushered English and Sammy inside and, after giving a suspicious look around her yard, closed it.

"Well, English, tell me what this is all about. I know it must be pressing for you to come all the way to Nairobi. I know how you hate coming into the city. What news could not wait until morning has piqued my curiosity even more, if that is possible."

"Yes, Commissioner, it is most alarming, but our drive was not a great one. We were in the Kibera slum." The commissioner looked surprised but did not interrupt. "We learned Kelly and her Grandmother had been taken captive. They wanted me to exchange myself for them."

The commissioner peppered English with questions. "What? Is she hurt? Who took them? You are not considering making the exchange, are you?"

"She is fine, and no, though I was willing to take her place, it proved unnecessary. Kelly's Bibi was a much tougher woman than the kidnappers had expected. She took matters into her own hands and freed them before we arrived. I have arranged a safer location for them both."

"That is good. Who took them?" She said, anger boiling just below the surface. She was nearly as protective of her people as English.

"It is a long story, and we do not know all the players, but we think we know the major ones." English indicated Sammy with a jut of his chin, and the commissioner acknowledged the driver. "Elijah's death was tied to an investigation he was working on. He had uncovered a smuggling operation. It took us quite a while, but we discovered uranium is being smuggled from the tsavorite mines through the Port of Mombasa."

"Uranium?" the commissioner interjected. "This is what Elijah was killed over?"

"It appears so," English replied glumly. "He was not the only one." The commissioner's eyes raised in horror as Safari described the events that had taken place, including the tribe's massacre and Michael Tsumbe's murder. She was sickened further as English listed the known conspirators.

"Lord Anson? One of the Americans from John's team? The Vice President? English, if this were anyone but you, I would think this fantasy."

"Unfortunately, it is not. These are very powerful and dangerous men. I attempted to call the Mombasa Police Commissioner, and they even had been monitoring his phone. That is how I learned of Kelly's predicament. They cut in on my call with him and said they would kill her at midnight had I not turned myself over to them."

"You are certain the Vice President is involved? I know he likes the occasional kickback, but this seems outlandish, even for him."

"He is the only one I have not yet been able to tie directly to the plot," English admitted. "However, he closed Tsavo after claiming the Waliangulu tribe had killed Lord Anson. We have seen Lord Anson alive and well with our own eyes. Elijah also had a chieftain's tsavorite ring hidden on his body when they found him. That is why we believe the bodies seen on the container scan and the blood found in it belong to the tribesman. The Vice President is the only one in a position to facilitate such dangerous machinations."

"Yes, it makes sense. How we will take down such an influential cabal is not a small thing. Do you have any thoughts on this, English?"

"Some. We informed John and the rest of the Americans what we discovered in Tsavo and our theory about how they ship it. All indications point to pirates taking possession of the uranium out at sea. This explains why pirates have been stealing from certain containers instead of commandeering entire vessels as they have previously. Once they obtain the uranium, it is likely transferred to another cargo ship flying a hostile flag or, more likely, a dhow. They are less regulated, as you know, and have a much easier time getting into and out of sanctioned countries. The Americans have a response team they can activate whose sole purpose is to interdict nuclear smuggling operations. That still does not solve the source problem. Stopping a pirating raid in international waters is one thing, but the Americans would not likely intervene on Kenyan soil."

The commissioner nodded her agreement. "International diplomacy is all well and good unless your Vice President is in need of removal."

English agreed. "Yes, we all have witnessed corruption in Kenya our entire lives. Never could I have imagined such a conspiracy. Had Elijah not been murdered, it might have gone undetected for a very long time. Each piece on its own seems innocuous. Tsavo being closed due to an uprising is not all that remarkable. The new radiation detection equipment at the port being vandalized is not entirely unexpected.

Lastly, pirates started taking less from cargo ships. This was actually celebrated as a victory. Little did we know it was far worse than if they had continued taking entire ships for ransom."

Commissioner Sambu agreed. "A very complicated, three-prong problem. Any chance you have a simple, three-pronged solution thought out?"

"Perhaps. We need to attack all three simultaneously, and that coordination will be challenging to arrange. I have a close friend in the Navy. He is a commander in naval intelligence. If I can get word to him about the situation, I am certain he can coordinate with the Americans to stop the cargo ship and the pirates to recover the uranium. The Mombasa Police Commissioner Abasi Chongoi can help secure the Port of Mombasa. I have discovered that he is a good man. We just need to get a message to him. Between the forces he trusts and the KRA officers I know I can count on, we should have enough to take control of port operations and secure all ingress and egress locations, even the unofficial ones."

"That is two of the three sites. What do you have in mind for Tsavo?"

English gave a nervous smile. "I definitely saved the best for last. Tsavo is the most difficult of the three, in my opinion. The guards we saw were well-trained and heavily armed. If I were to guess, I would say they were army or special forces. The Vice President has installed many of the army's commanders since he has taken office. I do not think we can count on them for assistance. The only other force I can think of which would be sufficiently armed *and*, using a liberal interpretation of their edict, within their jurisdiction is…"

"No, you *seriously* want me to contact my ex and convince him to take my word that Tsavo Park is concealing a uranium processing plant?" The commissioner folded her arms and shook her head at English's suggestion.

"Yes, Commissioner," Safari began, "even after you separated, you spoke highly of him. As far as I can see, the Border Guard is the only organization capable of securing Tsavo. You know it is the right decision, and you know he will do it if you ask."

The commissioner scrunched up her face in frustration as she conceded English's point. "You are right, of course. I will have to swallow my pride, which I am not fond of doing. How do you propose we coordinate this massive undertaking?"

"Do you happen to have a disposable phone?"

She shook her head no.

"Sammy, let me have your phone." The driver passed the phone to English, who gave it to the commissioner. "Only use this to contact me. The number is the only call logged on it. Call me when you have secured the Border Guard's aid. Sammy and I will travel to my naval friend's home and contact you when they are on board. I still need a method of reaching Police Commissioner Chongoi." Safari snapped his fingers as an idea struck him. "Do you have access to the KRA terminal system here, at your home?"

"I have my system laptop, but I have not logged in for quite some time. I use my office computer on the rare occasion I need to check on something. Why?"

"It is hardly used anymore with everyone having their own cellphones, but the system still has the messaging function enabled. If I see Thomas log onto the system at the X-ray scanning station, I can have him get a message to the police commissioner. I know they are monitoring his calls, or I would call him directly."

"Wait here. I will go dig out the laptop." The commissioner headed back upstairs to look for it. "Help yourselves to some food and drink," she shouted down to them.

English opened the fridge and grabbed water bottles for both of them. Sammy opened a package of crisps that was sitting on the counter and took a handful before passing them to English. They were finishing the bag when the Commissioner returned with her laptop and a power cord dragging behind her.

"Hopefully, this thing still works," her voice was laced with doubt. "Do you remember your system password? I have a few passwords I used to employ as standards for work-related applications, but I may have to try several variations before I am successful. It has been quite a long time since I have used this."

"I do remember some." The commissioner voiced an "ahem" at his use of the word some. "Elijah and I had several accounts to ensure any corrupt KRA agent would not easily track our activities," English explained. "I used one the other day to check on some scans of the containers involved in this smuggling. Someone might have associated one or more of these clandestine accounts with me, but I would wager they are still undiscovered." English checked his watch as they waited for the system to boot up. "I just realized Thomas will not be on shift for a few hours yet. Would you be averse to Sammy and me using the lavatory and cleaning ourselves up while we wait?"

Commissioner Sambu looked them up and down before allowing her nose to wrinkle in disgust as she teased the men. "*Actually*, I insist. I might even be able to find some clean clothes for you both. They are likely not perfect fits, but you will no longer smell as if you spent the evening wrestling an ailing buffalo. Follow me," she ordered, and they fell in line behind her.

She stopped at a bathroom on the ground floor. "Here you are, Sammy. There are towels under the cabinet and body wash in the shower. I will hang some clean clothes on the door. Do you need anything else?"

"No, Commissioner, asante," the driver said as he entered the room.

"All right. English, come on. You can use the upstairs shower, and I will go and hunt down some clothing for you both." English followed her to another bathroom, thanking her before closing the door. He started the shower and got in once the water felt warm enough. The filthy water cascading off his body into the drain sickened him. He washed in earnest once the caked-on muck was no longer visible in the effluent. It was surprisingly refreshing to be clean, and by the time he shut the water off, he felt like a new man. English wrapped a towel around his waist after he dried off and poked his head out of the room to find some clothes waiting outside the door. He grabbed them and went back inside to dress. It was a pair of jeans and a baggy sweatshirt. They weren't a great fit, but English had to admit the change was necessary. He gathered up his dirty clothes and headed back downstairs. The smells of coffee and toast wafting through the air greeted him as he joined Sammy and the commissioner. She was at the stove and turned to face English as he entered.

"I told you to eat something, and the pair of you

share some crisps. Neither of you will be of any use if you pass out," she chastised. The commissioner served up eggs and the toast Safari had smelled onto two plates, then turned back to pour two mugs of coffee. "Cream?"

Sammy nodded as English answered, "Yes, asante."

Safari went to place his clothes on the floor, but the commissioner stopped him. "Put those in the laundry room. Over there," she added, pointing her spatula down the hallway. "We can deal with those later." English complied and sat back at the counter when he returned. Sammy's food was already half-eaten by the time he started in on his own.

"This is very good, asante, commissioner."

"Please, English, it is just eggs, and for the millionth time, you may call me by my first name when we are not in an official setting."

"Yes, Elinah, samahani, it is a hard habit to break." English smiled. He had told Sammy and Kelly to do the same, but neither would address him with other than his title.

"That is better, *English*," she stressed the fact that she regularly used his first name. "Now, I think we had best go over our plans again. We have a great deal of coordination to work out and some formidable people who will do everything in their power to prevent it."

"Agreed. Measure twice, cut once, as they say."

The three of them planned and kept revising plans until the hour had come when Thomas should be starting his shift. English logged onto the KRA computer and opened the obsolete chat function. You had to know the username of the person you wished to contact. Fortunately, KRA had a standard configuration of first initial and last name for usernames, so it was easy to guess Thomas' information correctly. He typed in a message, "Thomas, this is Deputy Commissioner Safari. I need you to do something of utmost importance." The three of them waited impatiently for what seemed like an eternity in the world of texting and instant messages before a chime sounded Thomas' reply.

"Sir?" was the only word written in the chat.

"Thomas, can anyone else read our conversation?"

"No, sir. My coworker has not yet arrived."

Elinah smiled as she read over Safari's shoulder. "Well, at least a bit of good fortune has come our way."

"Indeed. Now I just need him to call me." English typed another message. "Thomas, write down this number." He opened his disposable and copied the number into the chat. "I need you to leave work immediately, buy a pre-paid phone and call me. Do not call this number from any other phone. Do you understand?"

After a moment's hesitation, a reply chimed. "Yes, sir."

"Excellent and," English added an admonishment before signing off, "Thomas, make sure to close the chat and turn off the system before you leave."

"Will do, sir. I will call as soon as I acquire a phone." The chat window closed on Thomas' end, showing he followed his boss's instructions.

English closed the program on their side and spun around in his chair. "Now we just need to wait for his call."

Elinah verified the next step in their plan. "Then you will have Thomas deliver a phone to the Mombasa Police Commissioner?"

"Yes. I think an official welcoming gift from the

KRA delivered by one of its officers should make it through to Chongoi's office. The guards would not stop a gift basket, and Thomas can pass the phone then."

The commissioner nodded her agreement. "Now, you and I must convince everyone else to do their part."

English smiled. "We should get to it then. I have a feeling convincing people to take on a large, well-armed nuclear smuggling ring in league with the Vice President might not be as easy as it sounds."

"Especially if you phrase it that way when you ask." Elinah smiled as she shook her head at the absurdity of it all. "Let me get my keys."

"Our situation has already improved. Ducking down in the back of your car is much easier than climbing back over the walls. I have a good feeling about this." Sammy nodded his agreement with English's words.

The three of them piled into the commissioner's car, she in the driver's seat and they in the back with a blanket pulled over them just in case her house was under surveillance. She drove through the estate district and let them know once they cleared the guard's station. Sammy then directed her to where his cruiser was parked. She pulled up next to it, and the pair exited her vehicle.

The commissioner took a long, hard look at the bullet-riddled cruiser, then solemnly stated, "Good luck, English."

"Good luck, Elinah. I will contact you the instant I have news. Thank you for this."

She smiled back at him. "Save the gratitude until this is over. If this does not work out, you and I will be out of jobs if not sitting in prison cells, or worse."

"That is why I am thanking you now." English nodded firmly once, tapped the roof of the commissioner's car twice, and joined Sammy in the cruiser after she drove off. "Well, Sammy, shall we see if we can convince the navy that they should be hunting pirates?"

The driver nodded yes with a smile as he turned the key, and the cruiser roared to life. "Where to, sir?" English began explaining where his friend lived, and they sped through Nairobi's streets just as the city was coming to life.

CHAPTER 16

English fought off the urge to sick up as he looked through his binoculars. The boat undulating beneath his feet made it difficult to keep his target in sight and retain his last meal. He swept the glasses across the ocean, focusing first on the cargo ship, then on the pirate vessels, and finally on one of the snipers whose job was to end this. How these men would find their targets when it seemed the Indian Ocean was dead set against it was beyond his comprehension. Their commander assured English their skill would overcome any obstacle. He hoped it was true. All phases of his plan needed to be completed simultaneously, or one or more prongs of the conspiracy might escape punishment. English wanted to take down everyone involved in the smuggling and dismantle the entire operation. Partly because of the obvious danger the uranium posed to the world but primarily as revenge for Elijah's murder. Once the teams received the go-signal, English would finally get justice for his friend.

Safari lowered his binoculars and looked around. The scene he had been observing became just a blur on the horizon. The vessel he was aboard was positioned far from the action. They did not wish to alert the pirates before enacting the operation. The larger US Navy ships were even further still, ready to hunt for the vessel the pirates were scheduled to rendezvous with once they had collected their treasure. The queasiness caused by the rocking subsided when he stopped looking through the binoculars, and the cool air was refreshing. None of it, unfortunately, ate through the tension of the moment. English resisted the urge to pace towards the aft of the ship and instead forced himself to remain planted at his vantage point. Once the wheels of justice finally began to turn, he was damn sure not going to miss it after all he did to get them moving.

Even though he wanted to dismantle this operation, English hated being stuck on this ship. Not only was he not a fan of the ocean's movement, but he had no role here besides being a KRA liaison to the Navy. He wanted to be part of the joint KRA/Mombasa Police strike team hitting the port. That is what he knew and where he could do the most good. Unfortunately, only two KRA assets besides Kelly and himself were proven trustworthy: Sammy and the commissioner. Sammy's knowledge of Tsavo made him the obvious choice to work with the border guard on the offensive there. The commissioner should have been the one on this vessel, but the captain had the outdated belief that women onboard ships were bad luck. There was no time to argue the point, and no other naval vessels were in the area or ready to be deployed.

Thinking about the captain's misogyny led English

to look back at the man in question. He was busily checking instrument readings over the shoulders of his crew and giving orders unheard from Safari's position far from the bridge. When the captain's eyes noticed English's gaze, he nodded. Safari nodded back, keeping the mask of professional indifference plastered on his face even as he seethed internally. The man would likely receive a chestful of medals if this operation was successful and even be promoted, ensuring his beliefs would survive another generation. English hated that he was contributing to this man's career, but there were no other options if he wanted Kenyan forces to be involved in the takedown of these pirates. The US Navy would eliminate the threat either way since John reported the smuggling operation. They would not knowingly allow uranium movement outside of approved channels but were happy to coordinate with a country whose shores rested on the Indian Ocean. Bilateral actions were very much in favor in the halls of the U.S. Congress. Its members dreaded being asked questions about the "U.S. Takes Unilateral Action" headline. Even if the patrol vessel Safari was observing from did nothing more than float nearby, it gave the politicians the ammunition they needed to defang the media's bite. The U.S. decision to interdict might not have been made so quickly without this vessel.

English turned back to observe the operation before his well-developed mask slipped, and his face betrayed how he felt about the captain—the past few weeks had nearly destroyed the political acumen he had carefully cultivated in his time since university. He had always known corrupt and otherwise unsavory men had risen to positions of power in Kenya. Still, its recent blatancy was overpowering his ability to maintain his pretense of abidance.

A sailor running up to man the deck guns alerted English that something was about to happen. It was confirmed when the ship's twin diesels fired up and began propelling it forward. He took a step back to regain his balance, but as soon as he had his feet again, he looked through his binoculars to see the last of the pirates aboard the cargo ship fall to a sniper's bullet. The snipers lived up to their reputation. Now, it was up to this vessel to capture at least one of the pirate ships to determine where they were planning on delivering their stolen cargo.

The pirates must have finally realized their men topside had been taken out. The vessels waiting by the cargo ship sprang to life and began separating rapidly. English saw the gunner place his hand up to his headset as he listened to the captain's orders. Once he heard and confirmed what the captain wanted, the sailor turned the gun towards the one pirate vessel heading in a different direction and began firing. Safari covered his ears after the first few shots, which prevented him from using his binoculars, but the explosion in the distance told English the gunner was successful. The man's beaming smile confirmed it.

The ship veered to intercept the remaining pirate vessels, slowly but steadily gaining on their smaller prey. English grabbed onto a nearby railing to keep his feet as the ship cut its way through the waves. Another round of shots blasted from the ship's guns and was answered by the thunderous sounds of a second pirate vessel being violently incapacitated. He silently prayed the captain remembered he needed at least one alive. His prayers were answered rather quickly as the captain's voice boomed a warning from the ship's speakers to the remaining pirates. All of them cut the engines rather than risk joining their former partners. English could see pirates sitting with their hands raised or on top of their heads while waiting to be boarded. Obviously, they had run-ins with the law before.

The U.S. Navy's boat came up on their port side just as English and a contingent of Kenyan sailors boarded the first of the captured vessels. Now that they were closer, English could clearly see how much larger the U.S. ship was. Their crew was three times the size of the Kenyan crew, so they would board the other vessels.

The sailors with English began questioning the pirates in a less than pleasant manner. He walked away before things got too violent, busying himself looking around the small vessel. Discovering a marine GPS at the helm, English scrolled through the device's menu and found some coordinates had been entered a few hours earlier. It had to be where they planned to take their booty once it had been collected. English searched around, found a charging cable, and took both back to the Kenyan patrol vessel. He felt no need to question the pirates. They likely knew nothing more than what to steal and where to deliver it. The GPS told him everything these pawns could *without* resorting to gratuitous violence. Even though he had no sympathy for anyone involved in this conspiracy, he did not feel the need to carry out extrajudicial punishments on those in custody.

English brought the GPS to the bridge, knocked, and waited for permission to enter. The captain was communicating with someone on the radio and held up a finger to indicate he would be with Safari shortly.

He addressed English once he finished. "Another successful operation, eh Deputy Commissioner? What can I do for you?"

"Yes, very successful, Captain. Any word on the other prongs of this mission?"

"Not yet, radio silence till the end. What do you have there." The captain nodded towards the device in Safari's hands.

"I found a GPS near the helm of the pirates' boat. It has coordinates stored in its memory. I think it is where they are meant to take their spoils."

"You don't say? Let's take a look."

English turned the instrument back on and navigated to the coordinates screen. "Here, this is where I believe they are scheduled to meet." He handed the GPS to the captain. "Perhaps the other boats had similar devices which would confirm this information."

The captain nodded his agreement. "Good work, Safari. Let's see if you're right." The captain picked up the radio mic and contacted the U.S. ship. After a few back and forths, the captain turned back to English. "You were right. All the ships had the same coordinates locked into their GPS. We're heading out immediately." The captain used the radio again to call his sailors back onto the ship. From his vantage point on the bridge, English could see the men returning, handcuffed pirates in tow. Before hauling their captives to the brig, one of the sailors threw something back onto the pirates' boat, and flames quickly engulfed it. "Ahead full," the captain bellowed, and the ship lurched forward, once again on the hunt. The U.S. vessel fell in alongside, and English was glad for it. Who knows what would be awaiting them at their destination?

Safari returned to the forward deck, hoping the fresh air and salty spray would distract him from wondering if his friends were all right. They did not, but at least it was invigorating. English began scouring the horizon with his binoculars. He knew it would be over an hour before they closed in on the coordinates, but keeping a lookout made him feel he was contributing. *Maybe I will see something interesting*, he told himself. Even his inner voice sounded doubtful, but there was nothing else for him to do, so he committed.

The minutes passed by at a gruellingly slow pace. No other ships could be seen; the waves were monotonous, and even the fish seemed to find this particular patch of ocean too dull to visit. Still, he scanned on, only occasionally looking at the crew and the U.S. ship shadowing them to see if others had located their targets. The boredom he saw looking back at him said they had not. Everyone had been on an adrenaline high after the excitement of taking down the pirates, but it had long since waned. Both crews wanted another dose or to call the mission complete and head home. English glanced at his watch. *Surely, we are getting close to those coordinates.* He hoped they discovered their quarry before the captains agreed with their men.

English came to full alert. A dark shape bobbed into the corner of his view at the very edge of what was visible. It was not much, but this was a most welcome sight after so much nothing. He trained the binoculars directly to where he thought he had seen something. Soon enough, a brown speck bobbed into his view, sunk out of sight, and just as quickly was gone again. It reemerged as the waves lifted it, and, in short order, he was able to identify it as a ship. A second vessel came into view soon after. He signalled for the gunner to come over and pointed out his discovery.

"I see a pair of ships in that direction," English pointed while handing the binoculars to the sailor. "Are those dhow cargo ships?"

The sailor scanned the area English had indicated. "Indeed they are, sir. Good catch. I'll inform the captain." The man returned the binoculars to English and then ran towards the bridge. Moments later, their ship had adjusted course and picked up a little steam. He looked back at the U.S. ship, which had altered its course to match theirs. If all went well, this would be over soon. Excitement began pumping in English's veins anew. He only wished the ship's speed could match his desire. They would be upon their targets at this speed in the time it takes to brew a decent cup. In his father's voice, he chastised himself, "A watched pot never boils, English, have some patience." Safari grinned. His father would be proud of the work he did this day. He just hoped their sister operations were going as well.

The dhows must have also noticed the two patrol boats heading in their direction as they fired up their engines and started moving. English wondered if the dhow captains thought they could outrun the patrols or if they hoped to be ignored by moving along. Safari smiled. The gods of the sea would be proffering these sailors no such luck. The captain's voice piping over the ship's speakers broke his reverie.

"Prepare for boarding!"

Men began running to and fro on the deck, taking up arms and laying boarding planks near the front of the ship. English ran up to the master-at-arms, "I can shoot. Do you have a weapon for me?"

The sailor looked Safari up and down, then shook his head in the negative. "Sorry, sir," he said in a voice that had done its fair share of yelling. "The captain won't allow a civilian to use one of his guns, especially someone he's not seen in action." The man added in a whisper after English deflated a little, "If you want to join the boarding party, I suggest you grab yourself a weapon of opportunity and be ready when we're given the order."

"Asante sana," English replied with a nod before heading off to find something with which he could knock someone over the head. He finally settled on a watchman's torch. He hit it against his hand and was convinced the mass of the four D-cell batteries would do some damage if necessary.

English returned to the boat's fore and mingled with the sailors gathered there. The master-at-arms was instructing the men and paused momentarily to give an approving wink and nod at Safari's choice. "Take them alive if possible. We need answers only these men can give. Any questions?" When no one interjected, he finished with, "Good luck, make your captain proud!" The men replied in unison with "Yes, sir!" and then readied themselves at the side of the ship.

The captain's voice sounded out over the loudspeaker again, "Cut your engines, or we will open fire!" The diesel smoke billowing from the dhow's stack dissipated to nothing, and the captain's commanding voice was heard once again. "Prepare to be boarded!"

The ship's crew slid two boarding planks from their vessel to the dhow and began racing to the other side. English joined them, making sure not to look down as he ran over the open ocean. The sailors broke into small groups and began searching the dhow for its crew and evidence of malfeasance. Safari attached himself to the group heading for the cargo hold and went below decks. He was quickly swallowed into darkness, but luckily, his *weapon* of choice had a power button, and he used his thumb to turn it on. The beam was bright. He hadn't tested it back on the patrol boat when he had chosen it. He had only been interested in its heft. English swung the beam back and forth methodically, looking for crew members waiting in ambush.

Safari's team pushed forward gingerly. They were not willing to sacrifice caution for expediency. English, being armed with only a flashlight, appreciated their wariness. The group crept forward, eyes following the light beam with intensity. The torch illuminated a light switch, and English flipped it on. He immediately regretted it as the crew hiding in the hole burst forth as one.

As shouts and machetes rushed towards him, English backpedaled as fast as he could, but they caught up. He was forced to use his flashlight club and connected glancingly with the skull of the man closest to him. Shots rang out from the crew behind him, and he dove to the side to avoid being hit in the crossfire. The man he had hit landed next to him a split second later. English pinned the man's machete-wielding hand to the deck and began raining blows down with his free hand. The wound English had incurred opening the gate at the crocodile farm tore open again, and he felt the warm blood running down. There was no time to deal with it as his ship's crew were battling those not struck down in the opening volley. English picked up his flashlight and the machete of his vanquished opponent and headed back into the fray.

Since the mob had raced past him to get to the sailors firing their weapons, he found himself perfectly positioned to assist his team. The sailors were having varying levels of success fighting. These men were trained to be sailors, not hand-to-hand combat specialists. Safari ran up behind the closest brawl and bashed the dhow's man in the back of the head with his flashlight. The man crumpled, and his breathless combatant nodded his thanks before they both moved on to help the next sailor. English made great use of his torch. The machete he kept as a last resort. More sailors were able to assist as their fights were settled. Soon, all of the dhow's crew were subdued, and after some celebratory handshakes and shoulder claps, they assessed the damage. Most of their crew suffered minor injuries, nothing a few stitches or a cast would not fix. Unfortunately, one sailor was lying motionless on the floor. English joined the men administering first aid to see if he could help. While two sailors performed CPR, Safari tore strips of fabric and tied them around the deep gash on the unconscious man's arm. It looked like he had blocked a machete strike with his forearm and nearly lost it in the process. English grabbed a baton from one of the nearby sailors, used it to make a tourniquet out of the fabric, and began cranking down on the wound.

The sailor responded to the CPR with a slight cough, and the men picked him up and made for topside. English heard them calling for assistance as they disappeared from view. He felt terrible that this conspiracy threatened another young person's life, which must have shown on his face. The sailor standing next to him gripped his shoulder. "He will be all right. They'll bring him to the U.S. ship. They have a doctor and the latest equipment." English nodded and returned to zip-tying the men they had just overpowered. While pulling his second set of cuffs tight, he noticed how badly his hand was bleeding and stopped to add a makeshift bandage to it. The sailor who had just spoken to him clocked the wound also. "You need to get that looked at, sir. We don't need another collapsing on us down here."

"You can handle them?" English asked, inclining his head towards the dhow's remaining crew.

"We'll manage." The sailor had an air of confidence that convinced Safari they could indeed deal with the men scattered about the hold. "Do me a favor, though. If you see the master-at-arms, send him our way."

"Will do." English managed tiredly before trudging up the stairs. He slogged his way towards the Kenyan vessel and waved the master-at-arms over upon sighting him. The man jogged over, looking no worse for wear even though he likely fought his fair share of the dhow's crew.

"What is it, Safari?" the sailor asked before seeing the blood-soaked rags tied around English's hand. "You all right?"

"I will live," English uttered wearily. "They need some assistance securing the crew below decks."

"We'll see to it. Go find a medic and get that hand seen to ASAP." Before English finished nodding his acquiescence, the master-at-arms was bellowing for sailors to join him below decks.

Safari turned back and stumbled his way to the Kenyan ship. A sailor greeted him with a first aid kit. The ship's medic pulled the improvised bandage from his hand with a tsk and immediately began dressing English's wound. "This will sting a bit," he warned before pouring some antiseptic over the laceration. Safari grimaced as his hand burned wildly. A quickclot bandage was slapped over the wound, and the medic hastily inspected his work. "That should hold for now, but you need to get some stitches when we return to shore."

English held up his hand to inspect the bandage and assured that he would. The medic smiled. "Good, now drink this water. You look like you've lost a pint or two." The man handed Safari a bottle and waited until his patient began drinking before moving on to another injured sailor. English sat heavily on the deck and propped his back against the ship's hull. He sipped his water while waiting for the crew to finish searching the dhow. Some of the fogginess he felt began lifting as the lost fluids were slowly replenished.

English went to stand when he saw the captain heading in his direction, but the man waved for him to keep sitting, and he gladly complied. "It was a successful operation, Deputy Commissioner. We secured both ships and the cargo the pirates were after, with only one man injured seriously. That's a good day's work."

"Bora sana, Captain. Any word on where the dhows were heading?"

"Hapana," he said, shaking his head disappointedly. "Our crew found no GPS upon searching, and the dhow's hands aren't talking yet. One of them will, once the master-at-arms spends a little quality time with them." The captain left the interrogation techniques up to Safari's imagination and, having met the questioner, he agreed that one of them would be forthcoming. "The U.S. Commander is coming over to share what they've found. Before he arrives, I just wanted to say you comported yourself admirably." The captain extended his hand to English, who clasped it with his left hand. "For a civilian, at least," the captain added with a smirk.

English laughed, but his only retort was to waggle a finger at the man. He was too tired to come up with anything clever. Luckily, the U.S. commander climbed aboard just then, and the captain waved him over.

The two men shook hands before the commander pointed his chin at English. "You Safari?"

"Yes."

"Great work. That was some solid intel you gave Collette. Uranium smuggling's a big effing deal."

English nodded his thanks. "Any signs where these dhows were heading?"

The commander shook his head. "Nah, but this style of dhow is popular in Iran. I'd bet dollars to doughnuts that's where they'd be headed if we hadn't rained on their parade."

It made sense, and English nodded his agreement. "Any word on the other operations, Captain?"

"We're expecting notification any time now." Indeed, as the captain finished speaking, a sailor ran up and proffered a salute. "Let's have it," the captain said as he acknowledged his subordinate.

"Sir, we've just heard from command. The other missions are reporting success also."

"Injuries?" English asked concernedly. The sailor looked down at Safari and then back to his captain, who nodded for him to answer.

"Nothing life-threatening is what was reported."

English breathed a sigh of relief. "Asante." The

news bearer gave a single nod as his response.

"Right, back to your post, sailor," ordered the captain.

"Yes, sir," the young man replied before sprinting back the way he had come.

"Good day all around," the commander announced. "Good working with you, Captain."

"You as well, Commander. Let's do it again sometime." Both men smiled as they shook hands.

"Safari," the commander said in a farewell that somehow managed to convey his respect.

"Commander," English replied as the man returned to his skiff.

"All right, Deputy Commissioner. How about we get you back on shore."

"Sounds good to me, Captain. Sounds good to me."

CHAPTER 17

English threw his cruiser into park and looked in the rearview mirror as he adjusted his glasses. "You are doing this to support Aailyah and honor Elijah," he told himself admonishingly as his desire to return home flared up. It had been nearly a month since the successful operation to take down the smuggling ring was conducted. Most of the major players had been apprehended or killed in the raids, but he was never able to connect the Vice President to the conspiracy. In fact, the Vice President was scheduled to hand out the awards today, and it gnawed at Safari that he could not make a case against him. "Conjecture is not evidence," he angrily parroted as he exited his car.

The lividity built as he stomped fecklessly towards the award ceremony. "Aailyah and Elijah, Aailyah and Elijah," he told himself in a calming mantra. He spotted Kelly and made a beeline for her. He tugged at the tight neckline of his dress uniform, and Kelly playfully swatted his hand away.

"Leave it be, Deputy Commissioner," she gently

chided. "It will be less than an hour," Kelly said as she straightened his tie.

English smiled. "How can you be so calm with that man," he nodded in the direction of the Vice President, "right here?"

"I am glad for him to see he has not broken me," she replied defiantly. "Not only did he fail to kill me, but you thwarted his plans. That must have cost him millions." Kelly looked the Vice President up and down. "It could not have happened to a nicer man," she added with a mischievous twinkle in her eye as she turned back towards Safari.

"He is a dangerous man, Kelly. Do not provoke him."

"Pot meet kettle," she rejoined sarcastically.

"I am *serious*, Kelly. He does not seem the type of man who will let something like this go unavenged. We still do not know the identity of the Brit who came after you and the dozens of others who slipped our net. I wish you would have remained at Alex's place with your Bibi until we rounded them all up."

"And how long would that take?" Safari hemmed and hawed, and Kelly reached up to place her hand gently on his cheek. "Oh, English. You are very sweet to worry, but I must live my life. I think you are higher on their list than little old me. Besides, if they make it past you, they still have to deal with my Bibi." She gave his face a light slap. "Now, snap out of it. We are here to see Elijah and Sammy receive awards, and the man they frustrated has to present them. Today is a good day." English reluctantly nodded his agreement.

"That is true. I guess we can hope he chokes while giving his speech." The pair chuckled in unison.

Kelly smiled, "Hope springs eternal." She

straightened up suddenly. "Commissioner Sambu. How are you?"

"Well, asante, Kelly. More importantly, how are you?"

"I am well, also. Thank you, ma'am. If you could convince the Deputy Commissioner of that, I would be most grateful."

English shook his head as he smiled at his assistant. He mouthed a thank you to her before turning to face his boss. "Commissioner. Thank you for attending."

"Of course, English. You should be up there getting an award, too." English waved a dismissal, but she stopped him. "You thwarted them, English. Had you not followed this so doggedly, it would have likely gone on for years without discovery. Who knows how many lives you might have saved? If that *ass* up there," she gestured to the Vice President, "had not been corrupt, you would be getting your due."

"*Elinah*, language," Alex playfully said as he came up behind the commissioner. English recognized the overly familiar tone in his friend's voice, and he raised a brow at him to ask an unspoken question. Alex broke out a coy smile as his shoulders raised slightly and his head tilted to the side, acknowledging his friend's insinuation was true.

The commissioner turned to face Alex. "I *was* watching my language. He deserves much worse than what I said." Everyone laughed in concurrence.

Alex turned serious as he looked over at the stage. "So, we all agree that our Vice President is behind this whole thing, right?" Nods and muttered affirmations answered him. "It's barmy that he's up there handing out awards for stopping it. I've not gone bonkers here, have I? I mean, this is absurd."

Safari shook his head. "No, you are quite sane, my friend. At least in regards to this one, *very* specific situation," he added sardonically. Alex feigned indignation before chuckling. "Unfortunately, it is the world that is crazy," English somberly added. Kelly placed a comforting hand on his shoulder.

Commissioner Sambu tipped her head towards the stage, "It looks like it's about to start." Everyone directed their attention there. Indeed, the players had taken their positions with the port director standing at the podium. He tapped the mic to verify it was working before addressing the crowd.

"If I may have everyone's attention. Please be seated." The emcee paused while people shuffled around to comply. "Asante. Habari za asubuhi. Today is a great day—a great day for Kenya and a great day for our port."

English looked around while the director droned on and caught John's eye. The two men gave each other up-nods before English returned to scanning the crowd. The assembly consisted of a few family members of the honorees, a handful of KRA and police, while the bulk were dignitaries or those looking to solicit vice presidential favors. The speaker's introduction of the Vice President snapped his attention back to the podium.

"Habari na asante," the politician said in response to the thunderous applause pouring from the sycophantic audience. The seating area immediately surrounding Safari was palpably silent, and the Vice President's ireful gaze noted each of them. He paused an extra beat as he focused on English, and anger registered on his face briefly before the statesman's mask slipped back into place.

Safari quickly tuned out the politician's platitudes. He focused on his friends sitting on the stage behind the man. Aailyah with her and Elijah's two children and Sammy, his smile wide as ever; they were the reason he was here. Sammy knew of the Vice President's suspected involvement but was shrewd enough to realize the man was untouchable. English had not told Aailyah that the man she shared a stage with was likely involved in her husband's murder, albeit indirectly. She had enough audacity to confront, or worse, this paragon of corruption. Elijah would be proud of how well his wife was handling everything since he had been gone, and English smiled slightly at the thought. Then he slowly turned his gaze to each of the other award recipients in turn — the Navy Captain and his first mate, the Border Guard Chief, and Police Commissioner Chongoi — and tried to surmise their thoughts by reading their facial expressions. It was to no avail. Unlike Sammy's facial expression, these men were models of stoicism.

A sudden eruption of applause pulled English from his musings in time to hear Sammy's name announced. He joined the crowd's clapping and added a sharp whistle, eliciting a broader smile from his driver. Sammy stood proudly as the Vice President draped a medal around his neck. The small man reached up to touch the award as he beamed at Apollo Butundu, his surrogate father. The man cheered wildly, eliciting laughter from English and a few others in attendance. The emcee moved on after waiting what he felt was an appropriate amount of time.

"Now we have Aailyah Botsole, who is receiving a posthumous award for her husband, Elijah Botsole. Elijah Botsole was another KRA member who gave his life in pursuit of justice in this matter. Aailyah." The speaker gestured for her to come forward. She stepped up to the podium with both children in tow. Safari's group was, once again, exceptionally boisterous in their ovation. The Vice President hung Elijah's commendation around Aailyah's neck, provoking another outburst of cheers from English. The Vice President darted an angry look towards Safari again.

Alex noticed and leaned over. "Oh, that man hates you, mate," he chuckled. "Looks like you've finally made it, English. Judge a man by the quality of his enemies and all that."

English kept his eyes forward but whispered, "Yes, I would say that bridge is burnt." Alex clapped his shoulder but added nothing further. Their group politely applauded the remaining awardees while biding their time until the event ended. After the last commendation was handed out, the Vice President made his closing remarks and exited the stage. Everyone stood, some to leave, others to try and exploit the rare chance to interact with the second most powerful man in the country.

English chatted idly with his friends as they waited for Aailyah and Sammy to join them, all the while giving side-eye to the Vice President. The man either noticed or unpromptedly decided to give another warning by directing a long, hard stare at Safari. English maintained his composure and casually returned the look.

Alex turned away slightly to avoid the direct attention while sucking air through his teeth. "Yep, he *definitely* hates you," he whispered. "Absolutely shooting daggers, mate."

"Hakuna matata, ndugu," English whispered back,

never once releasing the target from his glare. After a tense moment, the Vice President blinked and returned to his adoring toadies.

Commissioner Sambu disagreed, "No, Alex is right. That man is dangerous and has set his eyes on you, English." She cut Safari off before he could dismiss her concerns. "We need to think about you and your team's safety. I would put nothing above our *esteemed* Vice President," she hissed. "He only has two years left in office. I think we can work out an intergovernmental rotational assignment. I have friends in most customs and revenue agencies around the world. You can be safely removed from his influence while improving our relationship with one of our partner countries."

"I will not run from this fight," English replied tersely, still glowering in the Vice President's direction.

Elinah reached up and gently pulled English's face so he was forced to look at her. "I admire your bravery, English, I do, but it's not just you who is in danger here. You've seen what they did to Elijah and their willingness to go after Kelly. Think about your team here. Two years is not a long time."

Safari sighed a capitulation as he looked over at Kelly and Sammy, who had just bounded up to their congregation.

"Good. We'll discuss where you and your team want to go on Monday."

"Asante, Elinah," English whispered. The commissioner was surprised by his use of her first name, something he consistently rebuffed when she suggested it. She patted his shoulder comfortingly, and Safari willfully brushed off his moment of defeatism. "Everyone," he announced, waiting for his group to focus on him. "I would like to invite you all to my house to celebrate our brave heroes." English indicated Sammy and Aailyah with his hand. Their little group clapped and cheered once again, bringing smiles to everyone. "You, as well, Police Commissioner," he shouted when he saw Chongoi was near enough to hear. Abasi gave him a thumbs up to indicate he would be there without stopping the instructions he was providing one of his officers. English looked at his watch. "Right, see everyone around eight?" Agreements were given all around, and the little band dispersed to make their way back to their respective vehicles.

English pulled his tie off the instant he closed his car door. Disappointment hit him as he thought of leaving Kenya, but he knew Commissioner Sambu was right. As long as the Vice President was in power, it would not be safe to remain in the country, not for him and not for Sammy or Kelly. English knew both of them had entered the Vice President's radar. He was more worried for their safety than his own. It would not do to lose another close friend to this corrupt bastard. *Snap out of it*, English chastised himself and turned his cruiser over. There were preparations needed if he was hosting a party, and it did no good to wallow in despair over things he could not change.

The party was in full swing, music was playing, and guests had been eating and drinking for over an hour when English decided it was time to make a toast. Clinking a fork against his bottle of Tusker, the crowd slowly quieted enough for him to speak. "I would like to thank you all for coming. It has been a terrible ordeal getting to today. We have all lost a dear friend." English raised his drink to Aailyah, and everyone in the crowd followed suit. She nodded thanks and wiped away a tear. "Thanks to Elijah's dogged pursuit of the truth and the herculean efforts of my friends, we stopped an international uranium smuggling operation and made the world a little bit safer. To small victories," he concluded as he raised his beer above his head.

"To small victories!" the crowd echoed.

Just then, the power in Mombasa went down, plunging the city into darkness. Upset sounds and complaints began emanating from those gathered in English's garden but not from him. Instead, he hurried over to his favorite lounge chair and lay down. He raised his Tusker to Elijah and, for the first time in a long time, looked up in awe at the beautiful Mombasa night.

ABOUT THE AUTHOR

Rick Dietrich is a Nuclear Engineer who has travelled extensively around the world, working with governments to implement safeguards against nuclear smuggling. Having worked in a dozen countries, from major cities to small border villages, he has gained a unique perspective on the human condition. Rick incorporates this insight into his stories as he's busily scribbling away while waiting in stations, airports, or sitting in various modes of transportation. He and his wife live happily together with their rescue dogs.

www.ingramcontent.com/pod-product-compliance
Lightning Source LLC
Chambersburg PA
CBHW010609310726
48969CB00010B/2620